A Lure to a Kill

COL. LEE MARTIN

I.E.R. Media

http://www.colonelleemartinbooks.com

I.E.R. Media
http://www.colonelleemartinbooks.com

ISBN: 979-8-9902075-1-6 (PBK)

ISBN: 979-8-9902075-2-3 (EBK)

PRINTED IN THE UNITED STATES OF AMERICA

The McGowan Collection Series

Wolf Laurel

Provocation: Return of the Weatherman

A Hateful Wind

The Justice Club

Killing the Viper

Saving Eagle One

Blood Protocol: Avenging the Viper

Red Kings Rising

Sting of the Scorpion

A Lure to a Kill

This is the ninth novel in the Bruce McGowan Collection Series saga. It is directly correlated to the second book in that series, Provocation: Return of the Weatherman.

As the timing of true events is important for credibility in fiction, this novel is assumed to be set before the fire at the Basilica of Notre Dame and the outbreak of COVID-19.

Table of Content

Prologue

Chatting gaily about the wonders of Paris they had seen that day, her hand tightly clutching his arm, the loving couple strolled in the moist night air in perfect step with one another along Rue Soufflot without hurry. The fog had partially lifted, but as the glow of the streetlights struggled to penetrate the hazy mist, their faces were not totally discernible. Occasionally, the woman was heard to laugh at something her companion had said. It was obvious they were in love, acting as teenagers even though he was well into his sixties and her, the mid-fifties. At one point she stopped, grabbed his suit coat and pulled his face into hers, laying onto his lips a long, tender kiss.

Thirty feet behind them, a man in a trench-coat, the hood of it covering his head, kept pace with them, stopping only when they paused for the kiss. He had followed them every step of the way from the Le Petit Maison restaurant where they had enjoyed a long, romantic dinner of salade Niçoises and boeuf bourguignon with another American couple. After their main course, a solo violinist had come to their table and serenaded them with the lilting traditional standard, *La Vie En Rose*, while they completed their dining experience with a flaming bananas foster.

However, as they walked along the uneven street, both agreeing it was too early to turn in for the evening, they decided to pass on by their hotel and have a nightcap two blocks further down at Les Trois Cheveaux. After all, it *was* Paris, it was spring, and the night was comfortable regardless of the mist. Off to their left the opaque, yet unmistakable lights of the most recognizable structure in the world, the Eiffel Tower, added even more romantic ambiance to their evening. The woman smiled, drew in a satiating breath and slowly let it out. "Ah, j'adore Paris," she said softly.

Just inside an alley ahead of them, a be-speckled man with a white beard sat in a wheelchair off to their right well back in the shadows. Although the couple couldn't see him, he could see them. When they were within fifteen feet or so of the chair, the footsteps of the man behind them quickened. The twosome, suddenly feeling the danger upon them, turned at the same time just as the assailant shoved the blade of a six-inch dagger into the man's gut. As the victim's wife began screaming, he fell first to his knees and then onto his elbows. The thin blade having been thrust into the abdominal artery with the pinpoint skill of a surgeon, the assailant had known exactly where to place it. As quickly as the killer had made the thrust, he then stepped into the shadows of the alley to watch as the dying man struggled desperately to get to his feet. Bright red blood gushed through his fingers as he tried in vain to stop the flow. However, as pressure onto the wound proved futile, within mere seconds he let go a final gasp and keeled forward face- first onto the sidewalk. A pool of blood quickly formed beneath the victim's body, his still-open eyes gradually taking the form of a milky death stare. The man in the wheelchair smiled, sweeping his tongue over his lips as if to savor the butchery he had just witnessed. The cries and sobs of the woman who knelt over her husband's body resonated like dessert to his ears.

As the killer quickly vanished into the dark shadows of the alley, the man in the wheelchair blew into a tube which propelled the chair into a wheelabout, allowing him to follow as well. All the while he laughed loudly. "Ha, ha, ha, ha…and so, Mister McGowan, here is where you finally die. You are not so invincible after all, are you? Cry your heart out, dear Adriana. Cry long, cry hard."

Chapter One

There are mornings I open my eyes and for a split second think I'm the man I used to be…man of action, man of purpose, a man making a significant contribution to the citizens of this country, either with a badge affixed to my belt or as a clandestine agent tracking down the worst of humanity. But then rising from my bed, I quickly remember who I am now… a man in love with his wife enjoying the peace and tranquility that comes with retirement. I must admit there are days I miss it all. Oh, I tell my wife these retirement years are now the best of my life. And they probably are. But I'm sometimes just not all that sure in my mind that love, peace and tranquility are what I have to settle for at this point in my advancing years, even though I no longer have the energy and tenacity of a young Bruce McGowan. I know I can't turn back the clock and go back to being who I used to be. Even if it was humanly possible to relive my past, I know I could never find it the way I left it.

However, as much as I valued my years in service to our country, there was one thing I regret didn't happen. I hadn't ever taken a vacation, at least not with the lovely Mrs. McGowan, my wife of over seventeen years. I think the last time I traveled abroad for other than government assignments, hunting down and killing terrorists and the like, was when my first wife, Darlene, and my ten year old daughter, Caroline, took a cruise to the Eastern Caribbean. Sitting on a sandy beach in my trunks and flip- flops watching the surf flow in and out, in and out, in and out, I was absolutely bored out of my gourd. The margaritas didn't help. Having been an action figure most all my life, my brain and body have to be engaged. Okay, I do like to take a little time out to watch a bit of television or sit on our veranda and read something for twenty minutes or so, but unless I'm asleep those four to five hours I get every night, I have to be immersed in something that keeps me on the move. My batteries have to stay charged. Of course, my morning jog, my half dozen cups of coffee and the occasional ravishing of the still beautiful body of fifty-six year old Adriana McGowan as often as she lets me certainly helps. But it's that latter thing that actually keeps me young.

Staying 'engaged' at this point in my life doesn't mean I still have to be out looking for bad guys and finding the ways and means to put them away…or in the ground. I am what is called *retired*. Hard to even say that word. It's just that…well, being a combat veteran, former FBI special agent and counter-terrorist operative, my brain is always on fire with want of new adventures. I'm not looking to sky dive, go bungee jumping or drive a race car 200 miles an hour; I just want all my neurotransmitters to continue firing.

However, a few weeks ago, Adriana and I received a surprise in the mail. I like surprises…good ones that is, and this appeared to be a good one. Every time a Publishers Clearing House brochure or chance to win opportunity comes in the mail, my bride jumps right on it. "You never know," she always says. "Nothing to lose."

"Except maybe our privacy and the avoidance of countless phone calls, texts, emails that come our way as a result of them selling our personal information to every hacker in the business," I will reply.

"But," she argues, "I'm careful that nobody will get access to our bank accounts, passwords, social security numbers and the like. If we get contacted by those I perceive to be scammers, I ignore them."

"And how do you determine if they are or are not scammers?" I will ask.

"Have we ever been hacked or scammed in all the years we've been together?"

It was no use. I learned long ago I couldn't win an argument with my wife…not that we argued a lot. But any time we fire our shots at one another over a matter, she ends up placing more holes in my argument than I hers, leaving me without any ammunition. And she does that so tactfully.

Anyway, we got something in the mail from an outfit called Saint-Amaury, a French travel agency. It wasn't really an offer as there was no cost involved. We had apparently won an all-expenses paid, seven-day vacation to Paris, good anytime. "Yeah, right," I scoffed. "Another gimmick which will end up costing us an arm and a leg in the long run."

"But look what it says," she retorted. "Accommodations at the L'Anglais, all meals, air included. What more would there be except a few same-day travels we might want to pay for on the side?"

"Where did this come from? Did you enter into any contest to get this?"

"I don't think so. None of this sounds familiar. As you can see, it is a letter from the travel agency and not a brochure with offer."

"Well, there you go. It's all too good to be true. Let's look these people up."

I pulled from our coffee table my laptop, turned it on and Googled Saint-Amaury. After bypassing several links, which immediately came up, such as Yelp, Trip Advisor and the like, I found the Saint-Amaury website. It was a for-real travel agency based in Paris rated five stars in most reviews. There was a contact number and a pop-up photo of a pretty face of Suzanne with the written question below her name, "May I help you?" It was in English, so I wondered if she could speak it. My French was buried somewhere back in the ninth grade.

Adriana, who was peering over my shoulder, told me to click, "yes."

So, I did. In a few seconds, I was in a chat room with Suzanne. I explained what we had received in the mail, and she wrote, "Let me check on this for you."

A moment later, she was back with me. "What you have provided is real, Mr. McGowan. The contract number from your letter indicates that this is a paid trip and all you have to do is tell us your travel dates."

I wrote, "Where did this come from and how was this paid? Neither my wife nor I entered into any contests."

"It is not a result of a contest. A friend of yours paid for the trip."

"What was the name of my friend?" I wrote. And then, "It is anonymous."

"Well, there you go," I said to Adriana. "Like deja vu all over again. Last year after receiving the telegram from my 'cousins' in Scotland, I ended up kidnapped, coerced to locate WMDs and dumped in the Yemeni desert. Now an unknown *friend* has paid for us a vacation."

"It does sound suspicious, now that you mention it."

I wrote Suzanne a final note. "Let me get back to you on this. Thanks."

We sat for a few minutes without word, me rubbing my forehead with my fingertips, and Adriana with her head against the sofa back. "Could have been Mom and Dad," she finally said. "They know we've never had a vacation except two or three days at a time."

"Call them and see, although Suzanne wrote that it came from an anonymous *friend*."

"Let's think who else. Maybe it was someone from your action-man days with the state department."

"No. That wouldn't happen. I know my pal, Keith Lambreau, was very appreciative that I not only saved his bacon a couple of times in Yemen, but that we found the WMDs, and I got him hooked up with the lovely Ms. Compagno, the woman of his dreams."

Adriana pinched me on the thigh. "You never told me about her. An old girlfriend?"

"No. I'll tell you after-while. I've got this Paris thing on my mind right now."

"Well, you think some more, Skippy boy (Skip being my nickname back in the days of my youth). I'm going to check with Mom."

I nodded. "It's not Lambreau, anyway. With his ego, if he or the state department had sprung for this, he'd make sure I knew he put it in motion."

It wasn't Adriana's parents who gave us the trip, nor would my brother Joey have given it to us. The damn mystery was going to drive me nuts. One thing for sure, I wasn't going to jump into this trip deal without an answer. I was duped the year before by an ex MI-6 dude pretending to be my Scottish cousin and I'd be damned if I'd be duped again.

Later that evening over the dinner table, Adriana posed that perhaps one of our delightful B&B guests may have purchased the Paris trip. We had so many who thanked us for our hospitality with cards, baskets of flowers, Omaha Steak deliveries, and one couple even offered us an expenses paid visit to the country inn they had started-up in Vermont, patterned after ours. When the dishes were done and we settled back in the den with our glasses of Pinot Noir and a little classical music, Adriana spread out on the coffee table all the cards she had kept through the years.

"Here," she said, "you take this batch and I'll look at these." She picked up about thirty of the cards.

I didn't know where this idea of hers would get us, but I played along anyway. Maybe we could find that anonymous friend among the cards…or at least speculate on someone.

After we had gotten through about fifty cards and Mozart's *Piano Sonata No, 11 in A,* Adriana said "eureka." She remembered well the couple from a small village just outside of Paris called Batignolles who were touring the U.S. and placed our B&B, Wolf Laurel, on their list. Adriana began reading their letter to me:

"Dear American friends, we loved our time at your quaint and beautiful West Virginia inn more than any other places we stayed during our two weeks in etats-Unis (United States). Your breakfasts were delicious and grounds as spectacular as any we experienced on our trip. We would love for you to come visit us in beautiful Batignolles which you will find outside of Paris…"

The note also painted a verbal picture of their vineyards which were touted as the finest in Northern France. Yes, they had money and could easily afford to arrange a paid vacation for us commoners.

"In paraphrasing, Genevieve says she regrets that she didn't know enough English to write the letter and as I remember her husband, Jean-Louis, he could only say "good morning" and "how are you.""

"Do you think they're our anonymous benefactors? There was nothing pretentious or self-serving about them. Maybe we should send them a letter and ask them.""

"I don't know about that, Skip. If it's from them, they would want to remain anonymous, and it might embarrass or even insult them if we asked.""

"I suppose you're right about that.""

"But if we decide to go, we'll definitely put them on our itinerary.""

I smiled. "I can sense you want to go.""

"Why not? It'll be a free trip. We have never had a real honeymoon, much less traveled to Europe. I know you were probably in every European country when you were with the state department, but I've never even been across the Atlantic.""

"That's your version of begging, I take it.""

"Is that what it sounds like?""

"It sounds like you've made your mind up. I guess we're going.""

"Well, this came from a travel agency, not some terrorist pretending to be your Scottish cousin."

"You have a point, my dear. What could go wrong?"

She leaned into me, grinned and blew a tiny puff of her sweet, warm breath into my ear. It sent a surge of adrenaline directly to my loins. "Come with me, lover boy. There's another place we can go to talk this over."

And that is how we decided to take advantage of a vacation offered to us, all expenses paid, to La Ville Lumier, the City of Lights.

As it was the month of February when we received the invitation to Gay Paree, we decided that late April would be a perfect time to experience France. The old standard *April in Paris* kept invading my brain to a point where I began incessantly humming the tune. Adriana would catch me and smile. She was super excited, and for her, that day in April would not come anytime too soon. "I hope there will be warm rain showers at times and that the tulips will be in bloom," she said. "It would be the perfect romantic setting, straight out of *Moulin Rouge*. Can't wait to see the Eiffel Tower, the Louvre and Sacre Coeur…" She went on and on.

I think the last time I had seen her so bubbly was the day of our wedding. But while I loved seeing her so happily expectant, I was still apprehensive about our venture turning out bogus. To prevent that, I would do some additional investigation. For her sake, I hoped like hell it was something real. If not, I would still make our vacation happen even if I ended up paying for the whole trip myself. Adriana McGowan deserved nothing less. All through our marriage, she had put up with me traipsing all over hell and half the globe taking down international and domestic terrorists. Even in the early years of my retirement, I was asked to take part in missions where expertise and pure-damn ruthlessness were needed. From the state department's short field of retirees, I was always their first choice, called back to duty under code name Scorpion. And much to Mrs. McGowan's dismay, ninety percent of the time I responded. Sometimes I came home beat up, shot up and even fed up, vowing never to answer the government's call again. Except I did…more times than I should have. Yes, I owed her big and I'd be damned if I would burst her bubble by denying her this trip to Paris.

Chapter Two

The identity of the mysterious altruist, if that is what he or she was, continued to bug me. I've never in my life been the recipient of such an undeserved gift. Yes, I was, by agreement, paid one million dollars to kill a notorious terrorist of the Islamic persuasion, known as the Viper, but even though I would have arranged it for less, I did go through some hardships to earn it. And so did the talented hitman Atticus Steed, who actually pulled the trigger. I then stopped to think, maybe it was he who paid for our trip. He collected a million as well, thanks to my bargaining with the State Department. And then I had come to his rescue by collaborating to end the life of the Viper's vengeful brother whose bullet had nearly ended the life of Steed's wife. Yes, if not the French couple, probably Steed.

The next morning, I was able to get hold of the face in the chatroom on the Saint-Amaury website. It was four o'clock in the afternoon there.

"Hello, Suzanne. My name is Bruce McGowan from the states. You and I communicated yesterday on your website regarding an anonymous payment for our trip to Paris."

"Oh, yes, I remember. How can I help you?"

"You speak English very fluently, Suzanne."

"I should; I'm from San Francisco. I taught French at the university there."

"And then you decided to live in France and arrange

vacations with a travel agency."

"I've always loved Paris and vowed someday to make my home here."

"I'm glad you were able to follow your dream. But, to get on with the subject at hand, may I ask you a couple of questions?"

"You're going to ask who the anonymous donor of the money was that bought your trip."

"Yes. And?"

"Well, if I told you, the individual would no longer be anonymous."

"But do you actually know who it was."

"Yes, I have a name, Mr. McGowan, but ethically I am bound not to disclose the name. We had to respect the payor's wishes. I never met the person but did speak on the phone. The money was paid by cashier's check."

"Can you divulge how much was paid?"

"I think we can do that. 6314.609 Euro which is $7655 in American dollars. That includes the trip, airfare, your lodging at the D'hôtel d'Anglais, taxi, tips, all breakfasts and four dinners at the hotel."

"Most generous."

"Yes, but yours is not the only vacation package I've handled where someone paid for another's trip anonymously."

"Really. How many times has that happened?"
"With me…maybe three times. I remember handling a matter where a big wig paid for his secretary's trip separate from his in order to meet her

here. He asked that we remain discreet and that the payment not be traced back to him." I heard her chuckle. "I often wondered if his wife ever found out about it."

"Can you give me a hint as to whether the payor was a man, woman or couple?"

"I've…probably said too much, Mr. McGowan. No hints, okay?"

"Okay. I don't want to get you in trouble with the guy."

"Who said it was a guy?"

"Ah, then it was a lady."

"I didn't say that either."

"Well, I guess I don't know any more than when I received the letter. I don't mean this to be insulting, but I just wanted to be sure the trip was valid and that my wife and I weren't somehow getting scammed."

"Oh, this is a real trip and all you have to do is board the plane from where you are, and all the rest will be taken care of. And since I have you on the phone, what dates do you have in mind?"

"We talked about the week of April 23rd. Is that time frame open?"

"Let me see." She paused and I heard the clicking of computer keys. "That's open, sir. From where would you fly?"

"From Yeager Airport, Charleston, West Virginia."

"Okay, then. Bear with me. It will take me a few minutes."

As she was preparing the plan, I listened to a light

classical piece of French music while allowing everything I had discussed with Suzanne to digest. Were there any more questions I could ask? I couldn't think of any. There was no way I was going to get more out of her. For some reason, however, I believed the identity of our benefactor would in time be divulged.

"Mr. McGowan, you will depart Yeager at 10:05 on American Airlines 1254 on April 22nd and arrive at Charles De Gaulle in Paris…" She continued laying out the itinerary which included pick-up by limo and delivery to the hotel. The Hotel d'Anglais was American owned, Anglais being French for the word English. At least I was assured I could understand what people were saying behind the counter. Then I wondered if the maid was French and would be wearing one of those little baby doll outfits. I pictured in my mind someone that looked like Brigitte Bardot…as she was about fifty years ago.

"Mr. McGowan, did you hear the last thing I said?"
"Huh…what? Oh, yes. I'm sure it will also be in the brochure and itinerary you'll be sending."

"Correct. So, if no other questions, I want to wish you and your wife a safe and pleasant trip to our city.

If you can think of anything else, please feel free to contact us again."

Well, I started feeling a little better about our trip. I didn't mean to book it without talking first with Adriana, but as she had already said she wanted to see Paris in April, she would be pleased that I went ahead and pulled the trigger.

The last time I was in Paris, I didn't get to see much of it. As France had left the door open for Muslim immigration through the years, that also opened the door to Islamic extremist factions such as the Armed Islamic Group and elements of al-Qaeda. In 1999 as a member of our covert Department of State Counter-terrorism Team, I personally took out terrorist Aabdae-malikil from the Lach-e-Taiba militant group, Pakistan's largest, who had bombed a Paris Metro subway station, killing 38. As we found Malikil in an Islamic Mosque and not wanting to shoot up the place of worship, I waited three days and nights on a rooftop with my HK 417 sniper rifle for him to slip out. Once I had radio confirmation from our Pakistani mole imbedded in the Taiba element inside the mosque that my target was on the move, and as soon as his face became magnified in my scope, I put a round between his eyes. His entire head exploded like a ripe watermelon. That's what I remember about Paris. I guess you could say I painted the town red. I was hoping my upcoming Paris trip with Adriana would render happier memories, although I was pretty damn happy with the results of my last vacation there.

Adriana was overjoyed that I locked in Paris with Suzanne. I told her that although I was still unable to find out who paid for our trip, I was feeling a lot more positive about it. "Thank you, whoever you are," she said. "I wish I knew how to repay you."

"Well, we have a couple of months to prepare for this and I'm thinking you'll need that long to pack."

She laughed. "Uh huh, and knowing you, you'll be able to get everything you're taking in a bag the size of a lunch box. But, Mr. McGowan, we're going to go out and get you a couple new pairs of slacks, some nice dress shirts and a new sport coat. I'm tired of you going around in frayed jeans and that worn out blazer with the missing buttons you wear to church."

"But…"

"No 'buts' about it. You're going to look spiffy walking around Paris with me. We'll go over to Charleston tomorrow."

She was sounding more like my dear old mom every day. She was right, however. I had allowed my wardrobe to slide downhill over the past few years. But I'd be damned if she would make me put on a tie.

On the evening of March 21st, I placed into my new suitcase my two neatly folded new sport coats, my five new pairs of Ralph Lauren slacks, new Calvin Klein underwear for seven days (an extra pair in case I ate something that went directly to my lower intestines and out), and my two new ties. I was going to feel naked, or as they say in the great WV, *nekkid*, without my hardware. I never go anywhere without one of my big three: my Sig Sauer, my S&W .45 or my Springfield Armory XD. If I could somehow smuggle in my diminutive James Bond PPK, I'd even be okay with that. Even if I placed the weapon and ammo mag in separate locked metal boxes, I might have trouble picking them back up in Paris. The Les Police would frown on me toting it around on their streets.

My bag comfortably held everything I packed, but Adriana's two pregnant suitcases would barely zip up. When I mentioned we were only staying a week, she kindly reminded me that's why she reduced her wardrobe down to two pieces rather than three. "You men don't have to carry all the cosmetics and things like hair dryers, hair curlers and hair products like we women do. You just run a comb through your hair and splash on some cologne."

"Cologne? Was I supposed to pack some cologne?"

We made sure to pack our charging cords, medications, few that there were, and some reading material in our carry-ons. Adriana kept asking me if I could think of anything else and I told her maybe a box of Little Debbie's in case I didn't like the airplane food. That idea got nixed.

And so, we were ready. All we had to do was get up the next morning, roll out our bags and drive the hour and a half to the airport. Well, there *was* that one thing to accomplish before we closed our eyes.

"You can't wait till we get to Paris?" she said. "It will be all the more wonderful when we are in the City of Romance."

She was probably right, but considering it had already been two days since our last loop-tee-loo and as we were not only facing another eight hours on the plane but probably another couple of hours before reaching the D'hôtel, my pent-up fervor would be busting at the seams.

Chapter Three

We arrived at Charles De Gaulle just after six-thirty AM on the 23rd. With the travel time in the air and time difference, we seemed to have lost the better part of the 22nd. The limo driver was waiting for us at the taxi stand, a porky hombre in his early sixties with a three-day growth and smelling of B.O. and cigarettes. He did little more than growl at me, but he was peaches and cream with the lovely Mrs. McGowan. And his eyes seemed permanently affixed to her cleavage while loading our luggage. Then when he was seating her in the car, I saw him taking a long leer at her shapely legs as far up north under her skirt as he could. But it was when he asked, "Are you now quite comfortable, mam'selle" without giving me the time of day, I knew he'd be all over her if I weren't in the picture.

"That's *madame, Monsieur,*" she quickly corrected him.

"Of course, Madame. Pardonnez moi, s'il vous plait."

"Ce n'est rien," she replied, meaning "think nothing of it." Except, it could have meant, "Put your damn eyes back in their sockets."

Once both of us were planted on the rear seat,

I said to her, "Why didn't I know you were fluent in French?"

"Well, not exactly fluent, but I can carry on a limited conversation. My high school French kind of stuck with me. And then sometimes at the library I listen to books on tape in French. I've actually been brushing up on it the past couple of months."

"I'm impressed, Madame. So, how do you say, 'Keep your lecherous eyes on the road and not on my wife's body, you fat prick?'" I noticed he was still stealing looks at her in the mirror.

She actually laughed at that. "Shhh, you don't want him to hear you. Don't be rude."

"Well, isn't everyone here rude to Americans?"

"I don't think you'll find that. Didn't you see how nice the people in customs and the baggage handlers were?"

"Didn't notice. But I know up there behind the wheel is a freaking sleaze-ball. Be ready to experience more of the same on our trip, not to mention when we encounter the Muslim assholes which are all over the city."

"Be nice, Skippy. Let's just have a good time and expect the best out of our Parisian friends."

"Okay, you're right. I'm stereotyping based on what I experienced a few years ago as well as heard from people who have vacationed here."

"Oh, look. How beautiful is that…the Palais Garnier Opera House."

"Nice."

"Nice is all you can say? It's spectacular."

"Yes, it is, my dear. Just one of the magnificent structures you'll see."

"I can't wait to see Notre Dame, the Arc de Triomphe and walk down the Champs-Elysées. Are we going to cruise the Seine? And visit Sacre Coeur…"

I smiled as she went on and on like a child at Magic Kingdom. It did my heart wonders seeing her so excited. I put my arm around her and kissed her on the lips. In his rear-view mirror, the eyes of Pepe la Pew were now on *me*. Was he thinking I'd be slipping Adriana Wee Willie Winkle right there in his back seat or were those just the eyes of envy?

Within another ten minutes, stinky man dropped us off at our hotel where a uniformed bellboy greeted us and took our luggage into the lobby. The Hotel d'Anglais was nothing fancy, appearing a bit more palatable than a Super 8. But it would provide a bed to sleep in and a shower (we hoped) and wouldn't cost us anything. We planned to spend ninety percent of our time touring anyway.

The young girl at the check-in desk wearing a shalwar with kameez and a nametag that read Fatema had a packet for us which included vouchers for our breakfasts, the four dinners and complementary cocktails each afternoon at the small bar adjacent to the lobby. Now we were talking. But the entire place smelled like curry, which always makes me gag, and that set me to wonder if the entire operation was run by people from India or Pakistan. However, the name of the hotel was Anglais which gave the impression that it was owned and operated by Americans or English people. Then it came to me that behind the counter of most every U.S. motel, Dunkin Donut and Dairy Queen were Indians or Pakistanis. That's never bothered me, however, as many of them are friendly, accommodating and always have big smiles on their faces. And although I am prone to stereotyping, I'm no bigot.

The same bellboy took us onto a rickety elevator

and then to our room. I held my breath all the way up to the fifth floor. Adriana hadn't said anything, but kept darting her eyes at mine, giving me the impression she was expecting her Parisian lodging to have more than one star. But it was a freebee, I told myself.

The room had one full-size bed, a chair, a bathroom with shower the size of our hall closet and an outdated TV. Again, it was just a place to sleep and bathe. However, I could tell Adriana's heart had sunk. Although she was not used to living like Marie Antoinette at our home in West Virginia, in Paris, France, she was expecting more. Maybe there'd be a mint for each of us on our pillows.

"Don't worry, sweetheart," I said. "We won't be spending much time here. The City of Lights awaits." The bellboy pulled our luggage off his cart and went over to open the window. I took it that the fresh Parisian air was our air conditioning. At least it would help take the stench of curry away. "I can do anything else for you?" he asked.

"Thanks, but I think we're good."

Adriana nudged me and whispered, "Aren't you going to tip him?"

"Remember, the package included all tips."

And so, our empty-handed baggage toter gave us a toothy grin and left the room.

On the TV stand I was relieved to find a plug adapter for our cellphone chargers and Adriana's hair dryer. I had intended to pack one that I kept from other European trips, but forgot. And by golly, there were actually chocolate mints on the pillows after all. The place had just gained another star.

But, after we showered and prepared to go down to the lobby for what I knew would be only a continental breakfast, the d'hôtel quickly demoted itself to one star again when a blood-curdling scream was heard from the closet bathroom. When I hustled in to see what the matter was, she said, "I found a roach crawling on my cosmetic bag."

Well, I smashed the big bug, wrapped it in a tissue and flushed it into the Seine.

"Uh, Skip, do you think we can spring for another hotel considering the flight was paid for in the package? I'd feel a lot better about our lodging."

It was the first time I had heard any semblance of dissatisfaction with anything on the trip since we left home. She wasn't a complainer by nature, but I wanted to know that she was feeling clean and comfortable. As we'd likely never return to France, I wanted the experience to be as near perfect as possible.

If it was only about the roach, I told her that even in the best hotels in the world, one can find creepy crawlers. I also reminded her we would be spending only our nights at the Anglais as our days would be full.

"I know and for that reason, I agree we should not come out of pocket for another place. Most places are over 250 Euros and that would add up quickly. We'll stay, but not without a can of Raid or something equivalent."

"When we go out today, I'll get some bug killer."

As neither of us slept on the flight into Paris, we took a three-hour nap. When we woke, since we hadn't had anything since a breakfast sandwich on the plane, we decided to go find a cafe to have lunch. We took with us our daily itinerary. Unfortunately, we had missed a meeting with our tour guide for the day, which meant we also missed a two-hour bus tour of the city. However, the bus tour was only scheduled to give us a prelude of the attractions we'd be seeing each day either on a walk or trolly.

We found only a few blocks from the hotel a quaint sidewalk cafe which was straight out of a place one would find in a Doris Day/ Rock Hudson movie. After being promptly seated at a table, the radiant early afternoon sun fell warmly on our faces, doing much to take the April chill out of the air. Our garçon was a young man with dark hair, a prominent nose and a weak chin. "Bonjour, madame and monsieur. Puis-je prondre votre commande?" (May I take your order?)

Well, I thought we looked very American and wondered if he had just called me an asshole. With as little sleep as I got, I probably resembled one.

But Adriana replied, "Nous sommes Américains. Parlez-vous Anglais?"

"What did you say back to him?" I asked.

"I told him we were Americans and asked if he spoke English."

The waiter responded, "I speak a little. I can try or bring one of my people that speaks Anglais."

"As you heard, I speak some French; so, between us, we can get through the ordering."

"Parfait (perfect), madame. I will take your order now."

As the menu was only in French, I was totally dependent on Adriana's explanation of each item.

"This is smoked herring with potatoes and roasted almonds. Below it is burgundy beef palate. Then we have pate, which is their version of meatloaf…" "That all sounds pretty heavy for lunch. I'm sure there's a salad on there somewhere."

"How about a mixed greens salad with boiled eggs and olives with a bowl of shellfish soup."

"Ah, the salade niçoise and bouillabaisse," the garçon repeated. "Very good choice."

"And I'll have the same," she said. "Also, two glasses of your Chablis."

"Oui, madame." He then gave her a slight bow and turned away with a degree of pomp.

"Prissy boy, isn't he?"

"Be nice, dear husband."

As we waited on our food and wine, Adriana took out our vacation itinerary. Our benefactor had purchased a package that included daily tours that basically scheduled two attractions each day. For example, since we missed Monday's bus tour of Paris, we'd pick up on Tuesday with a walking tour of the Louvre in the morning and a stroll along the Champs-Elysées and its iconic shops, ending up at the Arc de Triomphe at the top of the hill. Wednesday was the Eiffel Tower and cruise on the Seine. On Thursday we'd visit the famous cathedrals of Notre Dame, Sainte Clotilde Basilica, Saint-Etienne-duMont and Saint-Estauche, then the Pantheon in the afternoon. Friday was to be a trolly ride up to the highest point in Paris, Montmartre, with its fabulous view of the City of Paris, a walk through the art village and a reverent tour of the magnificent Sacred Heart Basilica, Sacre Coeur. In the evening was dinner at the lovely Le Petit Maison on Rue Soufflot. Saturday was a free day unless we wanted to pay for a side tour and go with the group to Louis the 14th's Palace at Versailles. Sunday we were to end our trip…back to the great WV.

As it was barely two in the afternoon, we decided on doing something that Adriana had on her list, but not on the schedule…taking in the Moulin Rouge Cabaret Show. It wasn't anything I was crazy about. If The Eagles, Charlie Daniels or The Jersey Boys were touring in Paris, I'd have been all over them. Adriana knew that and had suggested I needed a bit more culture in my life. As she was probably right, I would go with her wearing my positive attitude. But then as I thought more about it, I figured the scenery, of the feminine persuasion that is, might be worth the 200 Euros a ticket.

We were fortunate to get our two tickets considering Adriana had called to reserve them that very afternoon of the show. There had been two cancellations. Much to my surprise, I really did enjoy the Feerie show. And it wasn't just about all those beautiful legs…all 120 of them belonging to the 60 gorgeous Doriss girls. It was probably the most colorful fanfare I had ever seen, what with the costumes, feathers and glimmering rhinestones. I also actually got into the music. It did my heart strong to occasionally take my eyes off the show and glance over to watch the face of my lovely wife, whose own flawless beauty rivaled any of the faces on the stage. Her laughter, the tears of joy that smudged her makeup, and her dazzling smile showcasing those perfect white teeth, I think I fell in love with her all over again that night.

Chapter Four

It was on Tuesday, that second day of our Paris adventure, when I first noticed the old man. I figured he was part of the tour group whose faces we'd be seeing throughout the week. You see, all we had to do was show up on our own at a designated place at a certain time wearing our plastic badge from the packet left for us at the hotel and the tour guide would walk us through the venue. There wasn't anything organized beyond that. My question was, considering the man was completely paralyzed, only able to propel his wheelchair by blowing into a straw, I wondered how he would navigate in difficult areas. However, I was sure each venue would accommodate even severely handicapped people, although no country I had visited did so as thoughtfully as the United States.

There was something vaguely familiar about him, except I was sure I had never seen him before. He appeared to be in his upper seventies, had a full white beard like Santa Claus, a red beret and was wearing glasses with coke-bottle lenses. Adriana remarked how sorry she felt for the man and wondered how long he had been in his immobile state. The only part of his body he could move was his head which enabled him to ambulate via the blow pipe. As he couldn't move his arms to even feed himself, I also wondered how he was able to take in his food and drink. Yet, there he was each day, trying to enjoy life and what the world had to offer as best he could, rather than lying in a bed feeling sorry for himself.

My question was answered while we were standing in line at the Louvre, when a man stepped up behind him, pulled from the bag on the back of the wheelchair a chocolate chip cookie and fed it to him. His caregiver, a Middle Eastern man in a checkered kaffiyeh, had a black patch over his left eye. Adriana smiled, seeming relieved that the old man had someone in his life to cater to his basic needs such as with the toilet, his bathing and of course at the dinner table.

I was enthralled with the Louvre, thinking I could spend the entire day there and maybe a second day. But being hustled through the place those three hours by Andre, the day's tour guide, almost seemed like a drive-by. However, I did take an inordinate amount of time to sit and study several pieces of art such as the ginormous Coronation of Napoleon as compared to the Mona Lisa which I found rather disappointing. Try as I might, I couldn't find any evidence of a smile, maybe a smirk, and it was smaller than I imagined. Probably would have fit nicely on our bathroom wall.

I think Adriana was a bit embarrassed viewing the naked statues of Greek notables such as Apollo, the Sleeping Hermaphroditus, with his exposed manliness, and Marcellus as Hermes Logios. When we came to the room that included the statue of Spartacus and his naked full body and rippling muscles, I commented it was like looking in the mirror after stepping out of the shower. She did giggle at that, but said the main difference was that Spartacus did not appear to be all that abundantly endowed. Interestingly enough, I actually thought the face on the statue strangely resembled that of Kirk Douglas.

The celebrated Venus de Milo I thought was over-rated; however, I was mesmerized by the guide's narration about the Canover called the Kiss of Cupid, the beautiful embrace between Cupid and the Princess Psyche and the romantic story behind it. Where Psyche lies unconscious from opening the forbidden vial from hell that Aphrodite gave her, Cupid brings her back with a kiss. I get all teared up, especially when I hear stories about real life characters like that.

All the while, I kept seeing the man in the wheelchair for whom both Adriana and I felt sorry. But we did see that his caregiver was taking good care of him, responding to his every need.

That afternoon we were largely on our own, having walked from the Louvre to the base of the Champs-Elysées where we began our venture up to the Arc de Triomph. After another light lunch at a cafe and a bit of browsing at several of the shops, we finally reached the Arc. It was pre-arranged that our tour guide, Andre, would meet us there and provide a brief history of the structure. After we had taken the elevator to the top and beheld the magnificent view of all the streets that intersected with the Arc, we stood somberly by the eternal flame. One person in our group asked if it was true that when the body of the celebrated unknown French soldier from World War II was disinterred and run through the DNA process, was he instead found to be a German. Andre dressed the woman down immediately, telling her it was a disrespectful suggestion, and he would not answer the question. It was the first rude comment we had heard from a Frenchy person since we arrived.

The first of our planned dinners was at a restaurant called Le Chateaubriand which was about seven blocks from where we were staying at the charming D'hotel de Roach. As soon as we sat down and the menus were placed before us, the waiter took a napkin, reached down between my legs and laid it on my lap.

"Don't be fumbling around down there, Gaston," I said. "Territory you don't want to get into."

"Pardon moi, Monsieur, but it is our custom to do this. And I believe you meant to call me *garçon* instead. Just so you know, my name is Frederick."

"Sorry, Frederick, I'm just not used to ritzy treatment such as this."

"Of course, you're not."

I took that as a shot, so it appeared we were starting to see the rude coming out. The waiter then said, "I shall return with some water to give you time to decide on your dinner."

When he had turned heel, I asked Adriana if Chateaubriand was on the menu.

"To my surprise, yes, it is," she said in jest.

"Then, without a study of the bill o' fare, that's what I'll have."

"It comes with shiitake mushrooms and potatoes seasoned in butter, salt and pepper."

"Perfect. Tell the waiter to bring us a carafe of Merlot as well."

When he returned to our table, he went into a soliloquy about the evening's specials. "Madame and Monsieur, tonight we have a very fine dish of marinated mussels in white wine and shallots, beef liver with paprika powder and Worcestershire sauce, and our traditional escargot, lightly creamed with sweet apple and carrots julienne served in a cream puff shell."

That's when Adriana looked at me with eyes that said, "Oh, here it comes."

I replied as nicely as I could, but also throwing in a pinch of humor. "Well, first of all, as to the liver, I don't eat anything that used to be a filter, and as to the escargot, snails in our country, I don't eat anything I'd scrape off the bottom of my shoe."

If looks could kill, his eyes told me I had grossly insulted both him and his menu. "Monsieur, these dishes are traditions of *our* country and should not be mocked. So, then what *will* you have?" *Bam!*

I swallowed any retort I had in mind at which point I was also saved by my wife. "We will both have the Chateaubriand and potatoes, Frederick. And could you please bring us a carafe of Merlot?"

"Oui, Madame."

"Hey, Frederick," I began. "I must apologize if what I said sounded insulting. It was just my attempt at a little humor."

Down his long nose he gave me a nasty look, which apparently came free with every meal. "*Very* little humor, Monsieur."

It was then I figured I was not going to be getting along with garçons where we dined. I hope he wouldn't spit on my Chateaubriand.

"You need to get along with the natives while we're here, Skippy. I don't want us to leave a bad impression on this country."

"As ugly Americans, huh?"

She smiled and patted my hand. "Nothing ugly about you, Spartacus."

As we sat enjoying our steak and wine, I made it a point to behave myself when Frederick revisited the table to check on us. He then began warming up to me and my mouth…mostly because I kept my mouth shut. But I did ask him if he grew up in and around Paris, if he went to school there and to tell us something about his family. He seemed to appreciate my interest in him, and I supposed he had forgotten all about my insulting his country's snails. He in turn asked where we were from in the states.

However, it was this particular night that I began feeling a bit of that uneasiness I get sometimes. It's kind of a 6th sense with me. I don't know where it comes from, and I don't know what it's about. I do know that it's often connected with danger.

The feeling began when across the room at another table, I saw the old wheelchair bound man again, this time with a cold stare affixed to my eyes. Dining with him was his companion with the eye patch. His one eye was on me as well. But then my eyes turned back to the old man. He was still staring. Could it be that he was in some kind of trance connected to his disability and my face was just something he focused on?

Every couple of minutes, One-eyed Jamal, as I started calling him, cut up a small portion of the man's meal and fed it to him. Then after every third mouthful, he gave him a sip of wine. The old man, I'll call Santa, seemed to have no trouble chewing and swallowing, but Santa's helper was taking care, assuring that he wasn't feeding his ward too quickly. Occasionally, the younger man would also glance over in our direction, but mainly kept his attention on Santa.

When we finished our dinner and paid the garçon, me leaving him a nice tip for having put up with me, we promptly left and began walking in the direction away from our hotel to take in the fresh night air. As the sidewalk was along the Seine, we both remarked how beautifully the lights of the city shimmered on the water. Traffic whizzed by us opposite the sidewalk, and I made the statement how close it was. I could feel the breath of the vehicle each time a car passed.

She had chosen a rather tight white skirt to wear that evening, which served to accentuate every vivacious curve of her derriere. As we continued walking, I slowed a bit, allowing her to stay a couple a steps ahead of me which in turn always allows me to appreciate that almost musical, natural sashay she has when she walks. As I had done on several occasions, I began singing, "Backfield in motion. I'm gonna have to penalize you."

"Stop it, Skippy," she always said.

And I usually did. I knew it embarrassed her, especially if there were people around. Nonetheless, I knew it flattered her and I think if I ever did stop it, she may wonder if I still thought she was a dish. No worries there.

We had gone perhaps the equivalent of five city blocks when I noticed a cargo van about the size of a Honda Odyssey approaching at a high rate of speed. When it was within about fifty feet, it suddenly veered off the street onto our sidewalk, heading straight for us.

"Watch out!" I yelled to Adriana, at the same time pushing her down the grassy slope toward the water. Then, just in the nick of time, I jumped down the slope as well.

Once I slid to a stop near Adriana who was lying on her back near the water's edge, I yelled again, "What the hell!"

When I found her to be unhurt, I scampered back up the embankment just in time to see the taillights of the van disappearing around a curve. *"You sonof-a-bitch!"* I hollered, shaking my fist. Of course, the vehicle was also well out of the driver's earshot.

I then grabbed Adriana's hand and pulled her up the bank and under a streetlight where I could see that she was alright.

"I'm okay, I'm okay," she said. Checking her clothing, she added, "looks like I've got a huge grass stain on the back of my skirt, though."

"I wish I had hold of that bastard's neck. He'd quickly find out what a French twist was. You're sure you're okay."

"I'm fine. Let's just get on back to the hotel."

We crossed the street and took the sidewalk back toward the hotel, praying that we'd not have another close call. The more I thought about it, the van did appear to be a Honda. However, there were probably hundreds of black Honda vans in the city.

When we got to the hotel, Adriana was still shaking. I put my arm around her and could then feel her relax her body. We took the shortcut through the hotel parking garage and sure enough, there were two black Honda Odysseys sitting in parking spots. As we passed by each one of them, I placed my hand on the hoods. One of them was stone cold while the other was still warm. But that didn't mean it was the one that almost ran us down.

Once back in the room, Adriana took off her skirt and placed it in the hotel laundry bag to send out the next day. "I hope they can get the stain out. I love that skirt."

I smiled. "And I love what's under the skirt." Although she looked tempting standing there in her pink silk underwear, I knew she was too rattled to tend to my needs. We didn't have dessert at the restaurant, and it was for sure I wasn't going to have any of the carnal kind back in the room.

Chapter Five

Adriana was sitting up in the room chair by the window when I opened my eyes Wednesday morning. Her feet were tucked up under her on the seat. She was looking down on the street below. It was just after seven.

"What time did you get up?" I asked her.

"I've been up most of the night. As I was tossing and turning, I didn't want to wake you."

"You weren't able to sleep?"

"I probably got two hours between midnight and 2 AM is my guess. I had a bad dream."

"Tell me about it."

"We were walking along a street…I don't know if it was here in Paris or where…but it was in a city. We were being followed by somebody. He had something in his hand, although I couldn't tell what it was. When we reached a dark part of the street, he sprang on us. Then I woke up."

I swung my legs over the side of the bed, sat up and laid my hand on her bare thigh. "Probably stems from when we were nearly run over."

She nodded. "We could have been killed. We were a second from death. If you hadn't pushed me…"

I squeezed her thigh. "Yeah. But we weren't. I may be getting older, but my reflexes are still like a cat."

She smiled, grabbed hold of my hand and pulled me

off the bed into her. "Come here, kitty kitty."

I knelt in the floor beside the chair. "You're going to feel this lack of sleep sometime about mid-morning."

"I know. But we have to meet the others at the rendezvous point at 9:30 or we'll miss seeing the Eiffel Tower."

"We'll cruise by it on the Seine or in our free time just go on our own. Actually, we've already seen it. Hardly a place in Paris where you can't."

"Nah. Won't be the same. I'll be all right. A shower in the bath closet will help. Afterward, we'll go downstairs to get our granola bar and coffee, then leave."

"You're sure."

"I'm sure. If I get really tired, I'll snooze on the cruise."

As omens go, I wondered if there was anything to them. I recalled having that uneasy feeling back in the restaurant the night before and now she had had a dream about us being attacked. I definitely didn't want her to be fearful the rest of the trip, worried about something dreadful happening. But our day's adventure awaited, and I would help her through any mounting fears as the trip continued.

We met up with the twenty plus other tourists at the Champs de Mars, a park near the tower, at nine-fifteen. The face or faces I looked for were not among them. I figured Santa was not good with possibly being bounced around in the crowd or taking the elevator up in close quarters. There may have also been concerns about whether he would need a restroom.

The elevator did not go all the way to the top,

which Adriana would sometimes say about me. It only took us to the second landing which was plenty high for me. Still on this platform, it was high enough to enjoy a panoramic view of the magnificent city. Across the Seine our guide pointed out the Trocadero Square and Gardens along with the Palais Chaillot and museums. The venue we would visit the next day, Montmartre and Sacre Coeur, sat majestically on the opposite side. And then we had that spectacular, arial view of the place we had visited the day before, the Champs-Elysées and Arc de Triomph.

As warped minds go, I reminded Adriana of the hilarious scene in the European Vacation movie where Rusty throws his beret off the tower that sailed like a Frisbee and the little dog in the arms of the woman standing next to him took a flying leap over the rail to catch it. That image being stuck in my brain, I broke out in laughter.

"You're sick, you know," she said.

"I know."

We knocked down a crepe or two along with a glass of vino at a cafe we found on the way to our departure point where we were to pick up our Seine cruise. Once on board we smiled and nodded to the familiar tour group faces we had seen at the other venues. A couple that we had talked with a few times was from the neighboring state of Virginia. Roy and Liz Farrell were our age, she a pretty brunette like Adriana, and he tall with dark hair, but greying like myself.

As we cruised by Notre Dame, and once again, the Eiffel Tower, Adriana and I chatted with Roy and Liz like we were old friends. He had worked at the Pentagon as a civilian and she was a beautician for over thirty-five years. I told them I retired first with the FBI and then from a job at the state department about eight years back. I didn't tell them in that latter job I hunted down and killed terrorists for a living. We also told them about our inn at Wolf Laurel, but now it was nothing more than our home. However, they were welcome to come visit any time.

In the last couple of days, I had probably taken a hundred fifty pictures with my Nikon. Now, considering we were cruising by hundreds of Paris venues that we could catch from a new perspective, I'd probably take fifty more that afternoon. As we passed under Pont des Art or the Love Lock bridge, the boat's guide told us about lovers who have for years fastened padlocks on the rails of the bridge then tossed the key into the Seine. This ritual signified that their love is locked in, never to be unlocked. I wondered how many of them lost that love with one another and returned to cut the lock off. My quirky mind thinks up stuff like that.

While we sat as a foursome on one of the boat's long benches, I was steadily clicking off photos. Besides snapping pix of iconic scenes and attractions, I took some of our new friends and other tourists that were in our group. As I panned the lens around the boat, I caught sight of Santa and his friend. But as soon as I began focusing the lens on them, Santa's helper, who had apparently been watching me, stood up and walked with his back to me to the opposite side railing of the boat. Most people would think it a coincidence, but as a seasoned behaviorist, my antenna immediately went up. Something was up with this guy…and somehow it had to do with the man in the wheelchair. It was time to put my investigative hat back on.

I did check the digital prints on my Nikon and saw that in random shots of scenes and people on the boat, his face was in one of them. So was Santa's. Sometime during that week, I would email the photos to my friend Keith at the state department to run a facial recognition search. The photo I'd be sending, however, may not prove all that profitable since the bill of the Arab's cap shaded the one eye and his nose. Still, technicians can do remarkable things with photos, even those that are grainy and blurred.

As we were again on our own for dinner, we decided to go to a hole-in-the wall restaurant next door to our hotel. I knew Adriana was still a bit shaken from nearly getting run over the night before and gun shy about walking on narrow sidewalks that ran alongside narrow streets.

Over the dinner table, I discussed with her my gut feelings about the man in the eye patch…and even Santa.

"You're thinking that this little old man who can't move anything but his head is some kind of threat?"

"I don't know about him, but his caregiver definitely didn't want his picture taken. When people drop their heads or turn their backs when a camera is pointed in their direction, they're either Amish or have something to hide. And this guy doesn't drive a buggy and wear a straw hat. I'm sending Lambreau his photo to check facial recognition."

"Oh, come on, Bruce McGowan, you're not going to ruin our vacation by playing G man games."

"Something doesn't smell right with this duo, Adriana, and I'm going to get to the bottom of it. I'm not so sure that van driver last night accidentally lost control of his vehicle."

"Now you're getting paranoid, Skip. Give up on this and just enjoy the rest of our week."

"Okay, sweetheart. I hear you. We won't talk about this anymore."

I did finally get my dessert later that night…that carnal kind I was looking for.

Thursday, we visited the beautiful cathedrals of Paris, beginning at 9:30 with Notre Dame, which is not only the most iconic church in the world, but one of the most inspiring examples of French Gothic architecture. We saw that Santa and his helper were among those on the tour. Although they always didn't stay up with our tour group, my eyes were frequently on them. For the most part I saw that *their* eyes were not interested in following us. They seemed to be more captivated with the stunning exterior architecture of the churches and the magnificent marble statues and columns, gold ceilings and crucifixes, and stained glass on their insides. It almost made me believe I had misjudged the two of them. Maybe I *was* being a bit paranoid.

When we had completed our tour of four cathedrals, and before moving on to the Pantheon, we as a group were carted by trolley to the Cafe de la Paix which is in proximity to the Paris Opera Garnier that we saw on the way from the airport. Although no lunches were included in the tour package, we had the option of eating there or scooting two doors down the street to a quaint little sidewalk cafe. Since we were given a gratis tour by some benevolent person or persons, whose identity I was still determined to find out, we decided to bear the expense. The Cafe de la Paix we found to be an elegant restaurant with fine cuisine and a price to match. The Farrells decided to join us as did about half our group. So did Santa and his six-foot Arab elf. As the wheelchairbound man was not able to ride the trolly, I wondered how he was getting around. Adriana wondered the same thing but reasoned that the tour company was probably making separate arrangements for him.

When we were seated, I immediately had to use the toilet. What we found to be inconvenient if not aggravating was that most of the restaurants had their toilets downstairs separate from the main floor. And they were pay toilets requiring coins…20 c Euro coins. In one restaurant the day before, when I was standing at the trough, a woman came in on me and after dropping her dainties, sat down on the commode behind me. Most of the restrooms in the restaurants were unisex potties with zero privacy.

Nonetheless, I slung my carry bag, not a man's purse, and my Nikon onto the back of my chair and followed the directions to the restroom provided by the garçon. I was elated that not only was it on the same floor, but there was one room for the monsieur and one for the madame. And no coin is required.

As the Farrells had shared a table with us, we had more to talk about…they were mostly about their adult children, and I was about my FBI agent daughter, Caroline, who I found out was assigned to an office in Alexandria only ten miles from where the Farrells lived. Even though our table conversation consumed everyone's attention, I would still look over and catch both Santa and his companion darting their combined three eyes in our direction. It didn't take me long to re-ignite my suspicions.

At two-thirty, our guide, Marcie this time, gave

everyone the high sign that it was time to saddle up. The trolley had just pulled back in and was waiting outside. I had learned in the last few days how to summon the garçon to bring our bill. "L'addition, s'il vous plait." "Very good, Skippy," Adriana said.

"Thank you."

Roy agreed. "You even seem to have mastered the proper French enunciations of your words."

"And thank *you*, Roy."

When our waiter brought the bill and I shelled out the equivalent of sixty-five American dollars for two salads, I reached behind me for my bag and camera. The bag was there but the Nikon was gone.

"Whoa, everyone. I have a problem here. My camera is missing. Someone must have lifted it when I hit the latrine. Did you see anyone get close to our table?"

Adriana said, "The three of us were engaged in conversation and there were waiters and patrons walking by the back of your chair all the while. I'm sorry, Skip, but I just wasn't focused on it. "

Both Roy and Liz shook their heads. He said, "If we had seen anyone grab it, I would've caused a scene. I'm sorry as well, Bruce, I just wasn't paying any attention."

I allowed my head to fall back. "Ohhh, all this week's photos were on it…something we'll never get back." But then I glanced over to Santa and his helper's table. They were gone. It then occurred to me: the caregiver had likely been worried I had captured him on my camera and wasn't taking any chances. Either he was a wanted criminal on the run or a terrorist.

Chapter Six

Although my Nikon was not a high-dollar camera, I had clicked off nearly 200 photos, scenes that we could never recapture. Also, I was intending to download those one or two pictures of the disabled guy and his sidekick to my laptop and forward to my Team Zulu buddy. Since they *and* my camera were missing at the same time, Santa's helper had become even more suspect.

Not only did I summon the cafe's manager to report my camera stolen in his restaurant, but I asked him to call the Paris police. Unfortunately, the time it would take to speak about the theft to the police would cause us to miss our tour of the Pantheon.

About ten minutes later two uniformed officers arrived and sat down with the three of us…Adriana, the cafe manager and moi. One of the officers who spoke fairly fluent English began writing up the incident report. He took probably ten minutes asking questions that covered our personal data, whether we were on a tour and where we were staying. Then he took a look at our passports. He also wanted to know if I might have been aware of someone checking us out. I debated whether to tell the officer my suspicions about my two suspects, because in the unlikely case that I was wrong about them, I especially didn't want the disabled man harassed. I shook my head. But then having the investigative nose that I did, I broke off our conversation and asked the cafe manager, called the directeur, if he had wall cameras installed.

"We have three, Monsieur…one at the front where the cash register is located, one on the side wall there (he pointed) and one at the rear of the cafe."

"Would you be so kind to check them out while the police are here?"

The officer with whom I had been speaking said, "I was preparing to ask him that very question."

"Oui. The tape would be in my office, and I can run it back for you."

"Thanks," I said.

We then followed the directeur to a room off the kitchen where sat a computer of sorts with three screens, one for each camera. He ran the computer back sixty minutes prior to the current time and we stood around him to watch. Momentarily, we were able to see ourselves entering the cafe and once we disappeared from that screen, we saw us being seated at a table toward the middle of the room as picked up by the wall camera. Unfortunately, the images were rather grainy, but we were able to make out Santa and his aide, wearing a black, lightweight jacket, having already been seated three tables over. The third screen providing images from the rear of the room was no help as it was focused on another part of the eating area. We watched the boring footage for nearly thirty minutes until we saw me get up to hit the pisseria. Within thirty seconds, Santa's helper rose from his chair and walked in the direction of our table, preparing to pass by the back of my chair. As luck would have it, bad luck that is, our garçon had stepped into the picture, shielding our view of the man when he was within grabbing distance of my chair. The officer asked the directeur to run the film back, not once but three times. Unfortunately, we were unable to see whether the man had snatched up the Nikon as he went by. Neither could we see anything in his hand as he returned to his table.

"It would appear this man is the only person who walked that close to your chair," the officer said. "But as you can see, our view is blocked by the garçon and there is no evidence that he pulled your camera off the chair back. Also, I cannot see anything in his hand as he returns to the table."

I shook my head. "I see that, but why would this man merely get up from his chair, walk by our table and then return within seconds to his table without going anywhere?"

"I see your point, but even if we can locate this man, we cannot question him without what is called probable cause."

"I understand. I guess I'm just SOL then."

"What is SOL?"

"Never mind. It's just a revered American expression."

We watched the tape further to the point where I paid our bill and then noticed the Nikon was missing. Even while I was sitting in my chair, no other person except our waiter had gotten so close behind me that the camera could be snatched without my realizing it.

The officer then said, "I am sorry we cannot be of further assistance. If we were able to see any theft on the screen, we would have the man."

And so, I was indeed SOL; but this didn't take the two men off the hook as far as I was concerned. If Santa's aide was a seasoned criminal, with a slight-of-hand movement, he could have pulled my camera's strap off the chair back and tucked the Nikon inside his jacket in two seconds without anyone noticing. As I was convinced it could only have been him, I would on my own do the digging the police wouldn't do.

We took a taxi back to the hotel where in our room, I pulled from our vacation brochure the list of names in our tourist group. The list was intended to get us all acquainted with each other, so that we could potentially make friendships that lasted beyond the tour. It consisted of everyone's names and the city and country in which we resided. We saw our names, Bruce and Adriana McGowan, above which were the Farrells from Chantilly, Virginia and so on. Most were husbands and wives, for example Chase and Diana Norquist, but there were also two singles, both women in their fifties. We saw them a couple of times all to themselves looking lonely as hell. Either divorcees or had perhaps lost their husbands. There were two couples with different last names, both male and female. However, I was pretty sure I was able to pinpoint Santa and his helper. Two men's names listed as a couple…John Drake and James Wilson. Their address was surprisingly listed as Paris, France. They were home boys. If these were my suspects, I was sure the names were bogus. Neither name fit Santa's aide who was obviously Middle Eastern. I never heard him speak to the wheelchair-bound man at any point over the past few days, but he was nevertheless attentive to his every need. If I just knew the location of their room…

Adriana was good with merely relaxing and possibly taking a nap that afternoon, we having been hustled through four separate cathedrals in four hours. This gave me an opportunity to venture on my own in and around our hotel to dig up more information on my suspects. Suspects as to what, I didn't know. For now, it was just about the camera.

I knew what the answer would be when I asked at the front desk the room number of John Drake and James Wilson. "I'm sorry, Monsieur, but we cannot give out that information for the security of our guests."

The best I could hope for was to catch them in the lobby when they came back from the Pantheon tour and covertly follow them to their room. Then at some point before the end of our trip, wait for them to leave for dinner somewhere and find a way to break in. Maybe make it happen that very evening.

As our hotel was close to the Seine, I took a walk on the sidewalk along the water's edge down to a pedestrian bridge where I stood watching cruise boats pass beneath me. Occasionally, some of the passengers would wave at me and I'd wave back. This particular bridge was not covered with padlocks, but lovers had still painted their adorations for one another in the form of hearts and initials on the concrete portions. However, there had also been graffiti artists at work, some who had painted symbols and words that appeared to be gang related.

It came so suddenly and unexpectedly, I nearly froze on my feet. However, it only took me a couple of seconds to realize that the first of three bullets had ricocheted off the bridge only inches from my head. After diving onto the concrete to get as low as I could, I raised my head just high enough to see more flashes from the open front window of probably the same black van that nearly ran us over. More ensuing bullets then struck the metal and concrete sides of the bridge. Low-crawling as best I could to the opposite side of the bridge, I encountered two pedestrians who had just stepped onto it. That was when the van sped away, leaving me sprawled out in the prone position in front of the couple. As they had likely not seen or heard the bullets striking the bridge, I'm sure they wondered what was wrong with the poor man lying at their feet.

"Ca va, Monsieur?" the woman asked, which I took to mean "are you alright?"

I nodded then got to my feet. "Pardon-moi, I fell."

I think they understood that and finding I wasn't the worse for wear, went on by me.

Returning to the hotel side of the river, I ran, not so much to hurry back to the room, but in case the shooter set up somewhere else, I'd be a fast-moving target.

I surmised my would-be assassin had used a rifle, maybe with a scope. However, if he did use one, he was a poor shot. Whatever the weapon, it had a silencer.

When I got to the room, out of breath and drenched in sweat, Adriana was sound asleep. I grabbed a Coke from the mini-fridge and threw myself into the chair. I made up my mind I wouldn't tell her someone shot at me. She would immediately panic, pack our bags and make arrangements for us to get the hell out of Paris that very day.

As I sat sipping my Coke, I ran everything that had happened that week through my head. Tuesday night's near miss on the street was intentional. The theft of my camera had everything to do with Santa's aide fearing he might be recognized. The two men had Parisian addresses, and I was sure, bogus names. The bullets that came flying my way were from a locally-supplied weapon. It couldn't have made it through airport security. If the two men were from the Paris area, they were probably getting to all the venues on their own. I had never seen them on a bus or trolley with the rest of the tour group or in a special vehicle provided by the tour company. I did know that Santa needed to be accommodated and that was likely happening via a handicap-equipped van. I had to find the vehicle to be sure. That evening I'd be checking out every black van in the parking garage, especially the one I had found with the warm hood. So, when all suppositions were analyzed, would I have enough evidence?

And then another thought hit me. I don't know why it didn't register before then. Knowing that somebody tried to run me down and then tried to shoot my lights out, I suddenly knew why we were given a free trip to Paris. Our vacation was not from some appreciative benefactor; somebody paid for our trip to lure me to my death. But why Paris? I figured that's where the would-be assassin lived. Maybe he couldn't enter the U.S. because he was a freaking terrorist. But who wanted to kill me now? I hadn't pissed anyone off in Paris. And I'd been out of action for years except for the deja vu thing when I was lured to Scotland by the bad dude there. That was all about WMDs. And the old prick had lost his life, leaving no one I could think of to be mad at me.

I was also now convinced that the bad guy in Paris was the Santa figure in the wheelchair. His caregiver/bodyguard was just his means to get rid of me. I then wondered if he was playing two roles… nursemaid and killer. He was being paid very well to change Santa's diaper…and to find a way to kill me.

The two attempts on my life occurred on the street near our hotel and on the pedestrian bridge. If it was

Santa and company targeting me, they had every opportunity to nail me coming or going from our room. But then I remembered at check-in, the clerk at the desk said the place was well secured with cameras on every floor. There had been a hell of a lot of terrorism in France, thanks to the Islamofascists. Even so, my real concern was now for Adriana. She could get caught up as collateral damage in this deadly game. People all over the world could be mad at me for good reason, but no one could have it in for her. I had unwittingly put her in danger by accepting this trip to Paris. And so, every time we set foot outside our room, we both were targets. I had never in my life of action needed a firearm more than I now needed one in Paris.

Chapter Seven

As someone was set on my demise, I was set on finding out who it was, although I had a pretty good idea. At dinner Thursday evening we shared a table with Roy and Liz. It was not a planned dinner like that of the next night, so the four of us sought out a place near our hotel that gave us a nice view of the Seine. Adriana looked delightful in her fresh makeup, blue jacket, and white pants. I didn't look so bad myself in my new Navy blazer, pink dress shirt, and gray slacks. My bride ordered the onion soup and a side salad while I tried the Quiche Lorraine. The Farrells went a little heavier.

Somewhere in the middle of the dinner, our conversation began focusing on two of the folks in our tour group. I asked Roy, "Have you noticed the old timer in the wheelchair and his caregiver? Of all the restaurants in Paris, they decided to come here as well."

"Santa Claus?" he responded.

I had to laugh. "That's what we call him."

"We were just talking about him earlier. He had a coughing spell this afternoon where he couldn't get his breath and the Arab-looking guy with the eye patch inserted in his mouth some kind of a portable intubating device to clear his airway. Whatever it was it worked in only a few seconds. I really felt sorry for him."

"They were with the group today?"

"Yeah. Why do you ask?"

"No reason," I lied. "They had missed a couple of venues, so I wondered."

There went my theory that the van from where the shots rang out was driven by the Arab guy. Was I wrong about them? If I was, I still believe the caregiver guy stole my camera.

Roy added, "I did talk with the old man after his spell to ask him if he was okay. Seems like a nice enough fellow. He's an American but has lived here for the last fifteen years. I'm not sure about the Arab guy, though. He didn't say much, but he did communicate with our guide about his boss's condition. I hear the old guy is a millionaire ten times over, so he can afford to be kept as he is. Apparently, he has more than one caregiver looking after him."

"Ah ha," I said under my breath. Maybe he also has more henchmen as well, one of which drives a black van and spits bullets at people. Running all this through my brain was starting to stress me out and I don't stress all that easily. The thing was, somebody connected with our group was watching me, following me and trying to find the optimal opportunity to put me in the ground. But why?

Once I acquire suspicions about people, I rarely lose them. I basically trust my initial instincts. And so, I wasn't giving up on my theory that somehow it was the old man who wanted me dead.

When we returned to our hotel, I dropped Adriana off to our room and told her I was going back out to walk off my dinner and creme brûlée and find a good cup of coffee. Although I did want some coffee that had a French twist, it wasn't my main reason for abandoning her. On the spur of the moment, I had decided to camp out in the lobby. Maybe I'd get lucky and catch the odd couple on the move. Even though the old guy was a resident of Paris, was he on the list as staying at the hotel? If so, I had not given up on the idea of breaking into their room at some point. I had to find something that would give me a clue as to who he was.

I had only sat in the leather lobby chair with my coffee for about forty-five minutes, when the door to the hotel opened. Four people entered. First came Santa man in his wheelchair, being pushed by his aide, then came two other Middle Easterners, both of which looked equally as ominous as One-eyed Jamal. The old man slowly turned his head in my direction, his eyes ever menacing. Although he had eyeballed me for the last three days, he would not acknowledge me either with a nod or a bonsoir. But the eyes showed contempt and anger. I thought "what did I ever do to you? And who are you, anyway?"

The other three men didn't look my way, but my eyes followed them through the lobby until they made a right turn into the first-floor hallway. I figured he wouldn't be staying on any of the upper floors as most handicapped people would not be put in a position to use the stairs in case of a fire or failure of the elevator. In his physical state, he wouldn't even be able to get out of his chair.

After they had turned the corner, I sprang from the chair and hustled to the hallway where I saw them entering a room five doors down on the left. At least I knew where they were holed up.

As there were now three such companions, bodyguards, enforcers or whatever they were, any one of them could have been driving the black van. Before I returned to the room, I walked to the parking garage to scout around for the vehicle. In the same spot where I had seen it before, sat the van. I again touched the hood, finding it hot. As the window glass was blacked out, I couldn't see inside; however, there was a handicapped sticker on the front and rear glass and a wheelchair platform on the rear bumper. No doubt about it…it belonged to one of them, probably owned by the old man. All my suspicions about them were now solidified. I knew then and there what I would have to do to protect the two of us. Before the next two days had come to an end, I knew Santa and his henchmen would be making their move.

"Keith, it's Bruce."

"Great to hear from you, old man. Where are you these days?"

"Well, currently Adriana and I are in Paris."

"You dog. I'm stuck here in Washington, and you're still gallivanting around the world, living the high life."

"How's Shirley? Is she still the vixen I left you with in beautiful Yemen?"

"Well, she's still a beauty, but no longer in Camelland. You know we got married, didn't you?"

"You sent me the invitation."

"We have a nice flat here in D.C. and happy as two love bugs."

"Good for you, buddy."

"So, what do I attribute this surprising call to?"

"I need something…and I need it before we leave Paris."

"I would think you have everything you need, Bruce

old boy…you've got all that history and architecture and the lovely Adriana. What more could you want?"

"The one thing I don't have and couldn't bring with me. A high caliber handgun."

"Whoa. What do you need that for?"

"It's a long story, Keith, but the bottom line is, I've got somebody on my ass who wants to kill me. Already tried twice."

"Who did you piss off this time? A better question, who did you kill to piss somebody off enough to want to kill you?"

"I have no idea, Keith, but somebody has tracked me down and arranged for my death in Paris, France of all places."

"Your reputation gets around, doesn't it?"

"I'm done with hunting down bad guys, including sand fleas."

"How can I help you with getting a piece?"

"Contact one of your spook buddies assigned here and have one dropped off to me. You have agency counterparts all over the world. I know you're got one or two here in Paris."

"How long are you going to be there and when would you need it?"

"Two more days. They have to make their move before Sunday when we fly back. I need you to make your call tonight and have it dropped off to me at my hotel first thing in the morning."

"Tall order, Bruce. I don't know if I'll be able to…"

"Imperative, Keith. I've got to protect Adriana and

I can't do it without hardware."

He was silent for a few seconds, but then he came back on. "I know a guy. Can't say his name over the phone. I'm fairly sure he can deliver. Give me the address of your hotel and room number. If I connect with him, you should get a knock on the door in the morning around eight."

"Perfect, my man. I think we leave on another tour at 9:30."

"Anything else I can have delivered…a case of bourbon, a gross of Russian caviar, a Porsche 911…?"

"A full box of ammo."

"You'll owe me on this one."

"Hey, how many times did I save your life in Sandland?"

"Okay, but this makes us even."

"I'll send you my address and room number via text. Thanks, pal. Say hello to our girl Shirley."

I returned to the room just after nine. Adriana expressed her concern as to where I had been for an hour and a half.

"I went down the street and found a Starbucks, then I sat in the lobby for a good while watching people come and go. Saw the Santa man who now has *three* strapping males with him."

"Nurses?"

"Well, I think they do a lot of other things for the old man at his direction."

"That caregiver who's been with him this week gives me the creeps. I didn't tell you, but I've caught him looking at me several times."

"He appreciates American beauty."

"Well, even though I've been avoiding eye contact with him, I can still feel his searing eye crawling all over me."

"As long as it's just his eye."

At six-thirty on that Friday morning, the sounds of city life on the Paris street below began to increase…car and truck motors, honking of horns and the occasional yelling out of a voice. Cities all sound the same wherever you are. We had been sleeping with the window opened which helped erode much of the ever-present, stomach- turning smell of curry. Of course we found that the longer we were subjected to the odor, we thankfully experienced anosmia or what is called smell blindness. The longer one is exposed to an odor, the less it is noticed.

I had been awake since five, but being careful not to disturb my sleeping beauty, I sat up in the chair by the window taking in the lights of Paris from across the Seine. We were fortunate to have been given a city view room where we were able to see the golden lights of the Eiffel Tower, which like a full, romantic moon when gazed upon, had filled and thrilled the heart of many a lover.

I showered around seven-fifteen and donned my clothes for the day, which was a Greg Norman golf shirt and gray slacks, then slipped out the door to go to the lobby for a cup of coffee at the continental bar. I didn't want Adriana to be awakened by someone knocking on the door, so I planned to wait in the lobby for the arrival of the spook which I was sure to recognize when he came in. I also didn't want Adriana to know

I would have a piece on me the next couple of days, which if not a cannon like a .45, I could conceal it under my jacket. I was hoping the gun would be something smaller and thin like a .380 or Colt Mustang 9 mil.

As I sat again in the same chair as the night before, I watched a few early risers leave for their day's excursions, but right up till eight o'clock, only two people entered the hotel from the street. Then, as if on key, at the top of the hour, a forty-ish man dressed in jeans, a light jacket, a Yankees cap, and carrying a small package walked smartly into the lobby. I could spot these CIA types a block away. I can't put my finger on it, but it's the way they carry themselves.

I quickly rose and then joined him at the elevator door. As we stood there, neither of us acknowledged the other, but after the door folded open and we allowed an elderly couple to step out, we stepped in. The door closed and he hit the stop button.

"Scorpion?" he said.

"How did you know?"

"I can spot guys like you in a skinny minute."

I almost laughed as it was exactly what I said in my mind about him. We G men must have a certain body code that makes it easy for other G types to detect. Maybe it's our smell.

"Thanks for the delivery. What do you have?"

"A Sig P365. Compact but packs a punch. As requested, a full box of ammo. Going hunting?"

"Maybe. I detected a threat. It's mainly to provide protection for my wife. Appears something is going to happen before we leave here Sunday."

He handed off the package and we shook hands. After pressing the button that reopened the door, he said, "Get them before they get you."

"I intend to."

"Drop it in the drink before you leave."

"Roger. Thanks."

Then like the spook he was, he vanished down the hallway.

I took the elevator back to our floor, and after quietly entering our 'suite', I went immediately to the bathroom. When I opened the package, I uttered to myself, "Sweet." I then loaded the clip and shoved the Sig into my pocket. It was a perfect fit; however, I would carry it in the pocket of my jacket. It was to begin raining in the afternoon, and the jacket was waterproof.

I loaded up the second clip as well, hoping I wouldn't have to go to it, and then dropped it into my left pants pocket. After disposing of the package, I put the box of remaining ammo in my shaving bag. When I opened the bathroom door, I saw that Adriana was now stirring.

"Morning, lover man. You're already up and dressed. I guess I'd better get my bones moving as well."

I kissed her 'good morning' as she swung out of bed. "Yeah, we will be meeting the tour guide in the lobby in just under an hour."

"It won't take me long to shower and dress. Can you go down and get me a breakfast bar and some coffee?"

"I'm on my way," I replied.

At nine-ten, we joined the other twenty or so tour

buddies in the lobby. Our bus was to leave at nine-thirty. The Santa man and his compadre were not among them. Even though our tour buses were handicap-equipped, being Parisians, I was sure Mr. Drake and Mr. Wilson as usual would be taking their own vehicle up to Montmartre. But, if the other two goons who had followed them in the evening before were the operators of the van I checked out in the garage, was there more than one black van in the picture? I supposed from what Roy Farrell had told me that Santa was wealthy enough to have a fleet of them. The thing was, I didn't know enough about these people to have all the answers. I knew one thing though: unless there was somebody out there the next couple of days with a sniper rifle and a clear, distant shot to bag me, I and my Sig were going to remain vigilant.

With my hole-puncher filling up my right-side jacket pocket and my extra clip in my trousers pocket, I felt a helluva lot more confident about our morning and early afternoon walking tour of Montmartre, its art village, and the Basilica of Sacre Coeur. A half-hour later, when we had reached the pinnacle of the mountain and disembarked, it seemed the entire world opened before our eyes. From the base of Sacre Coeur, I believe other than my Grand Canyon experience and the view of Ansel Adams' Yosemite from Glacier Point, the panoramic view of Paris was the most breathtaking I had ever seen. Adriana stood with her delicate hand over her delicate breasts for minutes on end. The centerpiece, of course, was the far-away Eiffel Tower, which appeared in scale as one of the diminutive replicas one would pick up in a souvenir shop.

We first visited the art village where I haggled with a painter over the price of one of his pieces, only to come away empty-handed. However, when I had turned my back to look at other artists' works, Adriana, who was well-taken with the piece, slipped in and paid the man what he wanted.

When it came to local color, we saw and heard among the people of Montmartre every face and voice that we Americans stereotypically expect from watching movies set in Paris. They were so lively and expressive that we could have spent ninety percent of our week upon that mountain watching and listening to them. And as Adriana assured me, almost every vendor or restaurant employee was immensely friendly.

The only rude look I had gotten that day was from the old dude in the wheelchair. It seemed everywhere we strolled, he and his Arabic companion with the one fierce eye were behind us. Were they waiting for a chance to do me in right there in front of hundreds of people? I wouldn't think so; however, accidents have been known to happen. Maybe he wanted a chance to puff into his plastic straw and run his wheelchair over me at some point. I guess that would be considered an accident.

The tour of the Sacre Coeur Basilica may have been one of the two or three highlights of our trip. As it is the most visited church in all of France, I could see why. Its Romanesque-Byzantine architecture appeared as the Taj Mahal with stone as white as whipped cream. But the most spectacular feature to us was the mosaic in the apse of *Christ in Majesty* where He is standing in white robes with His arms stretched out. Even Santa and his pagan helper seemed mesmerized, spending more than five minutes taking in its beauty.

We had an early afternoon lunch in the village at yet another sidewalk cafe, sharing a couple carafes of wine with the Farrells. There we talked about possibly taking our next tour of Europe together soon… maybe Rome or going on a cruise of the Danube. They were good people. Adriana was well-taken with Liz. I was sure they'd be communicating often when Paris was over.

Chapter Eight

Our bus returned us to the hotel just before three, which gave us a couple of hours to relax in our opulent suite before the planned meal with the rest of the group.

It was a night of good food and merriment at the Le Petit Maison. The elegant country French restaurant only five blocks from our hotel was promising to be the most superfine, French-typical meal we had enjoyed to that point. As soon as we saw each other at the hotel, Roy and I laughed. Not only did we have on the same Navy sport coat as the other, but we were also both in khaki slacks. Most everyone had decided to walk to dinner, even though it was raining and even though the hotel had offered a couple of its large vans. But walking in Paris in the spring rain somehow seemed typecast for the evening, if not just plain romantic.

Once we were seated and the spiffy little garçon, Rene, had taken our wine order, Adriana and the Farrells had a big laugh at what I said about him. "Good thing he's not outside in the rain. With his nose in the air like that, he'd drown for sure." However, toplofty or not, he was neither snooty nor rude. Just an elegant sort of guy was all. Adriana had to invite me yet another time to "be nice."

As we two couples were noticeably very much alike, we had all ordered the same dinners: the salade niçoise and the boeuf bourguignon. "Ah, a most traditional French dinner. Good choice," Rene remarked. It was a heavy meal, but we also found that the bill would be a bit heavy as well…over 113 Euros, equivalent to about $135.00 not including our wine and tip. But we all agreed that Paris was a once, maybe twice in a lifetime experience, so why not splurge a little.

And there they were across the room, once again with eyes on us, Santa and his one-eyed elf. I started to go over and ask for my camera back, but that was just a frivolous idea. We had never spoken a word to them the entire trip, which is very unlike me, always wanting to get something started. The fact that Adriana was with me did a lot to keep me from pushing envelopes that week.

Besides the delectable, stewed beef, we ordered flambé desserts of bananas foster and flaming sorbet, set to fire right at our table. As our attention was fixed on Rene's dessert preparation, I didn't see when Santa and his man left the restaurant. But as Adriana herself had noticed their eyes set on us for most of the dinner, she whispered to me she was relieved they were gone.

Our dinner which lasted almost two hours, mostly due to table conversations, finally ended around eight. I was thinking that we'd all walk back to the hotel as a foursome, but Roy wanted to walk down a little further to a bar he had seen the day before to get a nightcap. As they had acted like a couple of teenagers in love at the table, obviously caught up in the romantic aura of Paris, Adriana figured they might want to be alone. I needed to hit the latrine anyway, so we bid them adieu and a pleasant night.

When I returned from the pisseria, Adriana said she'd like to have just one more glass of wine before we began our walk back. I thought that was a splendid idea, so we took seats at the restaurant bar.

"I've really enjoyed keeping company with the Farrells on this trip," she said. "I'm so glad we got to know them."

"Yeah, nice couple. We have a lot in common. I hope they take us up on our invitation to come for a visit."

"Well, they're not that far away…maybe three hours at the most."

It was then we heard the sirens. Out the large windows of the restaurant we saw the emergency vehicles speed by, their lights making a strobe-like effect as they passed. Although we said nothing about it to one another, my sixth sense kicked in, this time with a feeling of dread.

"You look a bit pale, Skip. Anything wrong?"

"No. I don't know. Maybe. Just have this pit in my stomach."

"Something you ate tonight? I've got an Alka Seltzer back in the room."

"I'm okay. It's not a belly ache. It's…I can't describe it."

She took a last sip of her wine and said, "Come on. Let's go back to the hotel."

We held hands as we walked along the street. The gentle rain had nearly quit, so I folded up our umbrella. At one point she leaned close into me and then when we reached the corner of that block, she grabbed my sport coat, pulled me up to her and kissed me. That made it an even nicer evening.

However, up ahead of us on the street was where we saw the flashing lights of an ambulance and two police cars. As we closed in, we heard the wails. A woman was kneeling over what appeared to be a man lying face down on the sidewalk.

"Oh, my God," Adriana gasped. "That's Liz. And that's Roy lying there."

"Stay here," I said. I then hustled toward where two Paris cops stood. One of them stopped me physically and said something in French that I took to mean "don't go any further."

"Do you speak English?" I asked him.

"A little. You are American, I think."

"Yes, and these are our friends from a tour group."

"The woman is not understandable as she is grieving so much. Do you know their names?"

"They are Roy and Liz Farrell. She should have their passports." I then saw from the illumination of the nearby streetlight Roy's bright red blood covering almost an entire square of the sidewalk. "What happened here?"

"The man has a stab wound in his stomach. He is dead."

As Liz's cries continued, I saw in my peripheral vision, Adriana approaching. She then got down onto her knees to try consoling Liz; however, a second officer pulled both her and Liz to their feet. "I must get her statement," he said in very broken English.

"Can you give her a few minutes?" I asked. She's still in shock.

"Yes."

As one officer reeled out the yellow tape, another

knelt down with an EMT to check out the wound on Roy's body. Adriana and I stood off to the side with Liz. Her hands remained over her mouth as she wept bitterly. "Why," she kept saying over and over. For a few minutes, neither of us said anything, but finally, I said, "Tell me…what exactly happened, Liz."

"We were just walking and…and someone came up behind us. Roy turned and the man took a knife and…" She then began sobbing again.

"Were you able to see his face?"

"He had some kind of mask on his face. But…"

"But what?"

"That's when I heard the voice of another man saying *your* name, Adriana."

"My name? He said *my* name?"

"Yes. He must have thought I was you and that Roy was you, Bruce."

"Did you see the face of that man?"

"No. I think he was back there in the alley."

Adriana had a look of horror on her face. "He thought he had killed you, Skip."

"What exactly did the man say, Liz?" I asked her.

"He…he said something like you weren't invincible and told Adriana to cry hard and long. He then laughed."

"He mistook you two for us, mainly because Roy and I were dressed in the same clothing and the four of us are about the same age. The streetlight is kind of dim and it's fairly foggy as well. I'm sorry, Liz. Roy fell victim to a death meant for me. I feel responsible."

"But why would someone want to kill you?"

"I have no earthly idea. No one knows me here in Paris…or that I would even be *going* to Paris."

Two of the officers then approached Liz and the one who spoke better English asked her to sit in his car and provide her statement. Liz nodded and began sobbing again as she passed by Roy's body. As they moved away toward the car, the coroner then took over to examine his remains. Adriana and I stepped away and stood against the wall of a closed shoe store.

About twenty minutes later, Liz exited the police car and walked over to Roy's covered body. She then stooped down and laid her hand on his head. "Oh, Roy, what have they done to you? Just minutes ago, we were walking on this street, and I had kissed you…" Her sobs turned to wails. After a moment, she stood and Adriana went over to hug her.

"I don't know what to do, Adriana. I don't know where to go tonight. I don't want to go back to the room. But, I…I guess I'll have to stay here in Paris until they release his body. Then we'll both be going home."

After Roy's body was moved to the ambulance, the officer asked if he could take her to the hotel. She said it would be fine. Adriana said when we got back to the room, she would check on her. Liz gave her the room number.

After the police officers asked us to sit and talk in their car, we walked with them to the cruiser. The senior police officer asked for our passports and we handed them across the seat.

It was Officer Gouin who asked, "Monsieur McGowan, Madame Farrell told us the murderer thought he had killed you. She also thought he was mocking your death by saying something to you, Madame McGowan. Why would someone wish to take your life?"

"I have asked myself that same question, Officer Gouin. We are here on vacation where I don't know anyone, nor can I imagine anyone would follow me here from the United States."

"Have there been any other attempts on your life since you have been here?"

Adriana then spoke up. "A van almost ran over us on this very street a few nights ago, but I don't think it was intentional."

I didn't tell the officers about a sniper trying to put me away on the pedestrian bridge. They would wonder why I didn't report it. I should have of course, but I thought maybe I could get to the bottom of the attempts myself. Police involvement would muddy the water. Which led Gouin to the next question.

"Do you know of anyone in your tour group who you might suspect…someone who might have gotten angry with you for some reason?"

I shook my head. Again, if I told of my suspicions about the wheelchair-bound man and his goons, the police would question them and they would be gone without me finding out if they were the people who wanted me dead. In my gut, I knew it was Santa who was after me. I needed to find out on my own why. But in not divulging their identities, was I impeding their investigation and at the same time doing a disservice to Liz Farrell? I was in a real quandary.

"I don't understand all this, Monsieur McGowan.

There must be something you can think of that would help us out. Before you leave Paris, you will need to talk further with our inspectors. We are missing something."

Chapter Nine

With heavy hearts, we walked back to the hotel. I think both of us were too stunned by Roy's death to do any talking. I could tell that even though we only had two blocks to cover, Adriana was noticeably shaking. Her hand tightly grasped mine, and her eyes kept scanning the sidewalk, alleys, and behind us. She was obviously thinking what I was thinking. What if the killer realized it was not me who lay dead and stayed around to make another attempt? We watched every vehicle coming and going on the street beside us, wondering if a black van would suddenly swerve off the road onto the sidewalk. It was especially unnerving for Adriana, and she couldn't get back to the hotel quickly enough.

Instead of entering the front door of the hotel, I purposely walked us through the garage. When we passed the spot where I had seen the black van with the handicapped platform, it wasn't there. I didn't see it anywhere. I then thought, "Why stick around"? Mission accomplished. Santa and friend were back home. They had only been staying in the L'Anglais to follow me and gain an opportunity to take me down. They had done so...so they thought.

We didn't stop by Liz's room that night as we figured she would want to be alone to mourn; however, Adriana did phone her room to check on her. As she listened to Liz cry, tears formed as well in Adriana's eyes. Both of their hearts were broken and as I watched and listened to Adriana's conversation, I myself began spiraling downward into a somber, dispirited state of mind. I couldn't shake the realization that Roy was dead because of me. The question continued to tear at me…why? Who was it that wanted me dead?

Following her phone call with Liz, Adriana and I talked a little, again asking each other what this was all about. We both agreed that we were obviously lured to Paris by the killer who had sprung for the trip. It was not paid for by an appreciative guest of ours or by Keith who was thanking me for saving his life. Nor did the wealthy Atticus Steed arrange it.

After our brief conversation, we undressed and lay on the bed holding each other. Neither of us went directly to sleep as our minds and our moods were fodder. She went to sleep first and then my lights went out a half hour later.

Adriana had no desire to take the tour bus out to Versailles and neither did I; but I wanted to see if the old man in the red beret would be joining the group that Saturday morning. I told Adriana we would otherwise be bored sitting around the hotel if we didn't go and if we struck out on our own to do some local exploring, we would be exposing ourselves to possible danger. There was safety in numbers. Listening to my rationale, she finally agreed.

At nine the next morning, we stopped by Liz's room and rapped on the door. After knocking several times with no response, we figured she was either in the shower or had gone to see the coroner to learn when Roy's body would be released to fly back to Virginia. We then gave up and went downstairs to the lobby. When we met up with the others, our tour guide gathered us all in a circle and told us the sad news about Roy being killed. She said we needed to be vigilant and not go out anywhere that evening alone. We should take taxis or go to restaurants close by in groups of four or more.

One of the men in our tour group was a church pastor from Iowa and asked the guide if he could offer up a prayer for Roy's soul and the comfort of his wife. She thought that would be nice.

As it was 24 kilometers to the palace, it took us twenty or thirty minutes to get there. Upon our arrival, we were all congregated so that we could enter together. We passed through the Golden Gate and took a long look at the sprawling palace. It was the most majestic royal residence I had ever seen, and that included Buckingham Palace, the Alhambra, and America's castle, the Vanderbilt. "You know, it's even grander than the Inn at Wolf Laurel," I quipped, thinking it would put a smile on Adriana's face. Even though I had tried to add a little levity to her morning, her sad expression didn't change.

As it was now our turn as a group to enter the palace, I took one last look around to see if the old man and his sidekick had joined us. They would have arrived in the tour's handicap-equipped van or in theirs. But they never showed. Of course, they wouldn't, if I was right about them, being sure that I was. The old dude had no reason. As far as he was concerned, I was dead.

After our tour of the ornate, sinfully resplendent interior and magnificent gardens, we re-boarded the bus and made our way back to the hotel. There, we found Liz, who, as I suspected, had met with the coroner early that morning. When she opened her room door and saw us, she immediately broke into tears. She said Roy's body would be released the next day and she had already made arrangements to fly him out on Monday. Adriana asked me if she could stay with Liz to keep her company in the afternoon and we could bring her something to eat for dinner. I told her she should do that. I would be in my room spending time on my computer thinking about people from my past who could have it in for me. There could be hundreds of perps I had sent away when I was with the FBI as well as families of terrorist dudes I had put in the ground.

As I sat at the small desk in my room, I made a list in the 'notes' folder on my laptop. Most of the takedowns were of Arab terrorists, as they were who we were primarily focused on when I was an operative in Team Zulu. Perhaps Santa's Middle Eastern legman lost a brother or other family member to one of my bullets. But then I wondered where it was that the old man fit in. Maybe because he paid well, the man served him not only as a physical and medical aide but as a bodyguard as well. The old guy was supposed to be a multimillionaire and, in his condition, could be at immense personal risk.

I had downloaded on my computer photos of a few of the bad boys I had wasted or locked up, especially in my latter years of government work, as well as from wanted flyers provided by the Bureau, NSA, Interpol, and, of course, those compiled by my former state department employer, CTT. Some were domestic terrorists as well. Maybe seeing a photo of one of them would jar something in my brain.

I spent the better part of the afternoon looking at photos and reading flyers about perhaps three hundred bad dudes. By four o'clock, my eyes were burning, and my lids were heavy. I then shut down the laptop and stretched out on the bed.

Sometimes, eureka moments come to me unexpectedly, either from out of my unconscious or from stored memories that I thought had long since dissipated. And then sometimes revelations come out of dreams. It was that afternoon, having suddenly awakened from a nap, a dream caused me to sit straight up in the bed and yell, "Holy shit!" I had seen in that dream the man's face.

I then jumped from the end of the bed to the desk chair and turned on my computer once again. Going back to those photos, I scrolled about halfway down until I landed on the face of the man who I now knew had been trying to kill me. He was the most evil of all the nemeses from my past. The last time I saw him was maybe seventeen years before as he was lying totally paralyzed in a hospital bed, and I, with the muzzle of my pistol against his head, was debating whether to pull the trigger. Santa Man was the homegrown terrorist in the Weather Underground who I not only had arrested years before while an FBI agent, but in taking him down, unintentionally emasculated him by kicking him in the gonads. Out of the blue, a few years later, he re-entered my life by kidnapping my daughter, Caroline, to lure me into his compound, after which he intended to kill me. To make a long story short, after I escaped from his clutches with Caroline, the madman showed up at Adriana's and my outdoor wedding on the grounds of Wolf Laurel. In his attempt to shoot me, he instead shot Adriana, almost ending her life. That's when my FBI daughter Caroline put a well-placed bullet in his spine, ergo, the paralyzed man in the wheelchair. Oh, I didn't mention he was mad at me for another reason; I also put his mama in jail for the rest of her life. I later heard that she had died there.

Jonas Karn. The last I heard about him, he was not even supposed to be able to sit up nor even move anything but his eyeballs. And how did he escape perpetual care in a U.S. prison hospital and wind up in Paris, France, a multimillionaire? And it was little wonder I didn't recognize him. A man in his sixties looking eighty-five, coke-bottle lens glasses and that full, white Santa beard. But obviously, he still hated me enough to concoct the elaborate scheme of luring me to France to kill me. I assumed that the way he ended up in France, he would not be able to re-enter the U.S. Somebody had arranged to get him out of the States as he couldn't do it himself. It could be over the last fifteen to seventeen years; however, he was released from prison, much having to do with his immobility. Maybe the parole board had taken pity on him.

About the time I came to the revelation that the man in question was Karn, Adriana returned to the room. "What did you do all afternoon?" she asked.

"I spent a little time on the computer, had a Coke from the fridge, took a nap, and oh, there was that other thing…learned who the old man in the wheelchair is."

"What? You found out?"

"He's the man who interrupted our wedding, my dear…the man who shot you in the back. I took the photo I have of him on my laptop and, with my face alteration app, added a beard and thick glasses and aged him. It's him."

"Karn? Jonas Karn?"

"You remembered his name."

"How could I forget anything about that bastard?" A little unlike my darling wife to say that word.

"Yeah, somehow, he found his way over here and all these years later, still has a hard-on about me. He's our benefactor. Spends a little money to make a big kill."

"The thing is…he killed the wrong man."

"Yeah, how inept *are* he and his assassins? They drive a car at us but miss us; they shoot a half dozen rounds at me while I'm walking; they mistakenly stab the wrong man to death."

It was an oops moment.

"What do you mean they shot at you? You didn't tell me that."

"I didn't want to worry you. Yeah, yesterday, while you were taking a nap, I took a walk. I made it as far as the pedestrian bridge down the street and some potshots rang out from the window of a black van. It was when Karn and his bodyguard were at the Pantheon. That means he has more thugs working for him."

Adriana allowed her head to roll back. "God, what more? I'm glad we're out of here tomorrow. What else can happen before we leave?"

"Likely nothing. He thinks I'm dead, remember? That is unless he catches the news or has a friend still at the hotel who heard about Roy."

"Well, we can't take any chances that he found out. We're not stepping foot outside this hotel until we get our transportation to the airport tomorrow morning."

"The thing is, we know Karn is still out there. He might just take his vendetta to our very front door at home."

"Possibly. But unless he was paroled or served all his term, he may not be able to get back into the U.S. I have no idea how he even got out."

She sat down and placed her fingertips over her face. "This is all very distressing. Such an end to a lovely trip."

"Sorry, babe. How was Liz this afternoon?"

"I think my going to spend a little time with her helped. Mostly, I just listened to her reminisce about the good times with Roy…how they met, their marriage, their life together and all the fun they had with their kids. It was a catharsis for her. She had called their son and daughter last night to give them the horrible news. Not something anyone would expect to happen while taking a lovely vacation. She'll be torn up for quite a while."

"And it happened because of me."

"You can't say that, Skip. And she doesn't blame you. She just wants the bastard who did it to pay with his life." There was that word again.

"If I have anything to do with his capture, he will."

"No. The police will do their job. They'll locate Karn and he will go down."

"If he has all the money he's supposed to have, they'll know about him. Somehow, at some point, he'll go down."

"And *you* won't have anything to do with it. We're going home."

"Right."

Chapter Ten

Just as we were preparing to order a pissaladiere to our room, which, by the way, has nothing to do with the urinary system, actually a French version of a pizza, we heard a knock at the door. It startled Adriana to the point where she jumped. Although I didn't think it would be Karn or one of his boys, I opened the eye slot on the door and peered out. On the other side were a uniformed police officer and a man dressed in a suit.

"It's okay," I said to her and opened the door.

Our guests were Officer Gouin and what appeared to be a detective. Gouin put his fingers to his cap and said, "Monsieur McGowan, I must introduce you to Detective Lieutenant Allard of the French National Police from the Seine-Saint-Denis precinct. He would like to ask you some questions. May we come in?"

I waved my hand toward the room's interior. "Yes. Please do."

When Gouin entered and saw Adriana, he removed his cap and smartly dropped his head. "Madame," he said.

Lieutenant Allard, a nice-looking, dark-haired gent in his mid-forties, walked further in, politely clicked his heels, and nodded to her as well.

I said, "I don't have but the desk chair and the room chair by the window…"

Allard held up his hand and replied, "I would prefer you to sit at the desk chair, Monsieur."

"The old, third-degree, huh?" I quipped.

"Pardon?"

"Sorry, I'll take the chair."

"You may wish to have the Madame leave the room while we ask you questions," the lieutenant said.

"No, I don't wish. I'm sure you're here about the murder. She was there with me and can hear all your questions."

"But there are questions about *you* that you may not wish her to hear."

"She knows everything about me. We came upon last night's murder probably fifteen minutes after it happened. Why are you here to talk to me?"

"Because, Monsieur, the man who committed the murder intended to kill *you*. I would like to know why."

I didn't respond.

"Let me put it this way…I checked on you through Interpol. You have a history with many stories, Monsieur. You worked for an organization within your government that would make you many enemies. Your name appears connected with several fatal endings. Now are you sure you want your madame to hear these things?"

What he said surprised me. I didn't know how he knew this. I knew Interpol had a file on people like me in federal law enforcement, but what they *did* have probably amounted to less than twenty percent of every case I worked on with the counter-terrorist team, the super- covert unit it was.

"I know about my husband's history, Lieutenant Allard," Adriana answered for me. "There is nothing that would be shocking."

"I will ask you this now, Monsieur; do you know who wanted to kill you?"

Now that I knew for sure who it was, I was not going to keep it a secret. Karn had to be found out… and questioned. Even if I would be going after him myself, I needed them to do the leg work.

"Maybe. I have recognized a man in our tour group as someone who I had arrested while a government agent many years ago. He wanted revenge on me and kidnapped my daughter. To his misfortune, my daughter ended up shooting him and he became an invalid. He was placed in a prison hospital, then somehow ended up here in Paris. If I were you, I would look at *him*."

"A very interesting story. How would he learn that you were here? It would be so much a coincidence for him to be in your tour group at the same time you are here."

"I wouldn't know that. All I can say is he must have had people knowing when we were coming and going back in the states and figured since he lived here and knew we were to visit Paris, he'd be waiting on me." I didn't tell him that Karn likely paid for our trip to lure us here.

"You know that he lives here?"

"No, I don't. Just a guess. Like I said, he's not able to travel all over the world as he's paralyzed from the neck down. However, I understand that he had mentioned to the man who was murdered that he lived outside of Paris."

"I see. What is this man's name?"

"The man I recognized is named Jonas Karn. Have you heard that name? He has bodyguards and people who give him care."

"You are sure it is the same man?"

"Yes."

"But you did not recognize the man when you first saw him."

"That's correct. His looks have changed. He has thick glasses, a full white beard, and wears a French-looking beret."

"Is he going by that name in the tour group?"

"No."

"What name then?"

"I don't know. I haven't heard the tour guide say his name in front of the group."

Allard glanced at Officer Gouin. "Monsieur Gouin, you were at the murder scene last night. Do you have any questions for him?"

"I am only wondering how Madame Farrell is doing today. Have you seen her?"

Adriana nodded. "Yes, sir. I spent the afternoon mostly consoling her."

"That is very good of you, Madame," he said.

Allard then asked, "Monsieur, when did you plan to return to the United States?"

"We have a flight out of de Gaulle tomorrow morning."

"The Madame may have one, but you do not. I must request you stay for a few days. I am sure we will have more questions and when we do locate this man, you will have to identify him."

"That's out of the question, Lieutenant. We're both going back tomorrow."

"Then I must insist, Monsieur McGowan. I will make you a guest of our fair city. I do not wish to place you in custody, but I will."

"You won't do that. With the assistance of the American Consulate or Embassy, I will be on a plane in a matter of hours."

"You are subject to the laws of France while you are visiting here, sir."

"You can detain me for having committed a crime, which I have not. I don't like being threatened. If it were not for seeing my wife home, I might voluntarily stay a few extra days to help you with this man's profile."

Adriana then said, "Bruce, I can get home without a problem on my own. Not to worry. If all you'd be doing is sharing information with the Paris police to catch Jonas Karn, I am fine with you staying a few extra days." She then looked at the lieutenant. "But you, sir, must provide protection for my husband 24/7. If and when Karn gets wind of Bruce still being alive and finds out where he is, he won't stop before he tries to kill him again."

Adriana's agreeing for me to stay on in Paris surprised me; but I knew she wanted Karn apprehended as much as I did. The man who had almost killed her the day of our wedding, had indeed killed her new friend's husband.

"If I do this, it will be on two conditions: I'll need

to see my wife onto the plane in the morning and I request that you put me up in a hotel elsewhere…a nicer hotel at that."

"I can do that. I have arrangements with several hotel owners that they will give our witnesses lodging free of charge. We will also provide for your meals."

"Then I will agree to it," I said. "But if you have made no real progress in locating Karn by Thursday of next week, I'm leaving anyway. As much as I love your city, I will not make it my residence."

Allard nodded. "Tomorrow you make sure your wife is in the air and then get a taxi to the address on my card." He handed it off to me. "We have much more to talk about where it involves this Jonas Karn."

When the officers left, I asked Adriana, "Are you sure about this?"

"I'm sure. If the police will protect you, I'll be confident you'll not be in any danger."

"All right, then. It's settled," I said. "Let's order our dinner. Pizza and a movie. Like being back home."

"Except there are only eight channels on our TV, and the only movie being shown is in French without English subtitles, a real classic at that…*Mega Shark Vs. Crocotaurus.*"

I laughed. "Then check to see if reruns of Laverne and Shirley are on."

Sunday morning, we both checked out of the hotel with our bags and took the shuttle to the airport. As I could only go as far with her as the ticket counter, I stood as she checked her bags. Once that was accomplished, she was ready to go through security. For a few moments, we stood off to the side, embracing one another in a hug. She then took a short step back. With eyebrows arched and lips trembling, she searched my eyes back and forth. They were filled with tears. "You don't get yourself hurt and please stay close to the police officers. Give them what they need about this bastard and get on home as soon as you can." There it was again. I'd never heard her say the word *bastard.* She had either been around me too long or just plain despised Karn enough to call him one.

"I'll see you sometime next week. Talk every day?"

"Yes," she replied. "Call me before nine in the evening Paris time. Should be three my time."

"Okay. Be careful around the house. Be vigilant just in case..."

"He won't be coming my way and the police here will get him in no time at all."

I smiled and nodded. "You gotta get going. Your flight leaves in forty minutes and you have to get through this maze."

She kissed me long and tenderly and then pulled away from my hand. I knew she was concerned for me, still thinking about what happened to Liz's husband. That made her worry even more and she had eight hours to think about it on the flight just to New York.

Chapter Eleven

I had no problem with staying to help the police locate Jonas Karn as this man needed to be put away for good. Karn by himself was not much of a threat, however. It was his killers and his money to keep hiring killers that were. I knew that as long as he was alive, they would keep coming. But here was the caveat; I was only going to assist the police long enough until I had enough information on him. If I knew he was living in Paris or in its suburbs, I on my own would be going after him. I'd do things the Scorpion way.

After I knew Adriana's flight was in the air, I went to the rental counter to secure a vehicle. Assuring the Renault they assigned me had GPS, I then gave the agency my credit card information. However, before starting off, I loaded in the precinct's address. On the way to the police station, I was already missing Adriana. She may have been my wife of seventeen years, but she was still as young, fresh and gorgeous as she ever was. The best thing that ever happened to me except for the birth of my daughter.

In less than twenty minutes I pulled into the Seine-Saint-Denis precinct parking lot. After entering the front of the building, I was screened for hardware but them finding none, I was sent on through. My Sig 365 I had left in the car. After stopping at a desk with a police sergeant behind it, I asked to be directed to Lieutenant Allard's office. He spoke English. "On the second floor, first door on the right upon exiting the elevator."

When I entered Allard's office, I saw that he was

standing near the door talking with one of his technicians. "Come in. Monsieur McGowan. You did make it to us after all." His accent in the pronunciation of English words was thicker than I remembered from the day before, but his command of our language was very good. When he spoke, I had this image in my mind of Inspector Clouseau.

"I'm here as promised. Wifeless and homeless."

"Do not worry. I have arranged a nice room for you at the Saint-Loraine which is within walking distance from where we are. But for now, we need to go back to my office to begin a further interrogation."

"I think of interrogations as done to criminals. Suggest we just call it an exchange of information."

That's the first time I had seen him smile. "Yes, exchange of information." He then waved me ahead of him into his office.

After showing me to a chair in front of his desk, he said, "Coffee?"

"Do you have any French Roast?" It was my turn to smile. It was how I wanted our conversations to go…cordial and congenial.

The coffee was good, but I think it was more Colombian than French.

"And so, Monsieur McGowan, I did some digging, as you Americans say, into the name Jonas Karn and could find nothing. There are three Karns that I found, but no Jonas. One was a woman whose husband, Josef, died about five years ago; another was a young man named Peter Karn who lives alone; and the third is a French Naval officer who is currently on assignment.

His home is shut up for a year or until he returns from sea, according to the neighbors. The woman and young man were interviewed and neither have a relative from the United States named Jonas. None of them are very wealthy."

"Lieutenant, Jonas Karn didn't provide his right name on the tour, so I expect that he would not take residence under the name of Jonas Karn. He gave the tour agency fictitious names for him and his caregiver which were John Drake and James Wilson. You could run those, but you'd be just barking up a tree."

"Barking up…?"

"One of many American expressions. Sorry. I've also never known of a Middle Eastern man having anything similar to either name."

"I believe we will question the people at the hotel as well as the tour company. Perhaps somebody will know his identity."

"I thought about doing that myself."

"But you are not a police officer, and you must leave the investigation to us. That is one thing I must caution you against…getting involved in our investigation by 'digging' as you say."

"I don't plan to get in your way, Lieutenant, but I'm the target here. I'm not going to crawl in a hole and just wait for him to make his move on me."

"From what I understand, he believes he killed you."

"But Roy Farrell's murder two nights ago on that street will be covered in the newspaper and on television, if it hasn't already. He will know it was a mistake of identity."

"You are correct, Monsieur, and that is why he will need to be flushed out."

"Using my live body as bait."

"Not in so many words. But from your Interpol file, which contains information from FBI, MI-6 and your state department, you are or were a man who can take care of himself."

"I'm not afraid of this thing, Lieutenant; it's just I'm used to taking the offense rather than waiting on my adversaries to make the move."

"Your days of action are behind you, and in my city, you will not use the tactics you were so well trained to use. We will know your every move, Monsieur McGowan, just like we would have eyes on a criminal. But do not worry; you will not be treated as a criminal unless you become one."

Well, so much for the amicability I was looking for.

"I hear you loud and clear, Lieutenant. I'll tell you everything I know about Jonas Karn to include what both my daughter and I went through with this prick. But I expect you to tell me about anything you turn up. That's what I meant about *exchange* of information."

He nodded. "We will make this work. Now, I would like to hear what happened to you seventeen years ago regarding this man."

I gave Allard every detail I knew about Jonas Karn beginning with his Weather Underground activities back in the late 60s and early 70s. "Karn was hooked in with domestic terrorists such as Bill Ayers and Bernadette Dohrn who had actually declared war on America. Responsible for bombings at the Pentagon and in the U.S. Capitol building, their commie-related activities soon came to an end when the radical group was finally rounded up. I was a special agent with the FBI then. My piece of the action was Mister Karn. When he resisted my arrest and wanted to get personal, my size 10 neolite into his testicles changed not only his voice but his sex life. Why on earth would that make him mad enough to kidnap my daughter when he finally got out of prison thirty years later was beyond me.

"When I zoomed in like Batman to rescue her, I ended up getting shot in the back by none other than his mother. She was handcuffed in the back seat of my car. I didn't know she had a large caliber pistol in her brassiere. The bullet went through the front seat and into my back. I lived, as you can see. However, I was later able to get Caroline out of his clutches and see the end of the new and improved Underground gang with one catastrophic explosion of their bombmaking factory. Karn had escaped before the place went up, but then a few weeks later interrupted my wedding ready to plug me. Unfortunately, my lovely soon-to-be-wife, whom you met, took the round. Karn's spine then took my daughter's round which made him the quadriplegic you will find him to be, that is if you ever do find him."

"Then at some point, he had to be released from jail."

"Appears so, although I haven't had the interest over the years to keep track of him."

"Your story has much intrigue, Monsieur; like something from a novel or movie."

"As you told me yesterday, I've lived a storied life as a government agent."

"What did you do for your government after you retired from the FBI?"

"I worked for the U.S. Department of State."

"As…?"

"As someone who still wanted to make some money. I wasn't retirement age and still needed an income."

"That is not the answer for which I was looking."

"I know."

"Will I get the answer?"

"Probably not."

"You are a very evasive gentleman, Bruce McGowan."

"At least you recognize me as a gentleman."

He rolled his eyes which I believe is a universal symbol for "You're a putz."

"I will today be ordering an Interpol check, to include its 18 databases, on this Jonas Karn which should provide his complete criminal record, release dates and his last known address. This will be our start and we will follow up on all leads."

"And as I asked, you will keep me informed?"

"With general information. But when it will involve our police activities, I can share very little. Our investigation methods should not concern you. You will only receive the results when we are able to locate something as to the man. I want you to make yourself as comfortable as you wish, but remain available for more discussion when we need you. It will be very important that you not only answer our questions when they come up but be close by for identification when we bring him in."

If you bring him in, I wanted to say. But I actually said, "I'll be around, Lieutenant."

"Then you may go check in at your hotel and have a nice lunch."

I stood, shook his hand and nodded sharply as they did there in the land of fine wine and cheese.

The Saint-Loraine rated five stars in my book. I wished the flea bag Adriana and I had stayed in had been half as nice. My room was on the eighth floor and boasted a separate sitting room. The bath had both a tub and a shower as well as a full complement of fragrant toiletries. And sitting across from my kingsized bed was a 36-inch flat screen TV. I wondered how much the room was setting the National Police back.

After a short nap, I grabbed a ham and cheese baguette at the hotel's cafe and returned to my room to plan a little investigation of my own. I still had all the tour company's information in my bag to include their phone number, but I was looking for the actual address. Little can be accomplished over the phone, as I found out with them before we left on the trip. They could not or would not give me the name of the person who sprang for the trip for privacy purposes they said. Even if they would give it to me, I knew the name would not be Jonas Karn. The tour company had positioned a representative at the L'Anglais while we were there, but I wasn't sure if she was still on site.

As the address was not included in the packet, I went to my laptop. After failing to find it on their website, it took me the accessing of three or four links to finally locate one. It was through France's version of a Yelp site. The address was 14724 Marie de Medicis in

Paris. At least it wasn't a P.O. box, but it could well have been a hole- in-the-wall outfit sharing office space with a dozen other companies in one building, the company itself having a single individual working out of a lone desk. The phone number listed, however, matched the number I had called back at Wolf Laurel.

For the rest of that Sunday, I laid around in my very nice room, taking advantage of the minibar, then had dinner at a place called Le Rose. I knew Adriana would still be in the air, so there was no use in trying to call her. I passed out around 9:30 watching TV and then it only seemed like five minutes had lapsed until I woke the next morning at seven. After a nice long shower and a breakfast of scrambled eggs, bacon and English muffin, I took a short walk. It may have been the nicest morning I had happened upon in an entire week, what with the sun basking my face and the aroma of lilacs perfuming the air. It was what Paris *should* be in the spring.

At eleven, I was back at the hotel parking lot putting the address of the Saint-Amaury Travel Agency into the car's GPS. I then pulled away and began following the directions. After I found myself twice on one-way streets and having a score of near misses from drivers who only took traffic lights to be suggestions, I turned into a parking garage on Marie de Medicis Street. Upon entering the building at 14724 through the garage, I found myself in front of a direction board. Running my finger along the glass down to the S's, I found it. Third floor, Room 129.

I did see that it was a real business complete with a half dozen employees at their desks. A pretty receptionist who would have beautifully fit the baby doll outfit of that aforementioned French maid, asked me something in French. I replied, "Je suis Americaine," just as Adriana taught me.

"Ah, then good morning, Monsieur. How may I help you?"

"Yes. I just completed one of your tours of Paris and would like to speak to the person here who arranged it…maybe the young lady I spoke with on the phone."

"I hope there was no problem."

I wanted to say, 'The only problem was that somebody tried to kill me, not once but three times.'

"No, it was very nice," I really said. "I just have a couple of questions for her."

The receptionist took my name and tour information and then pulled me up on her computer. "Your tour host was Suzanne."

"Yes, I remember now."

"She is here. I will see if she is available."

I was impressed by how many of the French spoke English perfectly. But then I remembered that merry old England was just across the channel.

A few moments later, she said, "Suzanne will see you now. She is the lady sitting at the second desk there."

"Merci," I smartly said. I was getting the hang of this French-fried language.

When I walked over to her desk, she stood and took my hand. However, she held it so long, I wondered if she was ever going to give it back.

"Monsieur McGowan. I now have a face with a

name. I do remember speaking to you maybe two months ago and how funny you were on the phone."

"Yep, that's me; a veritable comedy act."

"I understand from Yvette that you and your wife did enjoy your vacation to Paris. I am so happy. That is what we like to hear. I will also be sending you a survey to complete."

Of course, you will…just like everyone else in the world. But I didn't actually say that either. I just nodded.

"What can I do for you, sir?"

"Well, I know that someone had paid for our trip, but preferred to remain anonymous. Since I'm here in your office, I thought I would ask you again if you had the person's name." While I was sitting beside her desk, she pulled up my tour information.

"Yes, it was paid by someone who did not want you to know his name. We cannot go against his wishes."

"So, the person was a *he.*"

"I suppose I can tell you that much. Yes."

"I have a very wealthy uncle who lives here in Paris, and I was wondering if it was him."

"Again, I cannot tell you that."

"I understand. You wouldn't want…" And that was when my theatrical talent kicked in. I touched my fingers to my brow and began to wobble in my chair.

"Is there something wrong, Monsieur? Do you feel alright?"

"Just a little dizzy. I…"

"Shall I call someone for you?"

"No, but I could use a cup of water."

I was counting on her concern for my well-being and that she would jump up to get the water. She did. And she did what I hoped. She left her computer screen up.

"I will get you a bottle from our refrigerateur."

As soon as she disappeared around the corner of the room, I leaned into her screen. Unable to read the words on the screen, mainly because it was in French, I clicked off a picture of it on my cellphone. And that was just in the nick of time, as Suzanne's form reappeared around the corner. I had quickly returned to my dizzy-man look, head down and fingers on my forehead.

"Here you are, Monsieur. I hope you do not have a medical problem."

"It's something that occurs sometimes…maybe low blood sugar."

"I can also get you something with sugar such as orange juice or a nice cookie."

I sucked down about a third of the water, then said, "Thanks, Suzanne. I think you have given me what I needed."

Slowly, I began rising from the chair and supported myself with my hand on her desk. "I guess I'd better go."

"I am sorry I could not give you the name of the good man who paid for your trip. It is policy, you know."

"I know and I appreciate your integrity."

"Is there more I can do for you?"

"No, Suzanne. I hope you have a good rest of the day."

"I hope you are able to make it out of the building fine. Is someone waiting for you in an auto?"

"No, but already I'm feeling stronger."

"I can have someone walk with you."

"You are very nice, Suzanne, but I won't need anyone."

After I left the Saint-Amaury office, I began feeling a little guilty for having taken advantage of such a nice young lady…someone who had a genuine concern for me. Just a *wee bit* guilty.

Chapter Twelve

I waited until I got back to the room to try figuring out the words on my cellphone screen. I thought maybe I could access a French to English site and translate what I was reading. For the most part, that worked. But what I was really looking for was a name imbedded in the French gibberish. I saw mine and Adriana's in a few places and others associated with the travel agency. However, maybe because my screen was so small, I almost missed the word *payeur* in the long document. To be sure I had guessed the correct translation, I looked it up. The English word was *payor*. And the name beside the word was Henri Cadieux. Was this an entirely different person or did Karn take a French name when he came to France? It had to be Karn because I knew I couldn't be wrong about his purchase of our trip being the connection. Allard had already found there was no Jonas Karn in all of Paris and its suburbs.

I had the upper hand, information-wise, over Allard and his people. The lieutenant hadn't known that anyone had paid for our trip and as such, couldn't know it was the lure that brought us to Paris and tied Karn to me. He was still scratching his head as to how Karn and I, with our history, could possibly have ended up on the same tour. He would still be following up with the hotel and tour company on the names John Drake and James Wilson. If he continued on that futile track, he would remain two steps behind me.

It wasn't a competition for me nor was I intending to withhold evidence. It was not even evidence at this point. Suppositions don't count. I wasn't all that sure that Henri Cadieux and Jonas Karn were one and the same.

When I looked up *Cadieux* on the internet, expecting to find a long list of people with that name, which I did, the first thing that popped up was the meaning of the name…' little fighter.' I guessed that Karn was every bit of that. He was a small man and a survivor. He survived me twice and a hospital prison. Now he was surviving as a quad in a wheelchair. Little Fighter might have been appropriate. I wondered if he knew the meaning of that name and that's why he chose it.

So, did I have enough information to find him? I would be most fortunate to find a telephone book, which was still utilized in France, and place my finger on his name. On the internet there had been a cool hundred Cadieuxs listed in the Paris white pages. I did find something interesting, however: an internet article about an upcoming party of celebration that was being thrown at the wealthy Henri Cadieux's home. Celebrating what? My demise? The article wasn't specific. And there was no photo of him.

But as I stared at the name, I kept saying under my breath, "Who are you, Henri Cadieux? Are you the maggot I'm looking for?"

I did see that Cadieux resided on a gated estate called Ramatuelle. As memory served me, there was a village or commune I read about in southern France near the French Riviera with the same name. I learned about it from an old Greenbrier native who had a bit of money himself and liked to vacation there. But, according to Google, the Cadieux Ramatuelle was a private estate on the west side of Paris not far from Versailles. It appeared the proprietor of Ramatuelle had his own modern but smaller version of Versailles to enjoy. If Karn *was* Cadieux, how the hell did he get all his money? When I encountered him, especially on the last go-round, he was not only lying in a hospital bed as immobile as a statue, but financially down and out for the count. I thought my last adventure in Scotland and Yemen was weird, but this was beyond my comprehension.

The gnawing dilemma was whether I should turn all this over to Allard, first coming clean about the probable connection between Karn's money and our trip, and then that I found him. But if I did that and he ended up collaring Karn, I wouldn't have the opportunity I was looking for to kill the man. He needed killing. It was time the bastard left the earth, or had it shoveled over him, once and for all.

But here's what I was thinking. Cadieux's party was slated for the coming Friday night, four days away, and I was planning to crash it. I didn't know whether I could stick around that long, but I figured Allard would want me to as long as I could in case he did nail Karn and wanted me to identify him. And then again, as I was staying at the upscale Saint-Loraine on the police department's nickel, I wondered how long I could ride *that* pony.

That afternoon I dug a little deeper and found out through an internet source the address of the Ramatuelle estate. Even though I had planned to slip in on the party Friday evening, I couldn't fathom sitting around in my hotel room for four days playing tiddlywinks. So, I jumped in the rental, downloaded the address and set out for Ramatuelle.

It wasn't hard to find. On the same two lane, winding road that led to Versailles, I found it sitting on a hill surrounded by a dozen acres and a tenfoot-high fence. The house, a sprawling stucco with six chimneys and a five-car garage looking every bit as palatial as the something the Hearsts might own, appeared to be about 15,000 square feet. What I would accomplish there I didn't have the foggiest, but I just wanted to know where the place was. I couldn't imagine it was Karn's; however, every piece of the puzzle that I had come up with told me Karn was within those walls. How he got there was anyone's guess. Did he mastermind a Brinks job, or did he inherit the place? His mother was an old crone living in a broken-down house in Colorado and unless there was another relative with a lot of wealth, I didn't know about who croaked and left him the estate, none of it made sense.

I had sat in my rental for something of an hour about three hundred feet from his ornate, iron gate when a black van followed by a large SUV approached from the east. Slowly, the gate opened allowing both vehicles to whisk through. I watched them through the iron fence all the way along the driveway until they reached the front of the house. Seconds after they came to a stop, the sliding door on the van opened and the driver dressed in black jumped out. That's when my tenacity paid off. When the van's ramp came down, a wheelchair bearing a man wearing a red beret rolled out onto the driveway. Bingo.

After 'Mr. Cadieux,' his driver and the two goons from the SUV began making their way into the house, I sat for a few minutes thinking about what I would do from there. I wished like hell I had had my Remington 700 sniper rifle with me with Karn in my crosshairs. I'd loved to have watched him roll out of his chair and splatter onto the concrete.

But as I sat there, I thought maybe I needed to play ball with Allard. Yes, I wanted Karn dead, but nobody goes to the guillotine anymore. The death penalty was abolished in France a few decades ago. I almost flipped a coin; heads I turn him in, tails he digests the bullet. I had four days to think about it.

Monday evening Adriana called. It was two-thirty her time. The first thing she said was "I miss you,"

"And I you. You made it home okay?"

"Actually, I just got home. I had two flight delays…one in New York and again to Charleston. I thought I'd *never* get here."

"But you made it safely."

"Yes. I didn't tell you I had a wonderful time with you in Paris. I hate it about Liz's husband, though. I'll be contacting her in a few days to see how she's making it."

"That would be nice."

"Although hearing my voice might restart her grief. When any friend of mine begins bawling, I start as well. So, how are you making it there? Is that lieutenant still giving you the third degree?"

"Not too much. He still wants me to stay around a few days to help him with Karn's profile. If and when they bring him in, he wants me to identify him."

"Do you know if Karn knows you weren't the man his man killed?"

"No, I don't. But if he reads or watches any news at all, he'll know."

"I pray he doesn't try again."

"He won't know where to find me. Lieutenant Allard has put me up in a different hotel. It's called the Saint- Loraine."

"When are you going to come home?"

"I guess when Allard has no more use for me. I might be here till Friday."

"That long? Oh, please tell him you need to leave before then."

"I may. We'll see."

"Well, I'll let you go now…overseas charges and all. Je t'aime, ma cherie."

"I love you too, Babe. Be safe."

"I will. Wish you were going to be here in our bed tonight."

"Won't be long, sweetheart. Bye now."

Maybe I wouldn't wait till the shindig at the Cadieux estate to go after him, that is if I did. I purposely didn't tell Adriana I thought I had located him, or she'd be pretty damn sure I would. And then she'd do nothing but worry.

Tuesday morning, Lieutenant Allard called me on my cell. "Monsieur McGowan, would you please come into our headquarters today? I wanted to check with you on something."

"I'll be there. I have nothing else on my schedule. What time do you want me?"

"Would eleven be fine with you?"

"Yes. See you then."

When I arrived in his office, I didn't find him as cordial as the day before. All he said was "Sit down, Monsieur McGowan."

"Sure. What's up, Lieutenant?"

"I was very explicit about you staying out of this matter except when I call on you to provide information, yet you go out on your own to investigate."

"What are you referring to, Lieutenant?"

"I contacted the tour agency that arranged your vacation to Paris. You had already been there trying to get information."

"Do you actually know why I was there and what I asked?"

"The people there told me you were trying to find out who paid for the vacation."

"So, what do you think that has to do with this case, Lieutenant?"

"I don't know. What I was told is that someone here in Paris paid for the trip. Do you have a relative here or perhaps a very good friend?"

"No. The trip just came from out of the blue."

"It is very strange to me that someone who you do not know brought you here."

"Let me ask you something, Lieutenant; did anyone at the tour agency tell you who paid for it?"

He leaned back in his chair and drew in a deep breath. "I am not sure whether I can tell you yes or no."

"Why not."

"I was asked not to divulge the name. The woman Suzanne said that was the payeur's wish."

"I thought you and I agreed we would be straight up with each other…to share information."

"As you said, what does it have to do with the murder?"

"You found out my benefactor's name, didn't you?"

"Oui."

"But you won't tell me."

"No."

I thought for a moment, took a deep breath of my own and let it out. "Okay, Lieutenant, we both are beating around the bush here."

"And I do know that American expression."

"We both found out who it was, and I think you have another question to ask."

"You are very perceptive. Why would Henri Cadieux arrange a vacation for someone he does not know, even though in my research I find him very wealthy?"

"Because he and Jonas Karn are one and the same."

Allard's eyes widened and he sat up in his chair. "You knew this and did not tell me. How did you find that out?"

"First, I deduced it. He paid for us to come here so that he could kill me. No one else could have done it. It took me a while to recognize him after all these years because his looks have changed."

"And again, you refrained from telling me."

"Yes. I wanted to be sure."

"I think you are trying very hard to keep information from me."

"Lieutenant, it's taken me almost the entire week to put this puzzle together. I don't tell people things I'm not sure of."

"One thing we have not discussed is what this Jonas Karn looks like now."

"The wheelchair is the first thing you'd recognize, of course. He has very thick glasses, rimless that is, and a full white beard. I called him Santa all week long without realizing it was Karn. In my hotel room, with the aid of an internet app, I took an old photo I had on my computer of perps I've nailed, and then doctored it up. When I added the beard, glasses and stupid-looking beret he wore every day, it was him. Now, do you know what Cadieux looks like."

"I have never met the man, nor have I ever seen a photograph of him in the paper or on the internet. I cannot tell what he looks like; however, it will be very easy for me to find out."

"How will you do that?"

"If he is the man you say he is, I will have my officers bring him in for questioning and identification. We will take his fingerprints and send them to Interpol. They have everyone's fingerprints in the world who has had them taken for a hundred different reasons."

"I want to be here when he's brought in, Lieutenant."

"I prefer it. You will be the one who will identify him and say he is or is not Jonas Karn. If he is, the fact that Madame Farrell heard someone in the alley say your name will make this a very good case for the procureur."

"Procureur?"

"I believe you say prosecutor in America."

"Then go get him, Lieutenant. I am ready to go home."

"Before you go home, the procureur needs to agree we have a case. If we do, your testimony as to his identity will be important."

"What are you saying, Lieutenant, that I'll have to remain here for his trial?"

"As a material witness."

"Not going to happen. I can be out of here on the next plane and you will not stop me. You can secure my affidavit or sworn statement to introduce to the court, but sure as hell not me personally."

"We will then, as you say, cross that bridge when we come to it."

Chapter Thirteen

And so, I had let the cat out of the bag about Cadieux, AKA Karn. Allard was destined to find out anyway. We had gone down the same but different paths to learn Cadieux's identity on our way to finding out they were one and the same. I was right to go ahead and tell him. Now I'd have to wait until the Paris police brought the man in. If all went like clockwork, Karn would be connected to the murder and duly prosecuted. He was already imprisoned in a body dependent on caregivers for everything he ate and every movement of his body. Going back to prison and not living a life of luxury, being waited on hand and foot, would be a fate worse than death. Maybe I was alright with that. A bullet in his brain would send him to hell, but living the rest of his miserable life back in a prison ward would be hell on earth. He could go to hell later.

It was somewhat of a relief to put what I had found out about Karn on someone else's back. Allard would carry the ball and hand it off to the prosecutor to make the case. What I worried about was that Karn was rich enough to buy himself out of any prosecution. There were dirty cops and dirty court systems everywhere. In a few days, it wouldn't matter to me, though; I'd be on my way back home.

The only thing I didn't want to happen was for him to send goons after me across the water. I had had enough people in my lifetime after me and people I loved got hurt. I could go ahead before the end of the week and just get it over with…take *everybody* down. I had through stealthy means, and by myself, taken out the most dangerous dregs in the terrorist community. Methodically and with meticulous calculation.

But I would wait. If Allard did not make his move on Karn, I would.

As on our tour the previous week, we were subject to the itinerary Saint-Amaury had scheduled for us, I decided to take advantage of a trolly tour of the city that lasted three hours. This time I could only take cellphone photos of sites such as the Arc de Triomphe, Notre Dame and Sacre Coeur, including the magnificent panorama of Paris from Montmartre. However, because the trolly would only be stopping for a couple of minutes at each locale, none of the images I would bring home would include interiors of venues such as the cathedrals and the Louvre. Neither would Adriana's beautiful image have been captured in any of them. Unfortunately, that's all we'd have to show for having gone to the City of Lights…that is, until I somehow got my Nikon back from it having been borrowed by the inconsiderate Mr. Cadieux and his man.

Tuesday evening, I feasted on a platter of succulent crab legs and cheddar bay biscuits at a restaurant near the Saint-Loraine called Le Bec-fin, washing the last of it down with a Parisian brew. Returning to the room around eight, I called Adriana to give her both a capsule of my day and my love. What Wednesday would hold, I hadn't a clue. I hoped it included the apprehension of the man who had three times in the past thirty-some years made me want to send him to hell. Maybe before I left town, this time I would.

It was one-thirty on that Wednesday that I got the call from Lieutenant Allard. "Monsieur McGowan, I will need you to come to my station to identify the two persons we secured from the Ramatuelle residence. Can you be here within the hour?"

"I can. Will be there in 20 minutes."

As I was already out and about, getting some toiletries at a pharmacy, I drove to his headquarters rather than walk. After finding a spot in the limited space parking area at the precinct, I placed my Sig once again under the seat and went inside. Because Allard was expecting me, he had one of his officers meet me in the hallway who let me know that Mr. Cadieux, his caregiver and attorney were in an interrogation room on the second floor. The officer was to place me in the room with a view next door. I would also be able to hear the conversation. It would be in English as Mr. Cadieux of course spoke it perfectly.

Upon being escorted to the room, I was seated in a chair facing a large window of glass. Immediately, after taking account of all the characters on the other side of the one-way glass, I recognized both Karn and his Arab companion. Besides Allard, there was another man in the room I took to be the lawyer and a recorder preparing to type in their conversations.

The officer who seated me in the viewing room then entered the interrogation room and whispered something to Allard. The Lieutenant's eyes quickly went into the mirror toward me, and he nodded.

"Alright, Monsieur Cadieux, we can now begin."

"Well, it's about time. We've been sitting here for a half hour."

I laughed. It had been years since I had heard his high- pitched, crackling voice which I caused to occur when I shoved his gonads up into his intestines with my shoe. The entire previous week, I had not heard him say a word, he likely fearing I would recognize that voice.

"Would you please state your name, Monsieur."

"Henri Cadieux."

"Your address?"

"15 Rue de Chateau, Versailles. It is called Ramatuelle."

"How long have you lived there?"

"About twelve years."

"What nationality are you?"

"I was previously American, now a French citizen."

"How was it you came to this country?"

"Lieutenant, these questions are a waste of my time. Again, I want to know why you saw fit to send a squad of officers to my estate and drag me here."

"We did not drag you here, Monsieur Cadieux. My officers delivered to you a summons to appear here, and you came to my office in your vehicle. As you were informed, we are investigating a murder."

His attorney then broke in. "What does this have to do with my client? He knows nothing about a murder."

"Let me continue," Allard said. "We will get to that. Who owned Ramatuelle before you?"

I heard Karn then blow out a puff of air, registering his disgust.

"It was my uncle, my father's brother, who owned it. I inherited it and his fortune, my being the only surviving relative." He then half-smiled. "A bit of a surprise, I must say."

It was to me as well. Lying on his back in a prison ward one day like a cockroach and a multimillionaire on wheels the next.

"I must ask you, Monsieur, why did you change your name?"

"Who says I did?"

"The records I have in my possession containing your fingerprints, Monsieur *Karn*."

Karn became flushed. "Oh, so you know about that."

The attorney again. "Lieutenant, as Mr. Cadieux moved here to France to assume his uncle's estate, he decided to become a French citizen. Because he wanted to begin a new life and blend in with the people of France, he took another name…a French name. He has also become fluent in the French language."

"Have you also decided on a new lifestyle and not one of crime?"

"I must object to that question, Lieutenant," the lawyer said. "Mr. Cadieux has been nothing but a model citizen."

Allard then looked at Karn's caregiver. "The man with you takes care of you, I see."

"He serves several functions. As you can see that I only have mobility of my head, he feeds me, helps with my bathroom chores and generally looks after my well-being."

Allard turned his attention to the man and asked,

"What is your name?"

"My name is Gamir."

"Gamir what?"

"Gamir al-Tajir."

And so, One-eyed Jamal had a name.

"Where are you originally from, Mr. al-Tajir?"

"Yemen."

"Oh, lovely," I said. Of course, they couldn't hear me. "I thought I was through with you people."

"This question is for both of you: why did you include yourselves on a recent tour? You live in the area and have much time to make a tour of your own."

"I'll answer for both of us since Gamir and I act as one person," Karn said. "There is a lot of history and other information one can pick up with having a guide. I just thought it was time I did that."

"Why did you give the tour people the names of John Drake and James Wilson and not your own?"

The question seemed to take Karn by surprise, but he had the answer, anyway.

"You must understand that having the money and clout that I have obtained can make you vulnerable to criminal elements and vultures who want to try taking it from me. I did so for security and anonymity. But again, what does my taking a tour have to do with anything? Is that against the law? And what does it have to do with any murder. I think it is time we left. No more questions."

"I am just getting to why you're here. Do you know one Bruce McGowan?"

That was when Karn's eyes and mouth really

opened wider. "I…I…yes, unfortunately. I think you probably know that. He arrested me years ago."

"And then you kidnapped his daughter to get revenge. I know the entire story."

"How do you know it?" Karn seemed to be getting angry.

"I have it all from the Interpol record."

I knew Interpol didn't have everything, just the record of him being captured and prosecuted. Allard's information came from me.

"Why did you bring McGowan up, Lieutenant?"

"Because he was on the tour last week with you. But I'm sure you knew that."

"No, I didn't," he lied.

"Do you not think it a coincidence that the man who had arrested you, not once but twice, was on the same tour with you?"

"I guess strange and coincidental things happen."

"Yet you did not recognize him."

"Lieutenant, people change. They get older, they lose their hair and grow beards like me. If I didn't recognize him, I'm sure as hell he wouldn't have recognized me."

The man had a point. I had no idea who he was for nearly a week.

"You asked me to get to the point on this murder. There was a man who was stabbed to death on a Paris street last Friday night. His wife was with him. In our interview with her, she said she heard a voice from someone saying something like, "Goodbye, McGowan.

You're not so invincible after all…" If you had a less than congenial history with Monsieur McGowan, it sounds to me like it's something you'd say."

Karn's face turned beet red with anger. "How dare you accuse me of killing him! Anyway, how could that happen? You're looking at a man in a wheelchair who can't move his arms. I know nothing about McGowan's death!"

Allard leaned across the table, I believe for effect, and stared into Karn's eyes. "Who said he was dead?"

Karn's head jolted back as though he had just received a shock…which he did. "What do you mean. You said he was."

"I said a man was murdered. I didn't say *him*."

I had to hand it to Allard. He was good.

"Well…you…you must've. McGowan is who we were talking about."

"The wife of the murdered man said her husband's assailant was about six feet tall like Monsieur al-Tajir."

"Are you accusing Gamir?"

"I'm only making a comparison. By the way, how did you obtain Gamir?"

"When I came to France, I needed some real help as you can see. Gamir was a hospital orderly who had experience with severely handicapped people like me. I hired him to provide to me 24/7 care. He is my protection as well."

"How many other 'protectors' do you have in your employ?"

"You have to understand that in my vulnerable

condition, I cannot fend for myself. I have three others who not only keep up the grounds but provide security for my estate."

Karn, being backed into a corner with all of Allard's insinuations, was being just a wee bit more cooperative. But then the question was posed that I saw coming almost from the onset of the interrogation.

"Why did you pay for Monsieur McGowan's and his wife's vacation trip to Paris?"

"What? I did no such thing."

"Why do you think I sent officers for you in the first place" That is how I got onto you, Monsieur Cadieux. Your name is in the Saint-Amaury file as the McGowan's payeur. That is what connects you with Monsieur McGowan today. You lured him to Paris with intentions of ending his life."

The lawyer jumped in. "If his name was placed in their file, it was done so fraudulently. And we will prove that. Monsieur Cadieux told you that people can make many attempts at defrauding those with money."

"What reason would someone have to do that... to pay all this money to a travel agency under his name?" Allard asked.

"We cannot answer that at this point. But I will tell you that you must charge Monsieur Cadieux at this moment or he is free to go. If you do charge him, you will have a difficult time proving that he murdered someone."

Lieutenant Allard sat stroking his chin, obviously wondering if he could connect all the dots to make a good case against Karn. He might be able to prove a connection between Karn and me as regards the tour, but could he prove that it was al-Tajir who killed Roy Farrell. And why Roy Farrell? Liz Farrell would be hard-pressed to testify that al-Tajir was the killer. She didn't get a good look at him. Neither did she see Karn in his wheelchair sitting back in the shadows.

"I know you intended to murder Monsieur McGowan on the street last Friday night. But it was a man named Roy Farrell that was killed. From my information, he looked very much like McGowan, same size, same clothes. You had seen him and his wife in the restaurant. He would have been walking on the street back to his hotel and you knew that. It was dark on the street and the fog had set in from the rain. After your man had stabbed Monsieur Farrell, you mocked the man you thought was McGowan by calling out his name. I believe we can prove it, Monsieur Cadieux. But today I will send you back to your home until the procureur and I prepare your case. You will not leave the Paris area to evade prosecution. If I know you have fled, I will order your arrest and incarceration immediately. Am I understood?"

Karn was silent in defiance, but his attorney replied, "Lieutenant, I am confident you will have no case against Monsieur Cadieux. He will, however, always be available to the legal system. We will now go."

As they began leaving, I left the viewing room as well. I'm sure Allard didn't want me to do it, but I stopped to stand in the hallway to be sure that Karn saw me when he came out. As he rolled past me, his eyes darted in my direction, then quickly back to his front. However, al- Tajir kept his eye on me until they were by me. I then walked toward the lieutenant's office. I had flaunted myself so that he would realize Allard hadn't lied to him and that we would meet again…for the last time in his life.

I was standing just inside of Allard's office when he came in. "You heard all that was said, I assume."

"Yes, and you did a very good job, Lieutenant. You asked all the right questions, caught him in lies and got him flustered. I know now that he wasn't aware he and his Arab goon had killed the wrong man. I thought his head was going to explode when you told him. Obviously, he doesn't read the newspaper because I know it covered Roy Farrell's murder. So, what happens from here?"

"I will need to get an official statement from you on video tape that you have identified Cadieux as Karn. I do not think it is necessary at this point that you remain much longer in Paris. I can reinforce your statement with the Interpol report confirming that Cadieux is indeed the American criminal Jonas Karn. With the evidence from the Saint-Amaury Agency that will confirm Karn's intent to entice you to Paris in order to murder you, I believe he can be indicted."

"I hope you're right. So, when can I return home?"

"I would like to ask you to stay until our soliciteur confers the charge on him and then you may leave. I would say this will be done by Friday."

"I read where Karn, AKA Cadieux, was going to have a celebratory party party at his house with his friends on Friday night. Now I wonder if he'll have it. You just took the wind out of his sail."

"I like your American expressions, and yes, I am sure his ship will be grounded now that he knows you are alive."

I looked at the clock on his wall, seeing that it was

ten minutes till four. "If you want to get that statement, I can stick around."

"Can we do that in the morning? I have scheduled to meet with the procureur at 4:30 today to go over this case and my recommendations."

"That's fine, Lieutenant. I hope you recommend prosecution."

"Most definitely. I believe we have a good case after everything is pulled together. There are many pieces of this puzzle that need to be put in place and all of the pieces must be there."

"I understand. What time do you want me here?"

"10:00 if that is okay, Monsieur."

"Yes, and you can call me Bruce, if you wish. Monsieur sounds a bit formal."

He nodded. "I will see you then…Bruce."

Chapter Fourteen

As I was walking to my rental, I saw Karn's attorney standing by the open sliding door of the black van talking with his client. He watched me all the way to my car as I'm sure Karn was doing from the inside. What a shocker to learn I was still alive. Once I slid into the driver's seat, the attorney walked to his own car. When I began pulling away from my parking spot, so did the van. Al-Tajir made sure he stayed behind me as I made the turn onto another street. I then turned off the street into the parking lot of my hotel. I wondered if he would follow me on in, but he went slowly on by. Now they knew where I was staying. I had no problem with that. I wanted them to know. Bring it on.

I wasn't expecting Karn's hoods to try anything inside the hotel such as bursting into my room while I was asleep. They'd wait till I left the building on a walk or follow me in my rental to where I'd be machine gunned down on some lesser-traveled street or forced into another car head-on. Maybe if they caught me on a walk, they might slip something sharp into my liver. As I recall, they'd done that before. Either way, I would be vigilant.

When was the last time I ever heard someone say "I was pretty damn bored in Paris" besides never? The thing was, I had seen most everything I had wanted to see and a few things twice, considering the afternoon trolly blitz. But I was getting washed out with no desire to look at anything touristy. I hoped to hell Allard and his prosecutor would be getting their act together and making their case against Karn…soon. However, case or no case, I planned to be in the air not later than Saturday morning. Still, that was three days away. I'd be stir-crazy by then. Perhaps I could take in a movie or a play. Better yet, go back to the Moulin Rouge. At least at the musical, there wouldn't be subtitles.

However, I probably did decide to push the envelope when I stepped out for a walk Thursday morning. If someone was out there watching and waiting, so be it. I wasn't going to spend any more time lounging in my room in front of the TV, overeating out of boredom or throwing down brewskis at the hotel bar. I didn't intend to gain ten or fifteen pounds on this trip.

It was 9:30 when I hit the pavement. I had in hand a fairly detailed street map of Paris which included some of the tourist favorites. It was another beautiful spring morning with chirping birds on the wing along the tree-lined streets, peonies in bloom, lilies of the valley and tulips colorfully merged in window boxes and a deep azure blue sky. It felt good to be doing something a little different and getting exercise at the same time. At home I enjoy cross-country jogging over miles of green pastureland, but it would be a little discourteous of me to be pushing and shoving myself along Paris's pedestrian- clogged streets on a run.

As I was depending on my peripheral and the occasional turning of my head to check the rear, a half dozen blocks from the Saint-Loraine I first saw the SUV. Traffic was slow anyway, so the black SUV was able to keep up with my brisk pace. After another block, I turned to the right at the corner. The SUV did as well. At the next intersection, I took a left and crossed over. He was still there. When I abruptly ducked into a men's store, the SUV virtually came to a stop, much to the dismay of the honking driver behind. I then watched through the store's window as the driver found a suddenly-open spot on the opposite side of the street. I kept watching to see if anyone was getting out, but the doors did not open. And so, I *wasn't* being paranoid. It was Karn's goons alright. How they thought they would make a move on me in front of hundreds of people was unrealistic. Maybe I would make it easy on them.

As the store proprietor appeared interested in me moving along and not standing in his window like a mannequin, I took the hint and left the store. Making an abrupt left turn down the sidewalk, I picked up the pace to the next block. With a half turn of my head to the right, I discovered the SUV had pulled away from the curb and was again following. And then I came upon an alley which I ducked down. I wanted them to see me going in. They did. There was nothing nor anyone in the alley except a couple of dumpsters. A split second before the SUV turned into the alley, I ducked behind the one on the left. The driver, no longer seeing me, sped up and continued until he was within about 20 feet of the dumpster. That's when I stepped out and smashed the driver's side glass with the butt of my Sig. The startled driver then lost control and ran the right fender of the vehicle into a brick wall.

A second later, I was at the broken glass door, this time smashing the driver's jaw with the butt of my gun. But then a shot rang out from the car's rear seat, sending the round into the frame of the driver's door, narrowly missing my head. I answered with three rounds of my own into the back seat area. The figure which I couldn't fully make out then fell over against the opposite side door. The front seat passenger who had made the mistake of not already having his gun out, was now fumbling into his shoulder holster.

I then yelled, *"Don't try it or the next bullet goes into your head."* He quickly raised both hands.

"Now grasp your gun with the fingers of your left hand and throw it out your window!" Without hesitating, he touched the window release to bring the door glass down after which he dropped the pistol onto the pavement.

"Alright, why are you following me?!" I barked.

"We are not follow…"

"Don't lie to me! You've been on my tail for the last fifteen minutes."

For a moment he merely glared at me. Then, after finding his set of balls, he replied, "I am looking at a dead man."

I remained calm but pushed my Sig past the unconscious driver until the muzzle was inches from the head of the passenger. "You tell that fat little maggot you're working for that this is his only warning. The next time you pricks come anywhere near me, I will send what pieces are left of you back to him in rubber bags. Now wake this guy up and get this SUV piece of shit back to Ramatuelle before I unload on both of you."

We stared at one another for a few seconds and then I turned away from the vehicle, walking quickly out of the alley.

"Well, *that* was fun," I said to myself. The day had suddenly taken an exhilarating turn. And what's more…I was no longer bored.

I then continued my walk, now less concerned anyone was following. A couple of blocks over I found a pub where I sat and ordered a baguette and a draft beer. No sooner had I given the garçon my order, my cellphone rang.

"Bruce." It was the Lieutenant. "The news is not good."

"How so?" I think I knew already.

"Try as I did, I could not convince the procureur's office to charge Cadieux…Karn or whatever we should call him. The deputy procureur failed to see where he could connect the dots."

I slapped the table. "Not good. What was his rationale?"

"He doesn't see the full picture. He acknowledges that it would appear Karn had lured his old nemesis, being you, to the city for some reason, but it was not you who was murdered. He further believes a jury would not convict because no one, including Madame Farrell could put either Karn or the suspected killer, al-Tajir, at the murder scene."

"It's what I was afraid of, Lieutenant."

"All I can tell you is I will not give up on *digging*, as you say, for more evidence. I will not let up on this man. I know he was at the scene when al-Tajir murdered Roy Farrell. Eventually, both of them will pay for this crime. However, I guess you can go on home to the lovely Madame McGowan."

"I believe I will. But I need to call the airlines to arrange a flight home."

"If you are not able to get a ticket to fly out this evening, perhaps we could talk more over a drink at your hotel bar later. I can tell my wife I'll be late."

"Or you could bring her."

"I will ask her. Let me know if you are successful."

"Will do. Au revoir, Lieutenant."

"Jacques."

"Au revoir, Jacques."

Well, that was a punch in the gut…but not unexpected. I would not have put it past millionaire Jonas Karn to have bought off the prosecutor. I didn't know anything about the guy, but I was betting he was in Karn's back pocket.

When I returned to the hotel, I sat down, turned on my computer and pulled up 'flights to the United States.' There were flights leaving all day Friday on American, Delta, United and a couple other airlines but they were booked solid. I could fly stand-by, but that list would be long as well. The first opportunity to leave Paris was Saturday afternoon on a 3:15 flight. I'd be on row 39 in the very back of the plane, middle section, middle seat, no window, outside the rest room, last to be served my cardboard sandwich and Coke, and likely squashed for eight hours between two 300-pound sweaty slabs of meat. McGowan's Law.

I could wait till Sunday, another three days away, and get a seat in business class four rows forward on the aisle. I thought maybe I'd book that. Hopefully, I wouldn't get bumped. And so, I had the remainder of Thursday afternoon, all of Friday and all of Saturday to while away my time.

At two-thirty, I called Adriana to give her all the news. Good news, we found Karn who was living under an alias by the name of Cadieux; bad news, the authorities would not be prosecuting him for Roy's murder. Something about lack of evidence. Good news, I'd be coming home; bad news, three more days.

"He won't be prosecuted? How can they not?"

"One of two reasons: either they realistically believe they can't make a case or Karn paid them off. He's rich enough to do that, you know."

"Scumbag," she said.

I laughed. She had been coming out with some words and observations lately that sounded mysteriously like the guy she lived with.

"What are you going to do the next couple of days…more sightseeing?"

"I think I've seen about everything I've wanted to see and then some. Will probably do some laundry, get drunk at the bar for two days, drive out and kill Karn…you know, neat things like that."

"That last thing…you'd better not be thinking it. Just let the creep live out the rest of his life a prisoner in his own body. That would be a living hell to me."

"He might be living like a slug, but he has people waiting on him hand and foot, literally dropping food in his mouth. I'd as soon kill myself than live like that."

"Just please don't hasten his demise. I don't want you to be hastening yours."

I had my fingers crossed when I replied, "Don't worry, darlin.' I don't have any such plans."

I actually didn't, but what else was I going to do till Sunday?

"Can't wait to have you in my arms again. If there's any way you can catch an earlier flight, hop on."

"Hmmm. Rest assured I will. I'll also be 'hopping on' as soon as I get home."

"Goodbye, bad boy."

When our phone call was over, I got back online to see if there was any change in Karn's plans for his Friday night bash. The same information was up, but this time there was a map as an attachment…as though none of his friends knew where Ramatuelle was located. I sure did, except I wasn't necessarily one of his friends. And, oh good, it was a costume party. Did that mean I was going to crash it? Better to sneak in wearing a disguise than for him to recognize me. Even though he wouldn't mind his henchmen finding me on his property and disposing of me, I doubt he would want that to occur in front of his guests. Things like that could get messy and he'd have some 'splainin' to do with Lieutenant Allard. However, as far as I was concerned, it was the perfect time for me to make an entrance at Ramatuelle.

I informed Jacques Allard that I was booked on a Sunday flight; therefore, I was good in meeting him for a drink in the hotel bar. He said his wife couldn't make it but wondered if seven o'clock would be okay. We set it up.

At six, I had a plate of poached salmon with a side of asparagus and new potatoes at one of the hotel's two restaurants, then sipped on a glass of Merlot until Allard showed at the bar. Yes, I know you drink a white wine with seafood, but I've been known to break a few etiquette rules in my lifetime. And I'm just not partial to white wines.

The lieutenant was right on time at seven and joined me at one of the bar's high-top tables. "Good evening,

Bruce. I see you already have a drink." He then snapped his fingers to summon a garçon.

"Oui, Monsieur," the young lady said. "Qu'est-ce que vous aurez."

"Bourbon et seltzer, s'il vous plait."

She nodded and turned about.

Jacques Allard was a bright-eyed man about forty-five, dark hair, maybe six feet, like me, and welldressed still in his gray suit from work. Looking a bit tired, he had put in over twelve hours that day, which he said was normal for him. After loosening his tie, he began our conversation. "I am sorry to be so brief today on the phone, Bruce. As I said, there was much going on in my office. I thought it would be better to meet personally before you went home as you may have some questions."

"That I do, Jacques. Foremost, how well do you know the prosecutor? Mainly, do you trust him?"

"The him is actually a *her*. I do not know her all that well as she has only been the procureur for two months. I have forwarded to her investigations on several hundred suspects."

"I don't want to infer anything or demean her character, but do you think she can be bought?"

"I think you mean that if there is someone who commits a crime and is wealthy like Cadieux, will she take money and not prosecute the person."

"Exactly."

"I do not think so. She seems to be very passionate about ridding Paris of crime in its streets."

"As the procureur receives the cases, does she

assign them to others in her department?"

"Yes. There are at least five assistant procureurs who would receive them. The outside world thinks Paris is a fairy-tale land where everything is wonderful; but I assure you, our city is like any other city with much crime and terrorism. Our department and the justice departments stay very busy."

"I'm sure. Would you be able to find out who received the Cadieux investigation?"

"I know who received it. But the ultimate decision rests with the procureur herself."

"Do you trust whoever received the case to recommend to her its disposition?"

Allard seemed to struggle with the question and shuffled in his chair. "Let me say I know of several matters we have recommended to be prosecuted that were, as you say, slam-dunk cases that went nowhere. This person has been suspected of receiving money from criminals before, but nothing has ever been proven."

"Aha! Then there-in may be our answer. How can you determine if that's the case here?"

He smiled. "We would have to ask Monsieur Cadieux."

"Is there a chance someone like me could talk with this deputy prosecutor? I figured since I'm a victim here, thankfully not a fatal one, I should have an opportunity to get answers."

Allard thought over my rationale for a moment. "I have never had anyone ask that question before. I do know the procureur team will often be in on our interrogations and ask questions of suspects *and* witnesses. I am sure a victim or witness can talk with *them* as well if requested. I will try to get you an answer."

"What's the man's name?"

"Gerard Devereux. He is on the fifth floor of our building in the procureur department. You may stop by my office tomorrow morning, and I will have an answer for you. But what will you ask him you haven't already discussed with me?"

"I want to hear from his own mouth why he made the decision not to take the case forward against Karn. An intelligent lawyer should be able to put all the pieces of puzzle together and come up with the same conclusion we did."

"An intelligent lawyer, yes."

His answer told me he had no use for Devereux. I definitely wanted to meet this guy. I would think of more questions if I got the chance to grill him.

We had mostly small talk from there on that Thursday evening, mainly about his wife and two children, and about what kind of place West Virginia was. He had never even been to the United States; however, he had studied much about it in travel books. What were New York City and San Francisco like? And Florida? What I liked about our conversation, he didn't press me to answer his question from a few days prior which was what I did for the state department in the area of counterterrorism and how many terrorist types did I end up planting in the ground. I respected him for not pursuing it any further.

But at nine-thirty and after too many drinks for the

both of us, we shook hands and he left. I liked Jacques Allard. Good policeman and extremely insightful. We had initially gotten off to a rocky start, but as the days went on, both of us mellowed out and became more genial. I also liked that he was quick to put all the pieces together and agree with me it was Karn AKA Cadieux and his goon who murdered Roy Farrell, thinking they were killing me.

Yeah, I wanted to see and talk with the man who recommended to the chief prosecutor that she turn down the case. I wondered if he even discussed it with her. Hopefully, Allard could set up a meeting between him and me. I had a stake in the case... maybe a half dozen stakes. I deserved an answer. Liz Farrell deserved an answer.

Chapter Fifteen

Was I seriously considering putting on a mask and busting in on Karn's victory party? I assumed the party was still on, but now it was to celebrate the fact that he wouldn't be indicted. However, I was still alive as his hoods failed to corner and kill me in the alley. One of them went home with a broken jaw. Another, who had three bullets in him, would take the eternal celestial dirt nap. That had to infuriate the fat little shit. And just maybe he had to rethink his statement that I was not invincible. Of course, that wasn't the case; I was just smarter than him.

If I did get past his security, what would I do once I got inside his estate? Would I actually end his miserable life? I don't like shooting people who personally can't fight back. It would be like killing a defenseless animal, which I also don't do. He needed to go down, but in what way? I couldn't just put a bullet in him. If I could somehow see to his financial ruination, I would do that. But I think what I had in mind more than anything was to get into his mansion house, rub elbows with his guests, eat his food, drink his booze and then confront him. I wanted him to know that I could get to him any time I wanted. But, since I had nothing else to do that Friday night, I figured I may as well have some fun.

However, Friday morning, at 8:30, Lieutenant Allard called my cell. "I approached Devereux a few minutes ago and told him you want some answers as to why he did not recommend prosecution. At first, he replied that he does not have to explain anything to anyone. But then I said that you, a tourist in our city, deserve to be told why a man who lured you here, planned to kill you because of old grievance, but was not charged with the murder of a man he thought was you. That is when he angrily agreed to spend only five minutes only with you and that would be the end of it. He will see you at 10:30."

"Thank you, Jacques. It may not do any good, but Mr. Devereux needs to look me in the eye and tell me directly why he rejected the case. Then he's going to learn a few new words from an American hot head. He does understand a little English, doesn't he?"

"He does."

"Good. I'll be there."

And I was. I first stopped by Allard's office and we exchanged a few words, then went to the next floor to the door that read *procureur*. The lovely receptionist with the dreamy eyes, not realizing I wasn't French, said, "Puis-je vous aider?"

I replied, "Monsieur Devereux, s'il vous plait." I was getting pretty dadgum good at French. However, I hadn't yet learned to say things like "Where's the toilet", "Can I get some fries with that?" or "How about you and I going out for a drink later?"

She smiled, picked up her phone and said something to the person on the other end I took to be Devereux. It took a couple of minutes, but then he came out. He was an unmade bed if I ever saw one. Long, greasy hair on the backside of his bald head, shirt tail hanging down over his belt, a wide, gaudy 70s tie and 225 pounds on a 5'8" frame.

"You are McGowan?" he barked.

"I am. Thanks for seeing me."

"I don't have long. What do you want?"

"Do you have a room we can talk in?"

He blew out a puff of air as though he were already put out. "In there." He pointed to the first of two rooms. Did I mention halitosis as well?

He sat down without offering me a chair, but I took one anyway. "You have questions for me?"

"I want to know why you recommended to your boss that Henri Cadieux, the man I knew in the past as Jonas Karn, not be prosecuted. You had every piece of evidence that clearly proved he was at the murder scene of Roy Farrell. He said my name, thinking that his goon had killed me. It all traces back to the trip he paid for that brought my wife and me to Paris. Lieutenant Allard was certainly convinced."

"I was not. I see no connection of Monsieur Cadieux to this murder. No one identified him or his man. And I cannot see how you are involved at all and am wasting my time speaking with you. You are not dead. He did not murder you."

"Mr. Devereux, I think you just don't want to understand how my history with the man I knew as Karn plays into the equation. For some reason, you're ignoring the evidence. Yes, you have to lay all this out to see how it connects, but you don't want to be bothered with it. A man lost his life and you don't seem to care."

"I care when anyone loses his life, but you did not bring anything to the police that convinces me Monsieur Cadieux had anything to do with murdering Monsieur Farrell. Our conversation is over now. You told me what you think. You must go." In that tight room, his foul breath was magnified times ten.

"I have a couple more points to make…"

"No you do not. Your time is over."

I stood and began moving toward the door.

"Yeah, I told you what I think, but I didn't tell you what I *know*. You're either a lazy piece of shit who won't prosecute the case because it's too much work or you are in Cadieux's pocket. How much did he pay you to drop the case?"

When Devereux jumped up, his chair fell over backwards. He then shoved his index finger hard into my chest and yelled, "That is an insult and if you don't leave in five seconds, I will throw you out of this office myself."

I grabbed hold of his finger, pressed it downward and dropped him to his knees. "You don't want to threaten me, you fat little bastard. I'll snap this finger off and shove it down your throat."

"I will have you arrested for assault."

"Assault? Prove it." I then released his finger and let him up.

When he threw open the door and ran to his receptionist's desk, what he said to her in French I took to mean "'Get the police up here." What she said back to him I thought sounded like, "Yuck. Go drink some mouthwash." But I could have been wrong about that.

I didn't know if the police ever came up or not as I left the building and began walking back to my hotel. It was how I expected my meeting to go with the exception of putting the man onto his knees. I thought I'd be fuming when I left, but although it would matter to Liz Farrell that Karn would not be prosecuted, it didn't matter to me any longer.

That same afternoon, I walked a few blocks down from the hotel and stopped at a novelty shop much like a store one might find in Myrtle Beach. I needed one thing…a mask. Should I buy a Lone Ranger type mask or one that was a caricature image of Richard Nixon, as though anyone in France would ever remember him? There was one of Truman Capote which adding a white beard would strangely enough resemble Karn. There were quite a few variations of the V for Vendetta character, Guy Fawkes. So, I chose one of them. With my black tee and black jeans, I brought to Paris with me, I figured I'd be looking sinister. Sinister was what I wanted to accomplish.

On my walk, I had forgotten to look for bad guys in black SUVs and vans; however, in retrospect, I figured Karn and his honchos would be busying themselves preparing for the party at Ramatuelle rather than worrying about me. Even though I had had a run-in with three of his very Middle Eastern looking goons who tried to whack me the day before, Karn may have thought I'd returned to the states by now. I had been wondering why Karn had specifically chosen Arab bodyguards. Other than the fact that they all were muscular, malevolent- looking dudes, why not hire some mercenary types from non-Arab countries like the U.S. or even right there in France? Maybe he was now dabbling in Islamic terrorism which was becoming ever more prevalent in France. But then I remembered, he had also engaged a few al-Qaeda terrorists back then who had found their way into the U.S. after 911 to help with the making of IEDs to kill soldiers on military installations.

Since I didn't have lunch, I enjoyed a nice midafternoon dinner of linguine and clams chased down with a Heineken around two o'clock under a canopy umbrella at a sidewalk cafe. Then, for the second time in two days whilst enjoying my dinner, Jacques Allard called me.

"You caused quite a stir in the procueur's department, my friend. I got paid a visit by the obnoxious Monsieur Devereux who after telling me you assaulted him, ordered your arrest."

"He said I assaulted him? I probably did so with words. I hope you asked him to show you his bruises where I beat him up."

"He had no marks on him that I could see, and he didn't show me any."

"Well, there you go. You just can't trust a maggot like that. By the way, I hope he doesn't show up in court looking like he just crawled out from under a rock like I saw today. The man is not exactly Monsieur GQ."

I heard him chuckle. "If anyone asks, my officers could not locate you this afternoon."

"You sent them after me?"

"I believe I sent them; I just cannot remember. Maybe I did…maybe I didn't. But I did inform Devereux that you had probably returned to the states on an afternoon flight."

I laughed. The guy was alright.

He then asked me "What are your plans this evening?"

"I think I might order me a pizza and a couple bottles of wine, spend time with my wife on the phone and watch a movie on the TV."

"I had thought you may wish to join my wife and I for dinner around eight."

"That sounded good, Jacques, but after assaulting Devereux and going on the lam to escape your officers, I'm a little tired. How about tomorrow evening?"

"I will check with my wife to see if she has plans; otherwise, it is fine with me."

"Great. Touch base tomorrow?"

"Yes. Have an enjoyable night."

I didn't like lying to Jacques Allard, but I wanted to paint in his mind the picture of me, a pizza, and a bottle of wine holed up in my room like a slug watching some porn movie. The thing was, if I happened to run into any trouble at Ramatuelle, I wanted it to be understood that it wasn't me who caused the commotion. It was Guy Fawkes. I had spent the evening in my room.

About seven-thirty I ordered a small pizza and wine. I wanted a record of it being delivered to my room. When it arrived, I gave the pizza boy an 8 euro tip, which is about $10.00 U.S. He spoke no English and so that he would remember me, I also gave him a red neck "mercy buckups" thanks along with the tip. "Hillbilly American," I'm sure he was thinking. I then ate about half of the pizza and poured a good portion of the wine down the commode. If the cops were called because someone at the party reported that Bruce McGowan had slipped in and shot someone, I was in my hotel room. I had physical evidence.

At eight-thirty when it was fully dark, I donned my mask, took the stairs to the lobby and zipped out to my rental which I had earlier parked on the street. There were security cameras in the parking garage that would have captured the numbers on my tag. It was then just over a twenty-minute drive from the hotel out to Ramatuelle. I was dressed all in black, to include my black jacket and new face mask. The Vendetta mask with the squinty eyes, goatee and smirky smile fit my personality to a tee. Would I be able to pull off the party crash considering all of Karn's security? I wasn't sure. However, considering my history of broaching premises to take down some serious bad guys, I figured it would be a piece of cake.

The white, palatial house, completely illuminated by ground to sky flood lights, loomed majestically upon the hill to my right. Across the road from the entrance, as many as thirty cars sat cluttering a grass field. I couldn't imagine Karn had cultivated that many friends; but, when you have money, you have friends.

As my headlights were already spotted by the large gate guard, I had two choices: either drive on by, find a spot in the woods to hide my rental, climb over the fence and sneak in or just go ahead and park with the others and walk directly in as though I were an invited guest. I was sure to be asked by the guard in French to show my invitation and in anticipation of that, I had practiced saying, "Excusemoi, Monsieur, je l'ai perdu" which translated is something like "excuse me, sir, I lost it." So, I parked my car and walked up to the gate guard as though I was one of them.

When I was within three or four feet of the man, who surprisingly was Caucasian, he showered the beam of his heavy-duty flashlight in my face. "Nom," he said.

I figured out that he was asking my name. I replied, "Guy Fawkes."

He then placed his light on a list of guests. A few seconds later, he shook his head and held out his hand. "Invitation."

I knew that one. That's when I answered, "Excuse-moi, Monsieur, je l'ai perdu." My enunciation was French-perfect.

"Je ne peux pas vous laisser entrer." I figured that one out as well. He wasn't going to let me enter.

That's when I looked behind me for other guests, finding none. I supposed everybody but me had already arrived. I then spotted the camera at the top of the gate. Slowly, I began moving toward the inside of the gate out of the camera's view and the guard grabbed my arm. *"Entree interdite!"* he shouted. That's when I gave him a throat chop which caused him to drop his flashlight. As he was holding his throat and gasping for air, I picked up the light and cold-cocked him on the side of his head. He went down like a fat kid on a seesaw. I then dragged him out of the driveway into a group of bushes. "Sleep well, dumbass."

It was about five hundred feet up the driveway to the house. At a brisk walk, I made it to the front porch in less than a minute in time to see the two late-comers entering ahead of me. I thought about going on in through the front double doors behind them, but decided instead to just watch and listen. As soon as they entered, a man with a loud voice announced them. "Monsieur and Madame Bouvier." I then heard the clapping. It made me wonder how the announcer recognized them, dressed as Louis the XVI and Marie Antoinette. So, I decided to get inside through another entrance.

After rounding a corner of the large house, I came

upon a brick patio, on the borders of which sat statues of fairies, goddesses and other characters such as Cupid complete with his bow and arrow and a four-foot version of the Venus de Milo. Leading out to the patio were two glass doors which I knew could be easily breached; however, just as I was preparing to take out one of the glass panels with the butt of my Sig Sauer, Count Dracula stepped out to light his cigar.

"Bonsoir," he said.

"Bonsoir." I knew that word as well.

I knew then that the door was unlocked as he had to get back in. When I stepped inside, I found I was in a study of sorts with a desk, three walls of expensive paintings and numbered prints, and the fourth containing shelves with more than three hundred classic books. I wondered if Karn was paying anyone to read to him. Certainly not any of his Arab boys.

Music and laughter suddenly burst from another room, and I discovered someone had opened the door to the study. A woman wearing a seventeenth century gown and mask shaped like a butterfly approached me apparently looking for something or somebody. She said something to me in French which I didn't understand and then she looked toward the patio doors. "Ah," she said. I guessed her husband, the Count, had slipped out on her. As she walked toward the patio, I went to the room with all the white noise.

It was a large room about the size of a church sanctuary with a massive chandelier, colorful wall tapestries and stained-glass windows on two sides of the room, which subliminally compelled me to compare it with a chancel. The music was loud, and it didn't surprise me at all its genre was American 60s and 70s. A haze of smoke lay on the ceiling like a fog. I would have guessed half the people in the room had a cigarette hanging from their lips. Of course, half the people in *France* were smokers. Although I didn't count them, I figured there were sixty or seventy people in the room, not counting at least three young men in tuxedos and masks, flitting from person to person offering goblets of champaign from their trays…and a man in a wheelchair being tended by a tall Middle Eastern man wearing an eye patch. Several couples in costumes ranging from Cleopatra to Charles De Gaulle, and a woman wearing a cowboy hat, buckskin clothing and a double set of pistols I took to be Annie Oakley, mingled throughout. Four or five couples were dancing to a disco number, one large bozo looking rather pitiful trying to emulate John Travolta.

The food was off to one side of the room and the dude who had been announcing couples coming in, said something in French which served to move the revelers in that direction. The beefier partiers were first in line.

Someone had dressed Karn to look like Julius Caesar complete with a wreath of laurel on his head, breastplate and sword which hung from the wheelchair. Cute, I thought. In hindsight, maybe I should have come to the party as Brutus and slipped a knife in his gut. But blowing on the sip-and-puff wand that moved his chair around the room, he tried to visit with as many of his guests as he could. I remained across the room as far away as I could as it was not the right time for us to come face to face. At one point he left the room with al-Tajir. At least I thought it was him as he was the same in stature and his dark olive skin peeked out from his long thobe. I didn't know if he was attempting to be a pirate or Rooster Cogburn in a dress.

I then took advantage of Karn's buffet, scarfing up a small plate of his hors d'oeuvres, such as smoked salmon canapés, brochettes, and baked camembert. I only knew the names of these finger foods because little cards were sitting in front of them. I left the escargots for the other guests.

Next to me, just inches away, elbowing his way through the line, a slovenly, overweight slob in a Batman costume loaded onto his plate one of every hors d'oeuvre on the table until it overflowed. It was his breath that gave him away. It could melt the chrome off a trailer hitch. I knew he couldn't eat with the mask on, so I waited until he found a chair where he could sit and balance his plate on his fat thigh. Devereux then took off his mask and began shoving food into his mouth resembling a human end-loader. Bruce Wayne, he wasn't.

I set my own plate down and after taking my cellphone from my pocket, began taking photos of the man with the phone's camera. After taking two or three, I caught sight of Karn rolling back into the room with the al-Tajir. I then positioned myself to where I could get shots of Devereux with Karn in the background. This was going to be good. It was going to make Jacques Allard's day. Except I couldn't send him the photos; I was never there. I'd have to find a way to get them to him.

It was then I found Karn's eyes focused on me. As he had visited with most all his other guests and I was alone, he was trying to place me. I thought maybe he also caught me taking photos of both Devereux *and* him. I then saw Karn say something to his man after which he sent a puff into his straw, turned his chair around and left the room again.

I went back to the table, retrieved my plate of finger food and found a chair in a corner of the room to feast on it. Having had half a pizza an hour earlier, I wasn't hungry. But I did want to try some of those exotic foods that I had never even heard of. When I had finished, I placed my plate with other people's dirty dishes and silverware. Before I stepped away from the table, I felt something steel-like in my back. When I turned my head, I came face to face with al-Tajir. I then looked behind me and saw he was holding an automatic. In a thick Middle Eastern accent, he spoke English. Having seen him most every day the week before, it was the first time I had heard any words coming from his mouth. "I don't know how you got in here, McGowan, but you will now come with me. Mr. Cadieux awaits."

Chapter Sixteen

With one hand on my shoulder and the other holding a gun, he escorted me from the room filled with guests into a hallway. That's where he pulled the Sig Sauer out of my waist band. He didn't know that at the same time he approached me and placed his gun in my back, I had lifted a piece of silverware from the platter of dirty dishes and stuck it in my jacket pocket. However, he now had *two* guns to my one butter knife.

As he kept nudging me along the hallway with the muzzle of his gun, I looked for an opportunity to disarm him. But, then another Arab, also dressed like an Arab, stepped from a doorway on our right, apparently the room in which I was being forced. When we passed through the threshold, there sat the fat little Caesar in the middle of the room waiting for me.

"Put him in that chair," he said to al-Tajir. And so, al- Tajir did so…hard.

"Ow," I said. "Watch the merchandise." I then shed my mask.

"And so, Bruce McGowan, you actually come to *me*. How convenient. I don't remember sending you an invitation; therefore, you had none to give to my gate guard. I hope you left him alive."

"He's alive, but he'll be sleeping all night. I have a question, Karn. You were in our tour group all last week, yet you never said a word to me like "did you have a nice trip or aren't you going to thank me for it?"

"You missed my point, McGowan; it was all about

anonymity. I'm sure you didn't recognize me or you would have said something. I thought that luring you here and watching you for a week would be like a lion drawing its prey into its clutches and playing with it before he devours it. However, how many times must the lion try to kill the prey before he succeeds? You're elusive, but as you find out now, not invincible."

"Your very words to Roy Farrell after you thought your camel jockey had killed me."

"That was a sore miscalculation on my part. Unfortunately for him, we mistook the man for you."

"Have you enjoyed the prison my daughter's bullet put you in?"

"I don't blame her for that, McGowan. She was only protecting her father."

"How the hell did you get out of jail, anyway?"

"Well, that is an interesting story. You see all these people of the Middle Eastern persuasion I have around me? They were allied with me and my Weather Underground brotherhood. Obviously, you didn't know that. Since you didn't take them down with my American cohorts, they grew stronger.

Being the special prisoner that I was, I had the best of medical care. The prison doctors moved me three times, each time to facilities that not only provided the latest in quadriplegia care but were less secure than the last. I suppose they figured that a man who could only move his head was not a flight risk. Friends such as you see here never forgot me. One day they just waltzed into my facility and wheeled me out. Because I was not worth much to anyone any more as a prisoner or otherwise, no one ever came after me.

"In the meantime, because my Arab friends enjoyed a deeply entrenched Islamoterrorist network, as you assholes refer to it, located right here in Gay Puree, this is where I ended up. And oh, did I mention I had one surviving relative on the face of this earth coincidentally living here, a fabulously wealthy one at that. He took me in. He allowed me to bring with me my trusted friend, Mr. al-Tajir you see standing there, who by the way is eagerly awaiting my command to kill you. Mr. al-Tajir has been a blessing to me. Every natural need that I have, he takes care of."

"Things like wiping your chin when food falls out of your mouth and your ass when…"

"*Shut the hell up, McGowan!* You are in no position to mock me. I am doing you a service by keeping you alive these few minutes left in your life."

"If I *do* only have a few minutes left, you're doing me a *dis*-service by making me listen to that nauseating voice of yours."

At first, he merely glared at me; then the glare turned into a smile. "You just ran out of that precious time, McGowan. As Mr. al-Tajir puts a bullet in your head, I will be getting back to my guests."

"Won't your guests hear the shot and wonder?"

"Notice what Mr. al-Tajir is doing."

I did. He was attaching a suppressor.

"Take him to the garage. I don't want his blood splattered on my expensive rugs. From there, you can drive his filthy carcass out into the Valley of the Bones. Let the buzzards feed." As he puffed into his tube and wheeled toward the door, he said, "See you in hell, McGowan." His cackle was nauseating.

As the second man at the door began escorting Karn along the hallway toward the party room, alTajir motioned with his gun for me to stand up.

"Look, Al," I began. "You have your gun and mine as well. May I have mine back? We can make this a fair fight."

"Out the door and down the hall," he ordered.

When I passed through the doorway, I turned left toward the big party hall.

"The other direction, McGowan."

So, I did an 'about face.'

"The elevator to the garage is on the right. Stop there."

After pressing the button, we stood waiting for a moment. I asked, "So how did Karn's uncle die and when?" I was interested to know how long Karn had been enjoying his inheritance. Why, I don't know.

"He died ten years ago of natural causes. The poison I fed him *naturally* caused him to die." He had a smirk on his face when he said that.

"You turned out to be a very bad man, Al. Did your mother hate you or something?"

The only response he had was, "The door is now open. Get in."

When I stepped in, he followed. Keeping the muzzle of his gun on me, he then pressed the *down* button. After a short trip, the door opened. "Step out," he ordered.

Always looking for opportunities in cases like these, I waited. Waited until he had turned his face partially away from me, having no peripheral vision on his left side. Suddenly, he let out a groan…the kind of guttural, breath-stopping groan one makes when he gets shot. But the fact was, he had just been stabbed. The butter knife in my jacket pocket had found its way into his liver. I had to jam it in hard, considering the blade was dull. With my left hand I grabbed the barrel of his gun and wrested it from his hand. Slowly he sank to his knees and cried out in pain while a pool of blood began forming on his thobe. Although I was sure he'd die an agonizing death within the hour, I went ahead and finished him off with his own gun…one round just behind his ear. Seconds later as he lay still in the floor of the elevator, blood began pouring from the back of his head. When al-Tajir's body was found, I was sure Karn would be on the phone to the police telling them it was me who invaded his house and killed his primary caregiver. He would testify to that. It was time to run.

Finding my Sig in his belt, I shoved it in mine. My fingerprints were on it. After sprinting across the yard toward the front gate, I saw that the gate guard was now on his feet and rubbing his head. When he saw me, he grabbed for his gun, but not in time to avoid another conk on the head. I extended his nap.

I wasted no time on the road back to the hotel. After parking my car, again on the street versus in the garage where there were cameras, I waited until I saw four people having been out for the evening preparing to enter through the front door. I was the fifth. Ducking down so that my face would be shielded by the others, we went in. I knew there was a camera on the outside of the building but was unsure there was one at the lobby desk. Nonetheless, I made sure the four of them were between me and any camera. Thinking there might also be cameras in the two elevators, I took the stairs to my floor. Once inside the room, I cast off my clothes down to my tee and shorts and settled in for the night. The box containing half my pizza still sat on the room's desk.

Sure enough just before eleven there was a knock at my door and a voice yelling "Police." Checking the peephole, I did see two uniformed officers and not two Middle Eastern goons wanting to cut me up in little pieces. Looking like I just rolled out of bed, which I actually did, I greeted them. "What can I do for you?" I asked.

"We are here to arrest you."

"For what?"

The lead officer replied, "I must first advise you that you do not have to say anything…"

"The Miranda rights. I know them. I didn't know they were popular here in France, though. So, what's the problem?"

"There is a complaint that you broke into a house and murdered a man in the west section of the city. It is at a large estate called Ramatuelle owned by a man named Cadieux who…"

"Do I look like I've even been out anywhere tonight?"

"I do not know whether you have or not, but we will now take you to our headquarters for official questioning."

They eyed the pizza box and half bottle of wine on the desk which I wanted them to do. "This is not to say you were at the house tonight; we still need to ask questions."

"Can you first call Lieutenant Allard. He knows me and can vouch for me."

"We will do that, but you must still come with us."

"I'll need to put clothes on. While I'm doing so, would you two like some leftover pizza? My supper in the room tonight."

"No, Monsieur. Merci. Thank you."

While I was putting clothes on, not the same ones I was wearing earlier, the lead officer called Jacques Allard. I didn't understand the conversation, but after a minute or so, he handed the phone off to me.

"Bruce, what is going on there?"

"I'm being accused of murder."

"I heard that. I thought you were staying in tonight with pizza, wine and TV."

"Your officers are looking at my half empty pizza box which was this evening's supper."

"Do I have to ask you if you went to a party at the Cadieux house and murdered a man?"

"Ask away, Jacques. No one can say that I was at his house tonight. If Cadieux or Karn says I was, he'll have to provide proof."

"Yes, he will. If you promise to not leave the hotel tonight, I will tell the officers not to take you in."

"Thanks for doing that. I have no desire to spend the night in a Paris cell. I like *this* bed just fine."

"As you will still be in Paris until Sunday, can you come by my office tomorrow?"

"Yes. And I'd like to take you up on the offer to

meet you and your wife for dinner tomorrow night if we're still on."

"We will do that unless there is evidence that you murdered someone at the Ramatuelle house." The way he said that sounded as though he were trying to be funny, but I knew he meant it.

Chapter Seventeen

After the officers left, I started thinking. It was a good thing they didn't want to go search my rental. That's where I left the two guns. And if I had been taken into their station for questioning, any sharp investigator would have done a GSR test on my hand to check for gunshot residue. It was imperative that first thing in the morning I get rid of the guns and the butter knife. I needed to do so anyway before I left for home.

I had developed a good relationship with Allard and would not be happy with myself if I ended up lying to him. That night I had danced around his and the officer's questions by *insinuating* I had been in my room all evening with my pizza and wine. The next day, I would be asked point blank if I had been to Ramatuelle and if I had killed Monsieur Cadieux's caregiver. Yes, I'd lie to save my neck. It wasn't worth losing my freedom and my wife when I spent the rest of my life in a French jail. And neither Karn nor his dead goon were worth it as well.

Even before having breakfast, I went to my rental car and drove to the south end of the Pont Marie Bridge and parked. There weren't many people out for a Saturday morning, so my presence on the bridge went largely unnoticed. For a moment I merely stood with my forearms resting on the stone reinforcement looking down into the waters of the Seine. An elderly couple out for their morning walk eyed me suspiciously, likely wondering if I was thinking of jumping. After they passed me, they even turned around to take another look. I then waited until they were nearly off the bridge when I pulled both pistols and the knife from my jacket pocket and dropped them into the water. Evidence gone.

After knocking down a plate of banana crepes back at the hotel cafe, I began walking toward the police station. I hadn't made an appointment with the lieutenant, but as I was sure he wanted to see me as soon as possible, I began hoofing it. Occasionally, I looked beside and behind me on the street to ensure that no one was following in one of Karn's black vehicles or trailing me as a pedestrian. I imagined Karn to be so angry that he would put me on his target list the first opportunity he could. Maybe a drive-by shooting or sticking a knife in my back when I stopped for a light at an intersection. But thankfully, his people were no-shows as I walked unmolested into the justice center.

The lieutenant greeted me with a smile and handshake but then pointed to the chair in front of his desk. "Have a seat, Bruce. Let's talk about this allegation against you."

"Where does it come from?"

"Your old acquaintance, now known as Henri Cadieux. He says you trespassed into his house while he was having a party for a few friends and his people caught you. They brought you to him and you two had a rather serious conversation. Even though you and he had a bad history, he was willing to let bygones be bygones. That's why he now admits he bought you and your wife a nice vacation. He had much to atone for in the past. However, you weren't willing to make amends and stormed out. When he threatened to call the police to have you arrested for trespassing, you stabbed his man and then took a gun from your jacket and shot him. His story is very specific and full of details. What do you say about all that?"

I laughed. "Do you know how all that sounds? Can anyone really believe from what I told you about our history that he not only wanted to forgive me for crashing his party but wanted to kiss and make up? He killed Roy Farrell. And if I supposedly killed his friend, where would I get a gun? The man hates my guts and wants to see me dead. We both know that. He brought me here to kill me. And in one last attempt to bring me down, he concocts this story. If he can't kill me, he'll try to have me put in jail."

"His loyal caregiver is now dead. How do you suppose he ended up that way?"

"Maybe one of his partying guests became too rowdy and got into a scuffle with him. To protect his valued guest, he comes up with the idea to pin the murder on me."

"Possible. But I do have to tell you, I have a responsibility to investigate all allegations. Not only will we be contacting Cadieux's guests to ask them if anyone saw you at the party. I will be floating your Interpol photo around. I also took the liberty to secure images from the hotel cameras to determine if you left the building last night. I was pleased to find you are not on any of them. They support your story that you had your dinner in your room. If none of the party guests claim to have seen you, you will be free to go home tomorrow."

"How can you get that done by tomorrow afternoon?"

"I have the list of the guests and our officers will take all day today to send your photo around. We will be able to determine whether they are lying."

"Strange to find myself being investigated. What happens if Karn pays a few of his guests to say they saw me there."

"I will have to charge you and send the case up for indictment. You won't be going home."

"Now that we got that out of the way, are we on for tonight."

"I have already made dinner reservations for the three of us at seven at Le Petit Soleil."

I was starting to feel guilty that I didn't come clean with Jacques. He was treating me fairly and with credibility. I didn't out-and-out lie about anything. I just kept asking questions and making comments about Karn's cock-and-bull story. There was no guest at the party who could identify me. But, if push came to shove and it was somehow found out I was there, I could identify Devereux. If the photos of him with Karn in the background landed in their justice system and then there was discovered a sudden spike in his bank account about the time Devereux decided not to prosecute Karn, his fat ass would be grass and Allard the lawn mower.

I found Vivienne Allard an immensely attractive woman, bright, multilingual like her husband and a delightful conversationalist. No sooner had we sat down than she laid the law down…no shop talk at the dinner table. That meant the subject of Karn would not come up and neither would the murder of Roy Farrell. Although I wanted to know more about the couple as a family, she immediately redirected the conversation to questions about me, Adriana, our home in West Virginia, and if we had a dog. As my nights had been a mixed bag of boredom and death, I needed to spend a night enjoying good food and drink, intelligent dialogue, and laughs with people like the Allards.

"Jacques told me he had the pleasure of meeting your wife before she left and that she is a very beautiful woman."

Jacques appeared embarrassed and tried to backpedal. "What I believe I said was that she was nice and very lovely."

"Whatever you told her, I'm sure she would be extremely flattered," I said.

"We have never been to America and would like to go someday. One place on our list will be your Wolf Laurel. It sounds wonderful."

"It is. The county we live in has rich, green farmland and I run all over it almost every morning. Got to stay in shape at my age, you know."

"Oh, I am a runner as well," she said. "Seven o'clock each morning you can see me pounding the sidewalk with our two dogs. Three miles, I go." And she was in extremely fine shape indeed. "Not to change the subject, but as I know you're retired, what was your work?"

"I spent 20 years as a special agent for the FBI and then I was hired by the U.S. Department of State. I worked there for another nine years or so. After that, I did a little freelance work for the government, as they say, at their beck and call."

"Doing what? I am sorry and don't mean to be intrusive; I'm just interested."

"I worked in counter-terrorism, profiling bad guys

who pose a danger to our country and its citizens."

"That sounds very intriguing. Like something one may see in a movie. Can you tell us about some of your experiences?"

Jacques placed his hand on her arm. "Vivienne, you are the one who set the table rules tonight. No talk of work."

I didn't discuss my function at Team Zulu further and certainly made it a point never to tell case stories.

The restaurant was unique as it served only about a dozen dinners. But their large dinner platters, which served four to six people, contained a little of everything, including mussels in white wine, creamy veal stew, steak tartar, roasted duck, and an out-of-this-world casserole. It was what we Americans called a family-style smorgasbord…just rake a little of everything onto your plate like at the Golden Corral.

Our dinner ended an hour before our conversation did. The three of us had a couple of after-dinner cocktails each, then the Allards decided it was time to go home. Ten-fifteen. As enjoyable an evening as it was, an emotional cloud came over me as I drove back to the hotel. My new friend, the French police lieutenant, could very well be compelled to arrest me for murder before I flew back to the United States. He would have about fifteen hours to make his case.

I didn't hear anything from Jacques Allard that Sunday morning, the day I was to fly out, nor did any officers of the law show at my hotel to arrest me for murder. Either none of Karn's guests had been bribed to say they saw me at the party or Jacques had shut down any further accusations against me by Karn. There were two reasons the complaint would die on the vine: any guests who said they saw me there would have to stand up in court and swear to it. I figured not even a healthy bribe would make a person perjure him or herself. Secondly, if Karn pursued the matter, all his past, including his life as terrorist Jonas Karn would come out. Millionaire Henri Cadieux would cease being a prominent figure in Parisian society.

My flight was leaving de Gaulle at two-forty but given the hassle of going through security and customs, I gathered myself up at eleven, had a quick brunch and checked out at the desk. My bill for the week had already been paid. Thanks, Jacques.

Left at the desk, however, was an envelope with my name on it. I wondered if it might be a 'Thank You' note from Jacques and his wife for the dinner I bought the evening before. I had insisted I pay for it much to their protest, but it was the least I could do considering he had befriended me and put me up in the swanky Saint- Loraine. Before I left the lobby, I went off to the side and ripped open the envelope. It read:

You took from me someone that I dearly loved. Now I will take the life of someone you love. I assure you my arms can reach across the Atlantic. You will mourn until you yourself will die. Goodbye, McGowan.

The message sent a fiery shard of adrenaline through my arteries. I've had threats made against me several times, which bothered me not in the least; but to have my loved ones' lives threatened made me both furious and worried. Karn had already targeted both Adriana and my daughter Caroline. He had kidnapped Caroline and inadvertently shot Adriana, the bullet being meant for me. But, as he was wheelchair bound in Paris and a fugitive from justice in the U.S., he would have to engage one of his American thugs to carry out the threat. I would have to caution both of my ladies to be vigilant. I didn't want to just call them from the airport to warn them. Adriana especially would be in a state of panic. However, as I was still a day away from home, I prayed Karn would not try to carry out his threat before I had a chance to personally inform Adriana of his intent. I should have killed the son- of-a-bitch along with al-Tajir when I had the opportunity, and all this shit would have been over. Not one of my better decisions.

As Karn had known where I was staying, I wondered if something of the explosive nature had been planted in or under my rental. However, even though the threatening note told that my loved ones would die, it also said I would suffer for a while until my life ended as well. I took it I was safe for the time being. But just in case the bastard was lying in his note, I checked beneath the car and under the hood anyway. Nothing. I then closed my eyes tightly and turned the key. No boom. Both I and the auto garage were spared destruction. But then in retrospect, I thought…how would any of Karn's men have known which car was mine anyway. As far as I knew, none of them ever saw me in it. I then backed from my space. It was a twenty-minute ride to the airport.

Chapter Eighteen

It was smart to leave the hotel when I did. The line at the airport was ten city blocks long…and that was just security. By the time I got through both customs and security and then arrived at my gate, the flight was boarding. My seat was supposed to have been 12B, but the airline, in its predictable wisdom, put me in seat 37E, near the back of the plane, middle row, middle seat. Again, McGowan's Law. Complaining didn't help. But, considering I had been away from my wife for one long week, eight more hours was a drop in the bucket. Then there was the layover and second flight from JFK to Charleston, WV. My hours in the air would be emotionally agonizing, however, as I would be worrying the entire time that Karn had already dispatched his cutthroats in the States to kill one of my ladies…or both.

The good thing was, there were no big, sweaty Bubbas on either side of me. The small grandmother on my right gave me a nice smile, talked a little about her grandchildren she had just visited in Paris, but then slept most of the way thereafter. The thirty-some-year-old beauty with the legs of a model didn't talk much but nonetheless kept me distracted. Then I remembered I had a daughter her age and a wife who…well, a wife. I also remembered I was worried about her. I tried to take my mind off my worries by engrossing myself in the three movies I watched. But, for the life of me, at the end of my flight, I couldn't recall the storyline or even the names of the movies.

Maybe it was all the anguish, fretful vexations and

over-thinking I did on the flight, but I found that the hours went quicker than I thought. Part of the reason was I had done something I rarely did…fell asleep. I think I was out about two hours when the suddenness of bright sun rays kissing the sea below us and flaring through a starboard window opened my eyes. The sweet voice of the flight attendant then told us to bring our seats back up as we were twenty minutes from touchdown.

As soon as we landed at JFK and I had cleared customs, I found a seat between two gates where no one else was sitting and called Adriana. How relieved I was that she answered. I had talked to her every evening of my second week in Paris, making love to her over the phone with my romantic voice, but this time, even though she was aware I was now back in the good old USA, she detected a sense of urgency in my voice.

"What's wrong, Skip? You sound a little strange. You're almost home."

"I'm just so happy to hear your voice, sweetheart. I can't *tell* you how happy. But I have to tell you something. Don't be alarmed that I'm asking you to do this, but I don't want you going out the rest of the day."

"But I'll be driving to the airport to pick you up in a little while."

"No. I'll rent a car and drive it to the Greenbrier airport. Then I'll get a taxi home."

"What is all this and why don't you want me to go out?"

I then told her the entire week's story and how I ended up killing the man named al-Tajir, Karn's trusted servant who had not only murdered Roy Farrell, but was trying to kill me. And Karn had now put out a hit on my loved ones, as per his note to me. "I don't know if he's just blowing smoke, but I'm not taking any chances. I'll be calling Caroline as well."

I thought she'd be frantic in her response, but there was an incredible calmness in her voice. "I'm not worried, Skip. Living with you, I've been in danger for years, but you've taught me to take care of myself, how to use a weapon, and to always stay open-eyed and watchful. Don't worry. I want to come and get you."

"No, please respect my wishes. When I get home, we can talk about how we can both stay vigilant."

"You should have killed the bastard when you had the chance."

I burst out laughing. There was that 'bastard' word again. "Yeah, just as I told myself a dozen times today."

"Okay, then. Have it your way. Just call me when you get to Charley West and are on your way here."

"I will. You stay put and keep my Smith and Wesson close to you."

"Be safe the rest of the way in. Love you, Hon."

"I love you, too."

I felt better about things. She reacted calmer than I expected. I knew she could handle herself and especially knew how to handle my .45. It was a cannon and a hell of a hole puncher. She also didn't scold me for going after Karn and the man who stabbed Roy, even after I promised her I wouldn't. And yeah, hindsight being 20-20, I should have left Karn dead.

"Hi, Dad. Haven't heard from you in a few weeks.

Are you doing well?"

"Fine, darling. I'm just returning from Paris."

"Well, lucky you. And you didn't invite me along?"

"I knew you wouldn't go anyway. Say, you got a few minutes?"

"For you I have more than a few."

"Let me tell you a true story." I needed to ease into the conversation.

I gave her the entire rundown of our lovely first week and not-so-lovely second, leaving nothing out, including bumping off al-Tajir." It took me about fifteen minutes to cover it all. "So now here I sit at JFK on my way home."

"Jonas Karn, huh? I thought we were done with him."

"If you had moved the muzzle of your gun just a few inches, we would be."

"Sorry, I didn't. I guess I was just in a hurry." She then chuckled.

"Be wary, Caroline. This slime ball apparently still has disciples in the U.S. as well as France. He's allied with Islamofascists and now has the money to fund their movements."

"I'll keep my eyes open, Dad. No one will try anything here at my Bureau office, but I'll be especially vigilant at home."

"I hope so. What are you folks carrying these days?"

"Glock G19 Gen 5s."

"Nice. Wear it to the gym, to the church house and

even Chuckie Cheese…everywhere."

"Not to worry. So, why didn't you put a bullet in Mr. Karn's head while you were there?"

"Exactly what Adriana said."

"She actually did?"

"I've rubbed off on her all these years later."

"Good."

"Well, I have to get down to my gate. Might have to fight to keep my seat. I'm sitting in 5A this time."

"You keep a lookout yourself, Dad."

"Always. I never know when somebody else might come from out of my past looking to settle a score."

"You all need to go live on a deserted island somewhere and leave no forwarding."

"Don't think I haven't thought about it."

"Bye, Dad. Love ya, old man."

My flight landed in Charleston at seven-forty, Daylight Eastern time. I was a bit worn out, but I still had to pick up a rental and drive the hour and a half to turn the car in at the Greenbrier Airport. Then my taxi ride would take another twenty minutes to the house.

I called Adriana as soon as the cabbie entered our gravel driveway to assure that when she heard it approaching, I wouldn't be greeted by a hail of bullets. After paying the driver, I thanked him and turned to find an angelic being standing on our front porch, illuminated by the porch light.

"I am so, so happy you're home and safe." She hugged my neck tightly and kissed me like we were brand new lovers. "Did you eat something?"

"I had a sandwich on the plane to New York."

"That was hours ago. Let me fix you something."

"No. I'm not at all hungry. Just tired is all."

"Well then, I'll start the shower for you."

"Got something in mind?"

"Maybe. It depends on how tired you are."

"Are you trying to seduce me, Mrs. Robinson?"

She laughed. "You picked up on that, did you? What was your first clue?'"

"I'm not as naive as you think."

"Well then, set your suitcase down and follow me."

Chapter Nineteen

Before I had my breakfast cereal and fruit, I took a run in the countryside. It would be the first time I was going to be apprehensive about leaving Adriana alone at the house while I was out for any length of time. But was I always going to be thinking along those lines? I often find myself doing a lot of thinking and even talking to myself when I'm jogging. One of the thoughts I had was whether Karn's note was for real or was he just trying to keep me on edge the rest of my life…or his…whichever ended first? If I ignored it and went about my life as usual, I'd be letting my guard down. And in doing so, I'd be exposing Adriana to danger. Did he really have killer disciples in the U.S? Whether he did or not, I wasn't going to let that question drive me nuts.

When I returned about an hour later, feeling wasted because I hadn't run in two weeks, I had my light breakfast and then sat down in what I refer to as my big easy. I then found the photos I took of Devereux on my cellphone camera. I intended to send them to Jacques Allard but wanted to wait till I arrived home to do it. Sending them while still in Paris would tell him I lied about being at the party and then I *would* be arrested for the murder. But, if I emailed or texted them to him after my arrival to the

U.S., two things could happen: first, I could be extradited back to Paris to stand trial for murder; but just as important to me was that I'd be throwing away my bonded friendship with Jacques and Vivienne, my being a suspected murderer *and* a liar. Jacques would feel deceived and betrayed and that would be a bitter pill for me to swallow. Something I didn't want to live with. But in all fairness, Jacques never asked me directly if I killed al-Tajir or if I was even at Karn's party. But I suppose in being evasive as I was, I was not being truthful.

But what if I found a way to send them to him anonymously and not from my own email or cellphone text? I wasn't any techie, so I had to get help from someone who could show me a way to get the photos to him without him knowing they came from me.

While I was sitting and viewing, Adriana came into the den and asked what I was doing. "Just looking at some photos I took on my cellphone." I was right in the middle of the pictures I had taken on my re-do tour.

"Oh, super! I didn't know you took these."

"It was this past week. I felt bad because I allowed our camera to be stolen, so on my trolley tour last week, I captured most of the venues we saw together. I didn't get them all, especially any indoor photos of the cathedrals or the city from the platform of the Eiffel Tower, but..."

"You got Montmartre and Sacre Coeur and that magnificent panoramic view. Good boy, Skippy. We'll make slides out of them." She then paused. "But what are these of?"

"They're the proof the authorities were looking for to nail me for crashing Karn's party and killing Mr. al-Tajir."

"Uh oh. Good thing you got out of Paris before they found these on you. Hmmm, there's Karn and there he is again. Who's the Batman?"

"That, my dear, is the deputy prosecutor I told you about who handled or mishandled the case against Karn and al-Tajir. I'm sure he was paid handsomely for refusing to prosecute the case."

"A slob if I ever saw one," she said.

"The bat cave is missing one of its Chiropterans. A slimy one at that."

For a good half hour, I sat and thought about how I could get the photos I took of Devereux with Karn in the background to Jacques Allard. I considered just downloading, printing and sending them in the mail anonymously. But they would be postmarked in the U.S., specifically West Virginia. I didn't want any inkling that they were mailed from anywhere in the United States or he'd know for sure who sent them. So, I came up with a scheme I thought was brilliant. I'd buy a burner phone, set up a ghost email account, send the photos from my phone to the burner, and then from the burner on to Jacques. Could it work? It sounded plausible, anyway. But first, I'd talk to an old friend in the State Department who I knew to be an IT genius.

At 10:30 that morning, Adriana came out of the bedroom dressed nicely in a business suit, smelling like one of those scratch-and-sniff perfume ads in our Belk flyers.

"Where do you think you're going?" I asked her.

"To a city hall meeting luncheon."

"Madam Mayor (which she was of our small town), remember the conversation we had last night? I don't want you to be a target out there."

"But I can't live my life hiding inside our house for God knows *how* long, never going out."

"I get it. I really do. But I also know this threat is very real. Karn's arms can reach across the sea and then some, especially with the money he now has. Any time you go out that door, one of his hired assassins could be sitting out there ready to strike."

"You're of course trying to scare me into staying home. Well, it's not working. I don't scare."

"Then, let me go with you when you go out. Two sets of eyes are better than one, and mine are well trained."

She sighed in resignation. "If it will make you feel better, fine. Take me to my meetings, shop with me at the grocery, sit and talk with the Vietnamese girl while she gives me a manicure and watch Becky while she does my hair."

"If that's what it takes to keep you safe, I will. When do we leave?"

That Tuesday was the first day of several days that I accompanied Adriana when she went anywhere. Whether Karn would make good on his threat, I didn't know. Was his threat real, or did he write the note to me as a parting shot, knowing its content would keep me rattled when I returned home and stay on edge until it drove me nuts? I knew he had spent years hating my guts, ever since the day I kicked the shit out of him and put him away for however many years it was until the legal system thought he'd learned his lesson and let him out. The fact that he put out the lure by purchasing us a trip to Paris with the intent to kill me proved his hate would never cease. So, causing the death of someone I love, knowing I would grieve bitterly until the day he had me killed as well, would satisfy his vindictive quest for blood. I had no doubt the threat *was* real.

It was a good week after I arrived home that I sent the party photos of Devereux and Karn via my new burner phone. I knew it was possible to trace their origin, but I didn't think Jacques would take the time to do that. He'd be more interested in the content. But then he'd also be wondering why someone would have sent them to him in the first place. A few days later, from out of the blue, the lieutenant called me.

"I assume you arrived home in good order," he said.

"Sure did. Monsieur Karn didn't have the plane shot down."

He laughed. "Now that you mentioned him, you will never guess who was at Karn's house the night of his big party, the one where you were alleged to have killed his bodyguard."

I knew where he was going with that, but I played ignorant. "Macron, the French president?"

"Someone not that high up, but around here, he thinks he is…Devereux. Your instincts were right about him. As he is friends with Cadieux, that is why he would not find the evidence against him credible in the death of Monsieur Farrell. I received photos from someone that clearly shows him with Cadieux in the background. They are now in the hands of the chief procureur, and I have suggested she look into charging him for criminal breach of his duties and obstruction."

"And obviously, he didn't see me at the party, or he would have insisted I be charged."

"But then he would have divulged he was there. He is what you Americans call a real skuzzbucket."

I laughed. "So, you like our American expressions, do you?"

"I think they are very funny and fit well in our society sometimes."

"I need to tell you something that was waiting for me when I left the Saint-Loraine to come home… a note from Karn telling me that I would soon be mourning the death of a loved one, then I was going to be a dead man myself."

"But he is here and you and your loved ones are there."

"He still has followers and assassins here…and of course the money to keep them funded."

"I am concerned for you and Adriana, Bruce. Are you taking measures to protect yourselves?"

"In spite of her protests, I am her constant bodyguard. I go with her everywhere and keep my eyes on cars with their windows down, bushes and every other possible ambush position. I'm armed, she's armed, and I suspect any stranger that gets within six feet of her."

"It is good to stay circumspect."

"You could do us a favor by bumping him off, you know."

"Bumping…?"

"Ending his life…but of course making it look like an accident, like bouncing his wheelchair down a long flight of stairs. Just get creative."

"Hey, friend, I have to remind you that sometimes our phone lines here are monitored. So, whoever is listening in, I'm not part of this conversation."

I chuckled. "Only kidding. If something does happen to him, *I'm only kidding.*"

"Well, I just thought you'd like to know about your friend Cadieux. I have also asked the procureur to reopen the Farrell matter to have Cadieux's activities reviewed, such as purchasing your trip, killing Monsieur Farrell thinking it was you, and mocking you by saying your name at the death scene. I am sure a different, very smart procureur assigned to the case can correlate everything. I also have your sworn statement and affidavit, so it may not be necessary for you to return here and testify."

"Me go back there? Only if your folks will pay for my trip."

"We will see." He paused; then I heard him draw in a breath and exhale. "I do need to ask you one more question, Bruce."

"Shoot."

"If you did not kill Cadieux's *loved one,* as he referred to him, why would he put a bulls-eye on *your* loved one? I would think because he was not successful in killing you here, it is you who would continue to be his target."

I'm sure I was noticeably quiet in response to his question. But then I replied, "I can't keep up the charade any longer, Jacques. You know, don't you?"

"That you actually do have blood on your hands? It was not difficult to figure out. I probably knew it all along. However, you were careful not to tell me directly that you were in his house."

"I suppose you think less of me now. And I'm sorry to have misled you."

"No, I do not think less of you; I consider you to be a careful and shrewd man. And you killed the man who murdered Roy Farrell."

"It was self-defense, Jacques. Karn discovered it was me behind the mask I was wearing and ordered al-Tajir to take me to the garage to send me to the bone yard. I just got to him first."

"You stabbed him with a butter knife and then shot him. That is what the coroner reported."

"Well, it seemed like a good idea at the time."

I thought I heard him laugh.

"And it had to be you who sent the photos of Devereux."

"Guilty."

"You must know if you come here to testify, Cadieux's lawyer will ask you directly if you were at Ramatuelle and killed al-Tajir."

"I thought about that. I wouldn't perjure myself."

"But such admission will harm the procureur's case."

"I thought about that as well."

"However, on the other hand, when all the evidence is presented, you going to Ramatuelle may be considered by the court as self-defense. He was an old nemesis who baited you to come to Paris so that he could watch you be killed. You were only defending yourself by confronting him as he was sure to have you killed before you left Paris."

"I'm banking on that. Again, I'm sorry I wasn't straight with you about Ramatuelle. I should have been up front."

"No worries. If I had been in your situation, perhaps I would have gone after him too. We can discuss your very bad decision should you decide to help the procureur at trial. I hope you do so. But, anyway, Bruce, I don't mean to break off our conversation so soon; I need to get back to work now. Much to do today. Au revoir."

Chapter Twenty

On the 10th of May, a Friday night, we went to dinner at one of our delightful small-town restaurants, ironically called the French Goat, and had a succulent duck cassoulet with all those wonderful sides and a carafe of Louis Jadot. Our quaint little village once won the title Coolest Town in America, mainly because of its unique, eclectic shops, artistic flair, and hip, vibrant atmosphere. When I left there back in the late sixties, the streets were filled with farmers in plaid shirts and bib coveralls, finely dressed southern aristocrats, many of whom were adult children and grandchildren of Civil War veterans, and cadets like me from one of America's most honored military academies marching through town to church on a Sunday night to the thunder of drums. There are a lot of hippy types now, but good kids, smart, ambitious, and polite.

Many of the visitors to this cool town are people very similar to those kids and could easily be recognized as tourists and appreciators of culture and history. However, noticeably out of place were two men at a table about twenty feet from us, not peculiar or atypical because they were dark-complected and had hair black as coal, but because of their manner. While they ate their dinner, they neither spoke nor looked anywhere but into their plates. Their faces were cold and had a look of callousness and urgency. I watch people. I watch everyone. When something about them seems out of kilt, I keep my eyes on them. Adriana says I'm rude when I do that. But my intuition about people and their behaviors is usually spot on. I had seen these kinds of faces before. *They were the faces of killers.*

We had eaten half our dinners, when I said, quietly and calmly, "Adriana lay your fork down and don't look around. Don't question me or even change your expression. We're leaving. I'm calling over the server for our check."

"Skip, what…"

In an even lower voice, "Don't say anything…just give me a smile."

She did.

I summoned the waitress with a raised finger. "Our bill, please, Lydia."

"Right away."

Still, neither of the two men was looking in our direction, but I knew peripherally they were.

I paid our bill, thanked Lydia, and then took Adriana's hand to escort her up from her chair. Without hurry, we left the restaurant, but once on the street, I took her hand again and walked her to our car. After seating her, I hustled around to the driver's side.

"Skip, what is this all about?"

"Just watch. Did you see the two men a couple of tables over from us?"

"I didn't notice anyone in particular."

"I'm waiting for them to come out."

"Do you think…?"

"Yeah, I do. And they not only know our car, but where we live."

I could tell she was now scared. "What do we

do now?"

"Keep an eye on them. Obviously, they followed us from home so they could get a good look at us. I'm going to move the car so that they won't know that I'm watching them. Then we're going to sit a while and wait for them. I want to see where they're staying."

I was pretty sure the two men just wanted to get a good look at *Adriana* to see what she looked like and not target the wrong woman. Karn himself had already made that mistake. I'm sure he warned his thugs to be sure. The little shit wasted no time carrying out what he wrote in his note. Adriana would die; I would be given that painful period of mourning for who knows how long; and then somebody would come after me.

We waited about fifteen minutes until we saw them come out. They looked at the place where I had parked when we came into the restaurant and then walked further down the street to a Tahoe. Momentarily, I saw the taillights come on and the vehicle pull away. I began following at a distance.

"How do you know these are bad people?" she asked me.

"Trust me, I know."

"I don't mind telling you, I'm a bit unnerved."

"Don't worry. They don't intend to do anything tonight. Tomorrow might be different."

"You were right in insisting to go everywhere with me."

"And I will especially be watching out around the house. You and I will not be alone until this threat is over."

"And when will that be?"

"When I have gotten rid of Karn once and for all."

"What will you do, tough guy, put a contract out on him?"

"I don't do business that way. If I can't do anything myself, it doesn't get done."

"You're here, he's there."

"Exactly."

She gave me that look. "You're not thinking of going back to Paris."

"Don't know."

"No." She apparently finished our conversation.

I followed the Tahoe's taillights another half mile until the vehicle turned into a motel parking lot. It was the first time I noticed the Michigan plates. Of course, it could have been a rental. If not, they had come a long way to do their dirty work.

So that they wouldn't realize I had been following them, I passed on by the entrance. A hundred feet later, I made a U turn and pulled into a separate entrance to the motel. After parking a dozen cars down from where they were just getting out of the Tahoe, I watched them enter the building. Could I have been mistaken about them, allowing my imagination to dictate? Could they have just been businessmen on the road? But they didn't act or look like businessmen. They didn't say a word to each other in the restaurant; and then there were those grim, nefarious looks on their faces. Businessmen let their hair down in the evening, enjoying a few laughs, a couple of beers, joking with the waitresses…not these guys. And businessmen aren't dressed all in black. They stood out for all the wrong reasons.

After taking down the Tahoe's tag number, I then pulled away from the parking space. On the way home, I stopped by our local county sheriff's detachment to see if my golfing buddy, Sheriff Sam Greene, happened to be there. But, at nine-thirty on a Friday night? Nah. However, another friend, Corporal Bobby Jaworski, the kid we called The Polish Pile-driver, was. Bobby was a standout wrestler in high school a few years back who went on to win the state middleweight wrestling championship. I took Adriana inside the HQ with me.

Bobby was standing by the copier when we came in. "Bruce, man," he called out. "You out again with somebody else's wife?" He grinned at Adriana.

"Shhh. Don't spread it around."

"So, what are you doin' here on a Friday night?"

I handed him the slip of paper with the tag number.

"Can you have somebody run this plate for me?"

"You get run off the road or somethin'?"

"No. Long-ass story, Bobby. Something I need to tell you and Sam about in the next day or so."

"Sounds serious."

"It is. Can you check it out?"

"Sure. Brenda, can you take care of this?"

She typed in the information and in a matter of seconds, printed out the response. "It's registered to Agresseur Enterprises in Detroit, Michigan," she said.

A company with a French name that sounded suspiciously like aggressor. So, they drove all the way in from Detroit to carry out their mission. What kind of business would two men in black have in rural Greenbrier County, West Virginia? If I was wrong and they had an explainable purpose other than ending the life of my precious wife, I'd eat my Glock.

"Can you and Sam come out to Wolf Laurel tomorrow, Bobby? Need to talk."

"You've got me intrigued now, Bruce," the deputy said. "Can you give me a hint?"

"There are two men in a Tahoe wearing that license plate that bear watching. I'll have more information for you when you get there."

"Okay, Bruce. I'll get hold of the sheriff right away and set it up."

"Thanks. Guess we'll see you tomorrow morning then."

I figured Adriana and I would be safe in our bed that night as the men in black would be putting together their plan, unless they already had. But we had a fool-proof security system that would go off even if the wires were cut. And I sleep so light that every little pop and crack in the old house wakes me up. However, I was more worried anyway about the daylight, especially when Adriana would walk outside. A sniper in the woods could pick her off the moment she set her foot on the veranda.

When we were operating Wolf Laurel as a B&B, our vehicles as well as the guest vehicles sat in the gravel parking lot to the front. Now that we made the inn our home, I got rid of the parking lot, planted grass and shrubs and had an adjoining two car garage built. Inside entry to the garage was at the end of our hallway. That meant we wouldn't have to go outside to leave the premises.

When we had returned home from the sheriff's office, I could see the fear building on Adriana's face. I placed my hand gently on the back of her neck. "Don't worry, sweetheart," I said. "I may have made too much of those guys. We're going to be fine tonight. I'm going to ask the sheriff for some security for at least the next few days. Maybe he can assign one of the deputies to camp out near our driveway."

As I expected, we had no uninvited visitors. But unfortunately, Adriana did not sleep. And because she didn't sleep, neither did I. We both watched our bedroom TV up until four on Saturday morning. That's when my feet hit the floor and I shuffled into the pisseria. I then made a cup of coffee on the Keurig and took it out onto the veranda.

The early morning hour was cool but not so much that it caused a chill. The hot coffee helped. Crickets and tree frogs sang loudly, telling me there was no human presence in the trees. I knew there would be none anyway. Off to the west, the Flower Moon of May was just setting. Even though lethargic and bleary-eyed from the lack of sleep, there was a freshness in my lungs. The coffee and morning air would combine to keep me going well into the late morning. Maybe I'd take a nap then.

But then I felt the sudden presence of someone behind me. However, it didn't feel threatening. Adriana had stepped out onto the veranda. I placed my arm around her and she huddled up into me. "You shouldn't be out here," I said.

"But you said there wouldn't be a threat."

"That was last night. It's now a new day."

"I just hate to be thinking about this…that someone might have me on his target list."

"You know I'll protect you. Maybe we should close up the house and go stay with your folks in Florida for a while. Neither Karn nor any of his enforcers would know where we are. You'd be safe and feel safe."

"We couldn't stay away forever, like people in witness protection. And I'm not going live my life afraid to come out of my own house."

"I hear you. And you're right. I'm going to take care of this. I promise."

She smiled and then swept her eyes up over the trees into the sky, the stars shimmering like diamonds on a velvet blackboard. They were so vivid and seemed so close that we could almost pluck them off. "So beautiful," she said.

"Yes, you are."

She then kissed me on the cheek. "We should go in. I want some of that coffee."

Chapter Twenty One

I had just gotten off the phone with my buddy Keith when, a little before nine-thirty, I heard tires on gravel in my driveway. I didn't expect it to be the Tahoe from Michigan appearing at our house in broad daylight, as that would not be their way of doing business. Instead, it was the high sheriff and deputy coming to visit as planned. They parked in front of our garage. I met them on the veranda.

"Morning, Bruce," Sam greeted. "You got coffee in there?"

"Sure do. You all come on in."

I took them to the kitchen and poured out cups of coffee from the old percolator. I only fired it up when we had company; otherwise, for Adriana and me it was the Keurig pods. They pulled out chairs and eased into them.

"What's going on, Bruce? Bobby here said you appeared a little rattled last night. Something about an SUV with Michigan plates?"

"If you have a few minutes, I want to start by telling you about a domestic terrorist I arrested years ago when I was with the FBI." They sat wide-eyed and attentive for the entire fifteen or twenty minutes it took for me to tell the Jonas Karn story. Sam was a deputy back in the early 2000s when Karn appeared at my wedding, and he remembered when the bastard almost ended Adriana's life with a bullet meant for me. Then after pouring them a second cup of coffee, I continued with

Part Two of the story beginning with the Paris lure. "Well, we took the bait, flew to Paris and found ourselves would-be victims of my old nemesis who was out for revenge. Thinking he had killed me, he planned a victory party of sorts, which I crashed. However, when he discovered me there, he ordered his trusted caregiver-slash-bodyguard to escort me to the garage and riddle me with bullets. But I turned the tables on the bastard, stuck a knife in his back and now he's got a headstone. Apparently, Karn was in love with the Arab dude. Now, via his threatening note, Karn plans to kill someone I love. He wants me to hurt inside like he's hurting. Then he'll come and put me out of my misery."

"Sounds like somethin' you'd see in a movie. Wild-ass story."

"My whole life's been like a movie, Bobby."

"And where do we come in, Bruce?" Sam asked.

"I figure these two men in the Tahoe are people that Karn has dispatched. They're here to try killing Adriana, to make good on Karn's threat. I don't think they want to be around long and will try something in the next day or so. They did their recon last night, likely following us from here to the restaurant to be sure they knew what she looked like. They'll be well-paid professionals and don't want any mistakes. I'd like you to post one of your deputies somewhere near Wolf Laurel to help me out. I'll be vigilant but would like to have another gun or two."

"And you're sure about these two?"

"Yes, and I'll tell you why. Their Tahoe is registered to Agresseur Enterprises. Earlier this morning, I called an old friend of mine from the State Department. I had him check out this company. It took him just fifteen minutes of research to come up with what I was looking for. Agresseur is a France-based import-export operation, the type of business which to me is always an immediate red flag, and he tells me its president is none other than Henri Cadieux, who is as you'll recall AKA Jonas Karn."

Deputy Bobby grinned and shook his head. "You gotta send this story to somebody in Hollywood. It's got more twists than a pretzel."

"Well, as you can see, I need your help. Like I said, these people are going to try something in the next day or so. They're not hired to lay around a week or two thinking about how they'll do it."

"Adriana's a sweet lady and the town's mayor at that. Not to worry, we'll look out for her. And if she needs to go anywhere, one of my people will take her."

"I can't tell you how relieved that makes me feel, Sam."

"And I sure appreciate it," came her voice from the hallway.

"Ma'am," Bobby greeted and stood.

Sam also did and added, "Well if it isn't the prettiest mayor east of the Mississippi."

"It's good to know there are guys like you out there protecting and serving," she said.

"That's what it says on our cruisers."

"Still, I hate to be the reason you're camping out here."

"I'll call one of my other deputies, probably Morris. His shift is about to start."

"Thank you, Sam. I'll need to go to the grocery before lunch."

After the officers left, I had an idea: "Adriana, do you still have that mannequin you got from Belk when they began replacing them a few years ago?"

"It's in pieces in the attic. Why?"

"When we're going out, she'll be riding shotgun with me and you will be in the back seat."

"A decoy?"

"Exactly. You need to put her together and dress her up."

The department store was selling the mannequins for twenty dollars, and she sent me there to pick up one. As Adriana made a lot of her own clothes back then and she was a perfect size six like many of the mannequins, she used it to put her patterns on. So, here I was standing in line with a couple of lonely, good ol' boys who wanted to pick out the purtiest of the models to take home with them. I guessed their inflatable dolls had sprung leaks from over-use.

Eunice…that's what we called her…came complete with a brown wig that interestingly enough resembled Adriana's own hair. Her eyebrows and lipstick were permanent. She was actually a goodlooking doll but a hell of a hard woman.

It was almost eleven-thirty when we backed out of the garage. After we reached the end of our lane, we caught sight of Morris Puckett's cruiser sitting back in the trees. He was in a good position to see anyone on Seven Bridges Road approaching within five hundred feet of our driveway. As Adriana, Eunice, and I passed by him, we gave each other a wave. Eunice looked sweet in Adriana's dark blue dress, her head turned toward me, her smile frozen. Adriana herself was scrunched down in the back seat, commenting how funny it would be if I were stopped by the state or county police and they found a dressed-up mannequin riding with me.

But our trip to the store was uneventful. I had watched closely for the Tahoe to ensure they hadn't picked us up. As the traffic was not heavy, I took account of every vehicle coming up on my side or following behind. Nothing apparent. Then when I pulled my Suburban into the store parking lot and took one of the spots, I looked carefully at every vehicle to assure the predators were not waiting for us. I then figured they had nothing planned that morning. We exited the vehicle. My hand gripping my Glock beneath my jacket, I escorted Adriana inside the store.

We spent about a half hour pushing the cart up and down every aisle, dropping food items off the shelves. Once we had paid and cleared away from the register, I told her to wait inside the door until I canvassed the parking lot again. No Tahoe. I then returned inside and walked her and the cart to our car. Eunice was still there, smiling like always.

On the way home, we again passed by Morris, who gave us a thumbs up, meaning no bad dudes were spotted, and then turned into our driveway. However, when we were within thirty feet of passing in front of the house, suddenly a single bullet drilled the windshield on the passenger side, smashing Eunice's skull to bits. Fortunately, Adriana was hunkered down behind me in the back seat.

"Stay down!" I shouted, at the same time grinding to a stop on the gravel.

As the round had come straightaway from the woods, I jumped from under the steering wheel and at a run, fired my Glock aimlessly into the trees. Once I reached the edge of the woods, I stopped behind a large oak to listen. That's when I heard them thrashing through the brush at a run in the direction of my ten o'clock. Seconds later, I heard an engine crank and build-up RPMs as if the vehicle were pulling out. As I knew the woods around our house, I figured they had entered our property via a firebreak from Seven Bridges that would not have been in Morris's line of sight. Obviously, they had seen him set up on the road. However, unsure where they were in the woods, I stopped to listen. Sound travels differently in the forest, reverberating off trees, often giving a false impression of where in reality it's coming from, therefore, making it difficult to pinpoint its location. So, I decided to run toward the road to intercept them. When I was within just a few yards of the intersection of Seven Bridges and the firebreak, I caught sight of their headlights through a section of scrub pines. As the driver then began revving up the Tahoe to pull from the firebreak onto the road, I stepped out from behind a tree and fired four rounds into the driver's side windshield. The Tahoe then suddenly veered off to the right and slammed into a huge poplar.

I figured one of my bullets had nailed the driver, but what about the passenger? Within seconds I was onto the vehicle at the driver's door. He had taken a round through the temple. However, as the other man in black had only sustained a cut on his head from the crash, he was still alive. I then ran around to his door and jerked it open. Obviously stunned and disoriented, he fell out onto the ground. But he still had enough left in him to reach into his shoulder holster.

"Don't do it," I warned, at the same time shoving another clip into my Glock.

But the man was still determined. When his hand landed on the gun and he began pulling it from the holster, I planted two rounds into his chest. I had wanted him alive, but there was no way he was going to be taken down without dying.

Morris Puckett, who had heard the shooting, was on the scene seconds later, skidding his cruiser to a stop on the side of the road. After jumping out with gun in hand, I said, "It's all over, Morris. They're both dead."

I then thought about Adriana. Knowing she had not been hit, I was still concerned about her. But as if reading my mind, Morris said, "The mayor's there in my car, Mr. McGowan. When I heard the shots, I flew down to your house and picked her up. She's a little shaken, but fine."

Adriana then stepped out of the car and ran to me. "Oh, Skip, I was so worried. Are you hurt?"

"No, but *those* guys are."

Sheriff Greene, the State Police and rescue squad were at the scene in twenty minutes. Of course, there was nobody to rescue.

"Looks like you took care of business, Bruce," Sam remarked. "That fella you told us about over in France is not going to be very happy with you."

"He hasn't been happy with me for a hell of a lot of years, Sam. There might be more coming just like them."

"And now you know how real his threat was. So, what are you going to do?"

"Short of going back to Paris to kill the bastard, I don't know. If it were just me, I wouldn't be so worried. I'm thinking of sending Adriana to her folks' house in Florida for a while."

"I'm the mayor of this town and have responsibilities, husband, dear. You're not sending me anywhere," she said.

"Sweetheart, go take a look inside that SUV. Karn and his people aren't kidding around. He's going to keep trying to make good on his threat."

She shook her head. "I've got all you brave boys protecting me and am not going to go hide under any rock. Enough said."

Back at the house, Adriana scraped together what was left of Eunice's head and pulled her body from the Suburban. The bullet was fired from a Russian Dragunov SVD sniper rifle which we found in the Tahoe. It had not only placed a nice, neat hole in my windshield but went through my headrest and into the rear seat.

To add some levity to the situation, we buried Eunice's remains in our backyard, placing on her grave a makeshift cross bearing her name and date of death. We had no idea when she was born (or manufactured). I couldn't remember any other funeral we had attended where we enjoyed such a good laugh.

Chapter Twenty Two

For the time being, I didn't see any further threat. However, once word got back to Karn that his two gunmen met their deaths on our property, he'd go ballistic. I could just hear him exclaim, *"What the hell do I need to do to bring Bruce McGowan to his knees? Can't I trust anyone to carry out my orders?"* Would he send more people out? He desperately wanted to put me in a position where I would be hurting. Perhaps his next attempt would be on Caroline's life. He knew I wouldn't be anywhere near her to foil his people's actions. I would again call her to be on the alert for anything or anybody suspicious.

Adriana called Liz Farrell a day or so later to check on her. She put the phone on speaker, and I listened in on the call.

"I miss Roy so much, I can barely get through most days. And every night when I close my eyes, I see that dark street and Roy being attacked by that terrible man. I wish I could find out where he is at any particular moment and go kill him myself."

"The man is now dead, Liz."

"How do you know that?"

"I have it on good authority that someone killed him."

"Oh, I wish I could find out who did it, whether he was a good or bad person. I'd kiss him."

"It was a good guy who did it."

"I don't know how you found that out, but I can't

tell you how relieved that makes me feel. Roy has been vindicated."

"I hope knowing that will help you heal."

"But then there was that other terrible voice I heard. It sounded so much like the voice of that man on our tour who was in a wheelchair. I didn't hear him talk much, but he had the same high-pitched voice. And the man obviously mistook Roy for your husband with what he said. Does Bruce have any enemies and if he does, how would this man know he was going to be in Paris? I've thought about that ever since I've been back."

I shook my head. She would just have to go on wondering.

"Not to change the subject, but how are your kids doing, Liz?"

"Better with losing Roy than I am. Just yesterday we spread Roy's ashes on the waters of Lake Hamilton, his favorite fishing spot. That was the first time I had seen them weeping since the funeral. It all just seems like a nightmare, Adriana…one that won't go away."

"I know, Liz. And both my husband and I feel for you. Maybe one day you'll feel like coming here for a visit."

"I'd like that. It'll be a while, though."

"Well, until then, anytime you need to talk, please do call me."

"I will. Pray for me. I need all the prayers I can get."

"You know I will, Liz. Take care."

When Adriana ended the call, she looked over at me with tears streaming down her cheeks. I pulled her tightly into me, her sobs causing my own body to shake.

By the end of May, life had returned to normal at Wolf Laurel. Even though the town's mayor was going out in the world without her husband, Sam Greene's deputies continued to hang close by. I was still worried for Adriana as I knew Karn would not let go of his quest to see me suffer. I didn't know why he was so dead set on ending the life of a member of my family versus just going ahead with killing me. I did stay in touch with Caroline, telling her to always stay wary. I worried as much or more about her as I did Adriana.

There was also news from Paris. Jacques Allard called again to bring me up on both Devereux and Cadieux. Based on the photos I sent, Devereux's association with Cadieux was investigated and it was learned he was in fact on Henri Le Creep's payroll having recently received the sum of 42000 euros which was something like $50,000 U.S. He was not only fired but arrested for conspiracy to commit bribery. A new investigation was initiated on Cadieux, and all the evidence presented before, to include my sworn statement tying in his history as the former Jonas Karn, his ploy to lure me to Paris to kill me, and the subsequent murder of Roy Farrell, would be part of it.

"And Bruce, I am not sure the case will get off the ground unless you are here to testify. Procureur de Barrere believes there would only be a 50-50 chance of a conviction if you were not here in person. We had secured Madame Farrell's statement before she left, and she provided the exact words that were spoken at the time her husband was killed. It was a second man at the scene of death who spoke those words, thinking he was taunting you. The man said Adriana's name as well. The madame's statement is also all important for the procureur.”

“When is the case scheduled for trial?”

“The 14th of June.”

“That’s just around the corner.”

“Yes, but there is another issue. When we were securing information on Jonas Karn through Interpol and America’s FBI, your government reminded us that Karn is an escaped convict, and the FBI is talking extradition. So, far I have been able to impress upon them the importance of prosecuting him and shutting down what we have found as the illegal businesses of extortion and prostitution as well as his funding of Islamic terrorist activities, specifically al Qaeda and Hezbollah.”

“I knew about his ties to al Qaeda from my own discovery seventeen years ago, but his other dealings must have begun there in France.”

“Yes. And as to the extradition, your government has partly agreed that if he is convicted here in France, they will drop their demand. If he prevails here, they will certainly extradite.”

“Which says he is behind bars either way.”

“Yes, but he is well into his years and severely handicapped. He will get special treatment and again serve his time in either a penal hospital or assisted living facility.”

“And still find a way to maintain all his illicit and terrorist activities.”

“Probably so.”

“Is he in jail awaiting trial?”

"No. Due to his handicap, the judge believes he is not a flight risk."

"Well, he was able to fly the coup when we locked him up in the U.S."

"That is what I argued, but it fell on deaf ears."

I then switched gears and told Jacques about the Detroit thugs Karn had sent to kill Adriana, true to his threat and that she had escaped harm.

"Did they get away after trying?"

"Let's just say I took care of the problem."

"With deadly results?"

"Definitely."

He chuckled. "True to form, eh Monsieur McGowan?"

"I do what I do to protect my wife."

"Do I count on you coming to testify?"

"It'll be a personal expense for me."

"The Minister of Justice and Court of Assize have agreed to pay for your travel, lodging and per diem expenses."

"Good…thanks. Adriana and I have talked about it, and she agrees that if the case is slated for trial and I am asked to testify, I should do it. So, you can count on me."

"That is good news for us, Bruce. Thank you. I will let Procureur de Barrere know. She will be pleased. It will be good to see you again. But I must go now. Business calls. I hope there will be no more attempts on Adriana's life."

"I'll be watching."

Over the next few days, Adriana and I talked more about my going back to Paris to testify in the upcoming State v. Cadieux trial. Even though Roy Farrell's killer was dead, the evidence had to prove that it was Henri Cadieux, AKA Jonas Karn, who set up the murder. All the pieces of evidence needed to be connected.

I told Adriana, "Even though Karn is going to be consumed with defending himself against the charges, his people will still be coming after you… and ultimately me. I can't have you here by yourself with me over in Paris. You're going to be vacationing with your parents in Florida. I doubt the trial will be longer than a few days, so that's how long you'll be away from the town's business."

"As much as I hate to admit it, you're probably right. I guess I can still do some things by phone, text and email."

"However, if Karn wants to dig hard enough, he may find out who your parents are, where they live and that you're staying with them. You will still need to remain hypervigilant."

"I can also alert the local police to look out for me."

"Just don't tell any of your friends or town employees where you're going."

I was pleased that Adriana was now receptive to leaving the state while I was in Paris. Otherwise, not a moment would go by that I did not worry about her. My entire focus had to be on helping the prosecution put Karn away.

Chapter Twenty Two

The Cour d' Assises pretrial process began on June 14th, but it was anticipated that the actual trial would not get off the ground until the 25th. Jacques Allard emailed me twice during the pretrial phase to advise what kind of case Cadieux was putting up. He had hired a lawyer well- known for his trial successes and who had already defeated two of the prosecution's motions before the court. Jacques told me that without my direct testimony, the charges of murder and conspiracy to commit would be dismissed by the judge. I reassured Jacques that he and the procureur could depend on my court attendance and testimony.

He told me to book my flight for the 22nd and once done, as promised, the Cour d' Assises would pay the cost. He and Madame de Barrere needed to meet with me for at least two days prior to the onset of the trial to go over my testimony.

My wife, the mayor, booked her flight before I did and notified her parents that she'd be coming to stay with them for a couple of weeks. Telling the town council that she would be away, per my suggestion she didn't say where. Just Florida. Procureur de Barrere's assistant took care of my arrangements with Air France from Washington Dulles, which meant this time, I would either be driving to Fairfax County, about three hours away, or grabbing a puddle-jumper from our local airport. I chose the latter.

On the night of the 20th, Adriana and I dined on a meal of shrimp and scallops at a new restaurant in town we had been meaning to try. What normally would be an evening of joy and laughter, our conversations with one another we found a bit solemn. Yet again we'd be separated as we had been on many occasions when I was working in counterterrorism. As we sat picking at our food, knowing she'd be leaving the next day and I the day after, she asked me if there would ever be a time in our lives when danger would no longer be lurking around the corner. I had long since been retired, yet it seemed there was always someone out there who the government either wanted me to take down or someone wanted to take *me* down.

"Maybe we sell Wolf Laurel," I suggested, "then move to some place like Montana where we know no one. The government won't be able to find me to pull me into another deadly game and the bad dudes would think maybe I died or crawled into a cave. We'd leave no forwarding address to anyone except Social Security and whoever was paying my government pension."

Her eyes rolled around in their sockets like two marbles. "Oh, great. I can see it now…me shacking up in a double wide in Montana with the Unabomber."

"What? My dear, not everybody who lives in the wide-open spaces turns into a revolutionary. We'd just…"

"We'd just live without air conditioning, modern conveniences, shopping centers and good restaurants. No, thanks. I think I'll just tough it out here in good old Greenbrier County. At least we have a Wal-Mart."

I had to laugh. She had actually compared me to the Unabomber.

We arrived home around ten and as I was still being protective on her behalf, especially at night when I'd have difficulty spotting danger, I had her keep her head down in the car until we were into the garage. Then, just in case someone compromised our security and was waiting for us inside, I allowed my Glock to lead the way. I hated we were living like that, but hopefully within the next few weeks the threat would be gone. I told myself that if Karn skated in the upcoming trial, wheelchair-bound invalid or not, before I left Paris, he would die at my hand.

As we lay in our bed glistening in post-coital sweat, the overhead fan cooling us down, she placed her hand gently onto mine. "Promise me you won't end up in a French jail or worse, come back to me under an American flag," she said.

"Now *that's* a morbid thought."

"Jonas Karn has tried too many times in the past two months to end your life. Now you will not only be back in the same city where his people can get to you easier, but testifying against him. He'll be even more determined to kill you."

"I'll be in a different hotel this time and the lieutenant will have his officers protecting me. He assured me of that."

"What happens if Karn gets off? I know you and you'll want to go after him."

"Have you been reading my mind again?"

"So, you *have* thought about it."

"What I *have* thought about is that even if he does go to jail, it won't *be* jail. He'll be back in some resident care facility where he'll still be dispatching his goons to carry out his vindictive threats. He'll still have his inheritance and his enforcers. You and I will never be rid of this maggot. He's made me his life's mission. And just as poor Eunice found out, *you* won't be safe either."

But for some reason, that last thing struck her funny bone. She began giggling. "Yeah, poor Eunice."

"Out there feeding the worms as we speak."

Then both of us began laughing. What we needed.

For the second time in the past two months, I was kissing my bride goodbye just before she went through security. This time it was at the small Greenbrier Airport. She would fly to Charlotte and from there on to West Palm. I hated we had to send her down south to stay with her folks, but I just had a feeling Karn would try again…this time knowing I wouldn't be around to foil the attempt. I could just imagine when I arrived in Paris; he would somehow communicate another message; this time, it would say something like, "You testify against me; Adriana dies. You can't protect her now."

I left home at eight-thirty the next morning, drove to the Greenbrier Airport, and caught the puddle-jumper to Dulles. My flight out to Paris was wheels-up at eleven- ten. I was elated that the Cour d'Assises and Procureur de Barrere had treated me well from the get-go by placing me in a Row 5 window seat. I never sleep on planes. Whereas most people *want* to be asleep when their plane goes down, I prefer to be screaming all the way to the ground…or in the case of a flight to Europe, all the way into the drink. But somehow, I did manage to sleep half the way there, mainly because I only slept for about two hours the night before, being worried about Adriana. She made it fine to West Palm where her parents met up with her. Still, I was set to wonder if any of Karn's bad boys were industrious enough to find out where she had gone. My mind had also been on Caroline; however, I didn't think she would be that high on Karn's list. And my daughter, as a stellar FBI agent, had turned out to be as dangerous to the underworld as moi. After all, she's the one who had shot and crippled Karn in the first place.

My flight landed this time at Orly which was closer into the city. I think it was probably in the early morning hours of the 23rd when we touched down, considering we were flying into the sun, losing hours all during our eight hours in the air. Math was not my strongest subject in high school, and I avoided it altogether in college. But I knew it was still the latter part of June anyway, whatever day it was.

As I had told Adriana, Jacques Allard had set me up in another hotel to throw Karn and his hoods off. He would be expecting me to be staying at the Saint-Loraine again since it was closer to both the police precinct and courthouse. However, The Le Fleur was twelve blocks away near the Eiffel Tower. Jacques had arranged a cruiser to pick me up each morning of the trial or whenever he or the assigned procureur needed to meet with me.

The Le Fleur was comfortable but not quite as swanky as my last digs; however, the restaurant was absolutely first-class. My lunch consisted of a delicious cassoulet. While finishing up the meal with a draft beer, I called Jacques Allard to let him know I had checked in. He wanted me to meet with him and de Barrere that afternoon. A police cruiser would be by to retrieve me at three. I had plenty of time to call Adriana. It was morning in Florida. I was pretty sure, anyway.

"I'm glad you made it there safely," she said.

"Now *stay* safe."

"Not to worry. Is all well there with your parents?"

"With Mom it is. It's good I came here when I did, though. Dad's not well. They didn't tell me he had a heart attack last week. He just got out of the hospital."

It didn't surprise me. I thought he'd be having one years ago. A man can't eat a pound of bacon and three or four eggs every morning and not suffer cardiac issues. Of course, when you're two hundred eighty pounds on a five-nine frame…

"Your dad needs to put his fork down every once in a while and do a couple of sit-ups."

"I'll be working on him while I'm here. How about you? Are you settled in?"

"Yep. I'll have some meetings with the prosecutor today and probably tomorrow. The case is already in pre- trial but will get off the ground in a couple of days."

"When you'll be face-to-face with Jonas Karn."

"I'm sure he'll be playing the sympathy card… "poor, pitiful me stuck in this wheelchair getting accused of murder when I can't move anything but my head."

"I'm sure the jury will see him for who he is once the evidence is presented. You'll make a great witness as well."

"The prosecution is going to have an uphill battle tying him into the actual murder. But then there's that charge of conspiracy to commit murder. Plenty of evidence that he set me up for the kill."

"But like you said, even if he's convicted, he won't

go to any penal institution. He'll end up in some perpetual care hospital ward."

"If I have anything to do with it, he'll end up six feet under."

"Don't be talking like that, Skip. You're there as a witness, not an executioner."

We talked a while longer, then said our mushy things to each other before the call ended. We had only been apart a day and I already missed her.

I was in my room when the front desk called a few minutes past three to tell me a police officer was in the lobby asking for me. After going down to greet the officer, I found that Jacques himself had come by to pick me up.

"Bonjour, Lieutenant," I said in my best French.

"You had a good trip here, I trust?"

We shook hands. "Yes. Thanks for setting it up."

I walked with him to his car which was parked in one of the check-in spots. He then slid in behind the wheel while I took the front passenger seat.

"Do you find the accommodations satisfactory?" he asked.

"Very nice. Again, thank you."

"We will meet in a few minutes with the State Procureur, Madame de Barrere, and her new deputy who will be prosecuting the case, Julie Durand."

"Julie being a woman."

"I think you will find both women tenacious and very eager to prosecute this case."

"Durand replaced Devereux?"

"Yes. A bit of irony that she is also the attorney who will prosecute him as well."

"Interesting. Is Durand up to speed on Cadieux?"

"Very much so."

"And does she know what you figured out about me?"

"That is something only you and I know. I have yet to share with her that you broke into the Ramatuelle estate and killed al-Tajir."

"I prefer it be said that even though I was uninvited, I walked into the estate through an open door. As Cadieux then discovered me, he told his man to take me out of his sight and kill me. I reacted in self-defense."

"If you keep this knowledge from the procureur and she learns of it, the case against Cadieux may be affected. Your credibility will be in question."

"I understand that," I said. "If it does come out, my invasion of his premises will not have anything to do with his conspiracy to lure me here in the first place. I was merely planning to confront him."

"If necessary, I will convey it to Madame de Barrere just as you have explained it to me. But I see we are nearing our building now. I believe you will be impressed with both ladies."

And I was…before we even began our conversation. Both Mesdames de Barrere and Durand were knock-outs. De Barrere was upper forties, pretty brunette with an hourglass shape and stately business manner; Durand had stylishly coiffed blonde hair, red-rimmed glasses that showcased her gorgeous green eyes, and a set of legs that were straight out of Playboy. But being the true-blue married man that I was, I didn't notice much about the ladies beyond their professional demeanor.

"Monsieur McGowan, hello." The chief procureur extended her hand. "I am Marie de Barrere. Welcome to Paris…again." Even though she spoke her English with a thick French accent, her words were crisp and succinct. "I hope you do not mind that we are meeting this soon after your arrival, but we have little time before the trial begins."

"I'm at your service, Madame."

"Please call me Marie. And this is Juliette Durand."

I shook her hand as well. Both she and de Barrere had firm grips.

Durand then said, "Monsieur McGowan, you may call me Julie. We have asked you here to personally capsule the history between you and Monsieur Cadieux. Lieutenant Allard has provided it to us, but we want to hear it from your mouth. There would be things you could tell us that he did not know." Her English was almost flawless; however, occasionally, her accent came through.

I began with my arrest of Karn when I was a special agent, referring to him only as Karn. I wanted the procureurs to get a mental picture of the man as Karn and not Cadieux. I told them I was not gentle with him which not only ended up altering his voice but affecting his ability to have children. I then took them through his kidnapping of my daughter and while rescuing her, shut down his return to the Weather Underground domestic terrorism operation. Still holding a grudge, he shot my fiancée at our wedding and then my daughter shot him. That is why he sits seventeen years later in his wheelchair as a paraplegic.

"That is a colossal story, Monsieur McGowan…"

"Since we're on a first name basis, Marie, you may call me Bruce."

"Fine, Bruce. And then you received the invitation from someone anonymous to come to Paris on a vacation. And you thought it was an act of kindness."

"I did. And I verified with the travel agency that it was real and was told it was a trip that was paid for by someone who obviously was appreciative of something I had done, but asked them to not divulge the name. My wife and I thought deeply about it and then decided to go. We later found out it was from the man I knew as Karn, and he intended to draw me into his web to kill me."

"And he was actually on the tour himself with his caregiver."

"Correct. My wife and I saw him in the restaurant watching me the night Roy Farrell was murdered. It was on the street not far from the restaurant that Roy was stabbed to death. His wife, Liz, heard a man with a high- pitched voice begin gloating because he thought he had killed me."

"Yes, we have her sworn statement. That is why I believe we have a good case against him for murder and conspiracy. If you testify just as you have told me this story, I believe we can put Monsieur Cadieux, the former Jonas Karn, away."

"Bruce, you left something out," Jacques said.

I was just about to spill the beans regarding

my sneaking into Ramatuelle and killing al-Tajir, when he continued. "…you know, about two of his Arab friends attempting to murder you on the street and then leaving you the note at the Saint-Loraine."

"Yes, and sending two more hit men from Detroit to my home in West Virginia to murder my wife."

"He did that?" Julie said. "I pray they were not successful."

"They weren't. They're taking a dirt nap as we speak."

The two women looked at one another. "Dirt nap?" Marie asked.

I chuckled. "Sorry, Marie. Just an American quip meaning they're underground…dead."

"At your hand?"

"Yes."

"This is an incredible case," Julie said. "In one sense it is obvious this Jonas Karn contrived to bring you here to murder you, but only you can actually connect him to Roy Farrell's murder. Even Madame Farrell could not identify the murderer as Karn's man."

"I understand that."

"That is why your testimony is all important in the case. Without you and Madame Farrell's statement, we have no case. And so, like any other witness, we must provide you protection during the trial." She turned to Jacques. "Can we do that, Lieutenant?"

"It's all arranged, Madame de Barrere. I will have an officer camping at the Le Fleur and driving Monsieur McGowan back and forth to the courthouse."

Chapter Twenty Four

No one could estimate how long the trial would last and it was also anyone's guess as to what kind of defense Karn's lawyers would put up. Julie Durand felt she had enough to go forward with the trial as did Marie. Having requested and received the travel agency's records, she had also subpoenaed both the director and the individual who set up our trip to Paris. Julie believed a guilty verdict would be a slamdunk, but the more seasoned procureur, Marie, was not so sure.

We met again on the 24th for about two hours. Julie grilled me with questions she believed the defense would ask. I had been on the stand many times as an FBI agent, ironically facing Karn and his attorney more than thirty years before when he was tried for domestic terrorism. I felt I was ready, but what was haunting me was not telling the prosecution about my crashing Karn's Ramatuelle party and then killing his trusted caregiver. Before we ended our practice session, I asked Jacques if I could talk with him in private.

The two of us then talked and came to an agreement.

When the four of us rejoined, I made my confession to the two ladies. I said, "Something you all need to know before we go to trial is that I attended Karn's masquerade party before I left Paris."

Julie and Madelyn looked at one another and then back at me.

"But not the way you think. It's bound to come out

and I can't perjure myself when it does. I had read he was having a celebration party, likely because he thought he had killed me. So, I decided to put on a mask and waltz in as though I had been invited. I can't tell you why I crashed the party as I'm not sure myself why I did it. He had attempted to kill me on two separate occasions only days apart and I guess I was just trying to be defensive. I wanted to get him off apart from his guests and confront him. In doing so, I guess I was planning to threaten him. But he brought in his caregiver-slash-bodyguard and told him to take me down to his garage out of the earshot of his guests and kill me. With a gun on me, he ushered me into the elevator. When the door opened, I distracted him, stuck a knife into his gut, then took his gun and shot him. What my admission does to our case I'm sure is not good."

Both ladies sat looking at me with mouths agape. I'm sure it was far from anything they had expected.

Julie finally said, "You're right. It will be a game-changer if the defense brings it up. I don't know what it will do to our case, but even though it is not related to the Farrell murder, the jury will not favor you. However, they may also think you were driven to this erratic act because your life was in danger. It's something Marie and I will have to talk about before tomorrow. If Karn's attorney is worth his salt, as you say, he will try to capitalize on it. He'll say his client is on trial for murder, yet *you* are the actual murderer."

"But I acted in self-defense."

"He will say that no one saw his friend try to kill you, just as no one saw him kill Monsieur Farrell."

I nodded. "I just thought I needed to divulge

this. Sorry if it sabotages the case."

"You did right in telling us this. It seems Julie and I will be burning a little midnight oil. However, I believe we can make this work for us."

Jacques and I left at the same time since he was dropping me off back at the hotel. "Well, you had to tell them, Bruce. They did not need any surprises. Nothing should be held back from the prosecution. "

"Hindsight being 20-20, I wouldn't have done what I did. I had just had enough."

"Which fueled your actions."

"I guess a whole new case could be opened on me for killing that guy."

"In essence, yes. But I will not pursue anything against you. Being a good judge of character, I believe you when you say you were defending your life."

"Thanks, Jacques." I shook his hand. "At least I got this off my chest."

He nodded. "Now go have a good night's sleep."

After I talked with Adriana and wished her a good night, I did.

Officer Herve Jordain was waiting for me in the lobby the morning of the 25th. The trial was scheduled to begin at nine. Jordain's English was about as good as my French, so there was little conversation on the way to the courthouse. However, I did understand that he was slated to be both my daily driver and protector.

Minutes after arriving at the grand building called the Palais de Justice, Jordain escorted me to the procureur room where Julie Durand was waiting.

"You ready for this, Bruce?"

"I am, and are you?"

"I feel good about our chances. Marie and I talked at length about your, shall I say, misjudgment and feel that if the subject comes up, the jury will be made to see that you had been under a death threat and reacted in a manner that may not have been rational, but understandable."

"How much of the testimony will I be able to understand in a French court?"

"The judge, the defense counsel and of course the American, Karn, are all bilingual. Any of the nine jurors who do not understand English will have on headsets where an interpreter will translate for them."

"Was it a good selection of jurors?"

"I believe so. They all seem objective. As Henri Cadieux is a very wealthy man and owner of the famous Ramatuelle, the case has garnered much publicity. There will be a courtroom full of reporters as well as some of Paris' elite citizens who have relationships with him."

"As long as none of these citizens are on the jury," I remarked.

"We made sure of that. A couple know of Cadieux, but none are friends."

At five minutes till nine, Julie and I took our seats in the courtroom. She sat with a neophyte co-counsel who was in the learning stage of his career, and I sat on a bench behind them. As soon as I sat down, Marie de Barrere and Jacques Allard came in together and sat behind me.

Momentarily, three other people entered the

courtroom: wheelchair-bound Henri Cadieux, AKA Jonas Karn, his new Middle Eastern caregiver, and defense counsel Arthur Lafevre. Karn's searing eyes immediately fell on me. There elapsed a period of several minutes when all was quiet. Finally, when all were seated, Judge Charles Sartre, appeared at the bench. The command "levez-vous" was given and we all rose.

The judge then began as in American criminal courts with charging the jury and issuing an admonishment to both the trial and defense counsel on rules of the court. The case was announced before the court by someone I assumed was a bailiff: "Cour de Assises, Conseil Constitutionnel frais Henri Cadieux, murder and conspiracy to commit murder."

"Arthur Lafevre for the defense."

"Procureur Juliette Durand, trial counsel for Cour d'Assises.

It was then that Lafevre petitioned, "Honorable Judge Sartre, as attorney for the accused, I ask the court to immediately dismiss the charges against Henri Cadieux as unfounded and meritless. The evidence does not exist."

"Monsieur Lafevre, the court has reviewed the charges and I will hear the case. Madame Durand, you may begin."

Julie stood. "Honorable Judge Sartre and members of the jury, the defendant you see sitting there in a wheelchair, paralyzed from the neck down, came to France fifteen years ago whereupon his uncle on his father's side, owner of Ramatuelle, took him in, providing care for him. Although you may feel sorry for him, he is in reality an American fugitive from justice named Jonas Karn, not Henri Cadieux. Monsieur Karn, as the prosecution will refer to him, engaged in domestic terrorist activities against his country, the United States of America, setting off bombs in government buildings. He was arrested by the man you see behind our table, Special Agent Bruce McGowan, formerly of the Federal Bureau of Investigation…"

Lafevre then stood. "Objection. How is this history relevant to the case against my client? And his name is Henri Cadieux."

"Your honor, the prosecution will show that it is indeed relevant as Monsieur Karn's terrorist activities against his country were the springboard of this entire case."

"Continue your opening, Madame Durand."

"Again, as Henri Cadieux is not his given name, I will continue to refer to him as Jonas Karn. Monsieur Karn was convicted and sentenced to ten years in prison. However, at such time he was released, he returned to his terrorist activities by reconstituting a domestic terrorist organization called the Weather Underground, collaborating with al Qaeda elements who had set up in several locations in the United States…"

Lafevre interrupted again. "I must object. There is no evidence of this, your honor…"

"I have excerpts from both Interpol and the FBI files to support this," Julie said.

"Please continue."

"Monsieur Karn has a long history of terrorist and other illegal activities in the States. Most alarming was Karn's kidnapping of Monsieur McGowan's daughter with the intent to draw him to a place in Colorado where he would murder him. Monsieur McGowan, with his law enforcement skills, was able to rescue her from Karn's clutches and then, as part of a federal task force, locate a bomb-making and munitions warehouse that was part of the Underground's operation."

I watched the trepidation on the faces of the nine jurors.

"You may ask how Monsieur Karn found himself in his current state. Monsieur McGowan and his fiancée were getting married on the grounds of their home when Monsieur Karn, who had learned of the wedding, appeared from the trees and fired his pistol at Monsieur McGowan. The bullet fortunately missed him, but unfortunately, his bride was shot in the back. That is when Monsieur McGowan's daughter, who is a federal agent, shot Monsieur Karn. The bullet severed his spinal cord, and the result is the man you see there.

"That is not the end of the story, mesdames and monsieur's. While in a prison hospital facility, one of Monsieur Karn's Muslim co-conspirators broke him out and arranged for him to flee to Paris. It was here he began under the care of his uncle. He then changed his name. And so, mesdames and monsieur of the jury, the man you see there is a fugitive from American justice who has continued his vindictive attempts to murder Monsieur McGowan.

"We also have records from the Saint-Amaury Travel Agency that show one Henri Cadieux paid for a trip for Monsieur McGowan and his wife to Paris. We had to subpoena the records as Cadieux chose to remain anonymous. Why would Monsieur Cadieux alias Jonas Karn gift an arch-enemy a free trip unless he wanted to have him here in Paris so that he could kill him?

Then, Monsieur Karn joined the tour with his caregiver so that he could keep an eye on Monsieur McGowan and find an opportunity to murder him.

"Monsieur Karn's looks have changed over the years, especially considering his full, white beard and thick-lens glasses, so Monsieur McGowan was unable to immediately recognize him. It was on the night of April 30 of this year that Monsieur McGowan and his wife were dining at a restaurant with another couple on the tour, Roy and Elizabeth Farrell also from the United States. According to Madame Farrell in her affidavit, everyone at their table recognized Monsieur Karn, the man on their tour, and a large Middle Eastern man who was identified as his caregiver, both of whom sat at an adjacent table watching them.

"By coincidence, Monsieurs McGowan and Farrell were similar in build, hair and other looks and were wearing similar sport coats. The Farrells and McGowans noticed that the man in the wheelchair and his assistant had left the restaurant after their meal. Roy Farrell and his wife left moments later to walk back in the direction of their hotel. In Madame Farrell's affidavit, a man approached them from behind and stabbed her husband. While Roy Farrell lay dying in the street, she heard a highpitched voice from the alley behind her laughing, saying words to the effect of "McGowan, you are not so invincible after all." Then he mentioned the name Adriana, who is Monsieur McGowan's wife, that she should cry long and hard. If you hear Monsieur Karn speak, you will notice he has a high-pitched voice.

"And so, mesdames and monsieurs, this is the incredible story that the defense cannot dispute. It was necessary to take you back those many years to connect a revenge-filled criminal, a fugitive from justice, with the gratis trip to Paris and to the murder of Roy Farrell. Monsieur Karn ordered his man to murder Monsieur McGowan, but instead killed the wrong man. On Monsieur McGowan's first week here in Paris, there were other attempts on his life as well. There was also an attempt on the life of Adriana McGowan at the McGowan home just weeks ago. The assassins were both killed. The car in which they were riding was registered to a company out of Detroit, Michigan, owned by…yes, the defendant who now goes by the name Henri Cadieux. There you have it, mesdames and monsieurs; you now have all pieces of the puzzle before you to prove Monsieur Karn AKA Cadieux conspired to murder Monsieur McGowan, but instead through his bodyguard and caregiver, killed the wrong man, Roy Farrell. I yield to Monsieur Lafevre."

Chapter Twenty Five

Lafevre then rose and walked toward the jury. "Mesdames et Monsieurs, before you are accused of a heinous crime sits a man of immense misfortune. Much of that misfortune he has had in his life was because of that man sitting behind the procureur's table, a ruthless criminal who wore a badge which he believed gave him license to destroy a man's life. I will now tell you a story about him and his vicious methods that would cause any man to be provoked to hate. There sits a man, a saboteur, sniper, and government-sanctioned hit man, who, in every recorded takedown, used his badge as a license to maim and kill at any opportunity. I have at my table a stack of cases I subpoenaed from several International Law Enforcement Agencies including Interpol, which keeps data on every crime and every police-related injury or killing of a suspect in custody. Do you know how many deaths and serious injuries of a questionable nature former Special Agent and government operative Bruce McGowan perpetrated? More than five hundred in twenty-eight years of combined law enforcement service."

Well, that was a surprise. I had no idea. But I'll bet one thing…nobody in the freaking courtroom had any thoughts of pissing me off. However, he was lying through his yellowed teeth. He had no such records. As a government counter-terrorist operative, my missions were mostly clandestine and only realized by two or three people, the President being one. But he continued trying to blow smoke up the jury's asses.

"As that was the way McGowan did business, I

could go through every case and give you specific details of his vicious handling of suspects and that doesn't include the assassinations…"

"Objection. Relevance."

"Your honor, I am only trying to show the jury how Monsieur McGowan's treatment of suspects including the maiming of Monsieur Cadieux, caused many to become so provoked they wanted to stop him any way they could."

"By murdering him," said Julie.

"I must sustain the objection as Monsieur McGowan's law enforcement history has nothing to do with this case."

"May I continue?" asked Lafevre.

"Yes."

"I think I have said enough about McGowan's character to give the jury a picture of what this man is capable of. However, there is the claim that Monsieur Cadieux conspired to bring McGowan here on a vacation to murder him. That did not happen. We believe it was someone else who used my client's name who arranged for the trip. No one at the travel agency will attest that Monsieur Cadieux was the one who paid for the trip. He is a very wealthy man and has been the target of several old enemies himself. We believe one of them set him up. We have presented a list of these suspects which we will expect the police to investigate.

"The defense will also claim that on May 5th, a Friday night at Monsieur Cadieux's residence during a party, Monsieur McGowan entered into the house uninvited and…"

"Objection, your honor. Monsieur Karn's party and

any allegations that Monsieur McGowan had entered his house have already been addressed by the police. The party and the witness' comportment and geste while here in Paris are irrelevant to this case. Monsieur McGowan is not on trial here. He is a witness who will attest to the events leading up to the murder of Roy Farrell."

"I would agree, counsel. Sustained."

I looked back at Jacques and Marie and caught their half-smiles. It appeared I had dodged the bullet, at least for the time being. However, I was sure that somewhere in the trial, Lafevre would try to get it in once again.

Lafevre continued. "The procureur has charged Monsieur Cadieux…and I ask that you refer to him as such…with murder and conspiracy to commit murder. The prosecution has failed to produce any witness who saw him or the person who looked after him commit the murder and we expressly deny the allegation. As others in the underworld of crime would know about my client's history, he would be an easy target as someone to blame. Monsieur Cadieux has lived a respectable life for the past twelve years as the master of Ramatuelle. He is remorseful for his past and has done much to make amends through his well-publicized philanthropic contributions. This is not the kind of man who conspires to kill anyone. Even though he was at issue with his government and went to certain lengths to make his point, he has ended no one's life. In contrast, Monsieur McGowan is hated by so many around the world who want revenge against him, we believe there has to be someone else here in Paris who not only arranged for his tour but is set out to kill him. Since there is no witness who can connect Monsieur

Cadieux to the murder and no one at the travel agency who can say it was he who set up the McGowan tour, the prosecution's case is built only on speculation. Since no evidence exists, your honor, we motion the court for an immediate dismissal."

Judge Sartre rapped his gavel and stood. "I hereby call a short recess of twenty minutes during which I will take your motion under advisement in my chambers."

Julie Durand turned her chair around and leaned toward me as Marie de Barrere and Jacques Allard came forward to huddle.

"I don't like this," Marie said. "Court has only been in session forty-five minutes and the judge is already contemplating the case. It is very unusual for him to do so, and I fear this favors the defense. Julie, you scored some very good points and I heard nothing but denials and accusations against Bruce from Lafevre. And there sits Karn looking at us with an evil grin on his face."

I asked, "Are you sure about this judge? Maybe he's been bought like Devereux was."

"I've known him to be a very honest and respectable judge in the past and he has provided a lot of what I consider fair rulings on both sides of the fence. However, as our system of jurisprudence has often proved to be unjust and dishonest at times, nothing surprises me."

Julie said, "On one of Lafevre's points, the travel agency will not help us much. Although they can say your trip was paid for by someone named Henri Cadieux, no one ever saw him. The matter was handled over the phone."

"But, can anybody on that jury buy the fact that

someone else who hates me is coincidentally out there wanting me dead and at the same time trying to frame Karn?"

"It's a flimsy defense, Bruce," Marie said. "No rational-thinking person will believe that."

Judge Sartre was back in the courtroom sooner than he said. "Monsieur Lafevre, I have considered your motion to dismiss and feel there is merit to continue the case. However, when the procureur's evidence is presented and I do not feel at some point in the trial it has value, I will reconsider. Madame Durand, you may call your first witness."

"Judge, before I call any witnesses, I want to present to the court a copy of Monsieur Karn's criminal record for the jury to review which will attest to his character."

"I object, your honor; Monsieur Cadieux's former life would be considered inflammatory and as such would prejudice the jury. Monsieur Cadieux is a changed man. His past is history and not a true reflection of who he is now."

"Sustained. What else do you have, Madame Durand?"

"I have the Saint-Amaury records verifying that it was Monsieur Cadieux who paid for the McGowan trip."

"Do you have a witness who can say that he or she saw the defendant?"

"No, your honor."

"What else?"

"I have Elizabeth Farrell's sworn statement that she heard her husband's killer or someone with him taunt the dead body he thought was that of Monsieur McGowan and make a sardonic comment to who he thought was Adriana McGowan."

"Is Madame Farrell in the courtroom?"

"No, your honor."

"Let me see the statement."

Julie walked it to the bench. The judge studied it for a moment and nodded.

"I will place this into evidence. Anything else?"

"Not at this time."

"Do you now present your witness?"

"Yes. I call Officer Jon Thibut to the stand."

After Thibut was sworn in, Julie began her questioning. Officer, you were at the scene of Roy Farrell's murder, were you not?"

"I was."

"What did you find?"

"When I arrived on Rue Soufflot Street, I found Madame Farrell bent over her husband in tears. I examined the body and saw a knife wound in Roy Farrell's abdomen with much blood running onto the sidewalk." His accent was thick, but I understood each word.

"What did Madame Farrell say to you?"

"She told me as she and her husband were walking in the light rain, a large man in a raincoat with a hood came up behind them. They turned around when they heard him approaching and then the man stabbed her husband. She said she screamed out and then a man's voice from the nearby alley began to speak loudly."

"What did she say the man said?"

"She…"

"I have your report here, Officer Thibut. Can you read it to the court?"

He examined the report for a few seconds and then said, "…and so, Mister McGowan, here is where you finally die. You are not so invincible after all, are you? Cry your heart out, dear Adriana. Cry long, cry hard."

"Is that word for word?"

"That is what she told me."

"Thank you, Monsieur. No further. Your witness, counsel."

Lafevre walked from his seat to the witness stand. "Thank you for being here, Officer Thibut. I just have a couple of questions. Did Madame Farrell tell you what her husband's assailant looked like? Height, weight, facial features?"

"She said he was tall but did not see his face. The hood of his raincoat covered it."

"Did the killer say anything while he was standing over the body?"

"She said he just stabbed her husband and walked away. It was a few seconds later she heard a voice saying what I read to the court."

"Did she say there was anyone who may have seen the murder of her husband?"

"She said no one else was on the street. But she does not think the voice she heard came from the murderer. The voice was high-pitched and…"

"I didn't ask you for that, Officer. No further."

Julie then stood. "Cross, your honor."

When he nodded, she approached from her table and asked, "You were about to say how Madame Farrell described his voice."

"She said it was of high-pitch. His laughter was like a cackle."

"Thank you, Officer Thibut. No further questions."

I thought we scored with that. I was anxious for the jury to hear Karn's high voice. That's what happens to somebody who gets his nuts kicked up into his intestines. A result of some of that ruthlessness Lafevre was mentioning.

The remainder of the morning consisted of arguments before the judge regarding the defense's introduction of character witnesses for Karn. Lafevre's list included over a dozen. Julie argued that two or three were enough, but her adversary insisted that each witness was important to their case.

I had lunch with Julie at a deli on the same street as the courthouse. She said the afternoon was going to be overkill with all the character witnesses. She was anxious to get Karn himself on the stand as I'm sure Lafevre wanted the same with me. Karn would continue trying to play the pity party to the jury. On one occasion during the morning, his caregiver stood to place a blanket around him. Karn looked at him and smiled, showing his appreciation. We had to admit that the jury took notice.

Court was back in session at two at which time Lafevre began putting his parade of witnesses on the stand. By the fifth witness, I could see that the jury was getting bored with all the praise Karn's handpicked and probably paid friends were giving him. He was not only a benevolent man when it came to charities but one who was always giving of himself to the community regardless of his handicap. A good friend, an honest, spiritual, tender-hearted man; we heard it all. The needle on my vomit meter was way to the right.

Julie Durand only chose to cross-examine one witness, a beefy man about forty-five who said he had known Monsieur Cadieux for over fifteen years. Thinking that he had not been totally forthright about his association with Karn, she began pushing his buttons. "Monsieur Landon, where did you first meet Monsieur Cadieux?"

"At Ramatuelle when his uncle passed away."

"You said you first met Monsieur Cadieux fifteen years ago, but the uncle passed away ten years ago."

"Maybe I was mixed up about the number of years."

"But you knew his uncle."

"I was friends with him before Henri came to stay with him."

"You are an American. How long had you been living in France at the time?

"Maybe fifteen years. Yes, that's where the fifteen came from."

"What brought you here?"

"Business."

"What kind of business?"

"Import-export."

"Can you be more specific, as in what company?"

"The company's name is Agresseur Enterprises."

Aha! I motioned for Julie to confer with me. When she came to my bench, I whispered a few words to her. She then returned to the witness and asked the first of several well-pointed questions. "Monsieur Landon, are you sure you did not know Monsieur Cadieux as Jonas Karn before he came to Paris?"

Landon became noticeably flushed. "I…met him here in France."

"Would it change your story if I told you that there were two men driving a car registered to Agresseur Enterprises out of Detroit, Michigan, who attempted to kill Adriana McGowan, Monsieur McGowan's wife, only a week ago? And the owner and CEO of that business is none other than Henri Cadieux. I believe that you actually knew him before you came to France. So, tell me, were you involved in his reconstituted Weather Underground seventeen or eighteen years ago?"

"Objection. Your honor, I object to this questioning of Monsieur Landon. Counsel is attacking my witness' credibility, insinuating he is connected to the alleged attempt on Madame McGowan's life. He has already said that he met Monsieur Cadieux here in France."

"Your honor, there are obvious discrepancies in his testimony that need to be addressed."

"Objection over-ruled. I will allow her questions." Maybe I was wrong about the judge.

"Think again, Monsieur Landon. Did you ever meet Monsieur Cadieux when he was Jonas Karn? And were you involved with the Weather Underground, a domestic terrorist organization? You are under oath."

"I may have met him before I came to France. It

must have had something to do with the business, I can't remember."

"Again, were you a member of the Weather Underground?

"No."

"Are you currently employed by Monsieur Cadieux?"

"We have become friends and…"

"Answer the question."

Landon paused to look across the room at Karn.

"Yes."

"In what capacity?"

"I run errands for him whenever he needs something."

"What kind of errands?"

"I pick up things for him when he needs them."

"Have you ever worked for him as a bodyguard?"

"Sometimes."

"Remember you are under oath, Monsieur Landon; has Monsieur Cadieux ordered you to strong-arm, threaten, or end anyone's life, such as Monsieur McGowan?"

Lafevre then jumped up. "Objection, your honor, we resent this line of questioning. Monsieur Landon is a character witness and not on trial here."

"I don't see a problem with asking the question since Monsieur Landon is in the defendant's employ. The witness must answer."

"No. Hell, no. I've never been asked to do such a thing."

"Thank you, Monsieur Landon. Your honor, I have finished with this witness." Julie then glanced at Karn and sat back down.

She was feisty and in looking at Karn's face, I presumed she would now be another of his enemies.

After Lafevre had put on his tenth character witness, the judge himself had had enough. He said, "Counsel, I see you have two more witnesses and if they will have the same words of praise for your client, will their testimonies be necessary?"

Lafevre, realizing Judge Sartre's impatience, replied, "I think we will not call them, your honor." He then said, "The defense rests."

I did notice that halfway through the afternoon, two venomous-looking Middle Easterners came into the courtroom and sat on the bench behind Karn. At one point, Karn's primary caregiver turned around and whispered something to them, which prompted them to look over at me. Could it be that I was in for more trouble? I then slipped Jacques Allard a note telling him to check out the two goons dressed in kaffiyehs, or Muslim headdresses. He then looked in their direction and nodded.

At five minutes past four, the judge announced that court would end for the day and to be back the next day at nine. Before he stepped down from the bench, he charged the jury to not discuss the case outside the courtroom nor watch or read any media.

As Marie de Barrere had earlier left the courtroom, Julie, Jacques, and I walked out together. As best he could turn his head, Jonas Karn watched us depart all the way out through the double doors.

When the three of us had stopped to talk in the hallway before leaving the building, Karn, his primary caregiver and two goons that I had earlier spotted stopped before passing by us. Karn couldn't resist making a comment. "Well, McGowan, I see you've survived another day."

"Is that a threat, Karn?"

"I'm just interested in your future."

"I'll bet you are."

"You can't win this, you know," he said.

"I'm not the one on trial."

He and his entourage then moved on without further word.

Jacques commented, "What a piece of…" He then stopped what he was about to say out of respect for Julie.

She finished his sentence in French. "Merde."

I laughed. "You don't have to translate. I got it." Of course, I thought the English word equivalent fit better.

Jacques then said sarcastically, "Yes, there goes that nice, congenial, and benevolent Monsieur Cadieux that all those witnesses praised this afternoon. "

"Benevolent, my ass," I scoffed. "I will bet if you checked his finances, he has never contributed one euro to charity."

"And Julie, I was impressed with your handling of Monsieur Landon," Jacques added. "It makes me wonder how many other of the witnesses are on his payroll."

I nodded. "Not only did the jury appear bored with them, but I'm also sure they didn't believe one word of their ballyhoo. And then considering Lafevre's reputation, I didn't think he came out swinging in his opening. His defense was rather milk-toast compared to your delivery."

"I have always considered Lafevre to be an honorable man, but unfortunately he has a *dishonorable* man for a client…and I'm sure he knows it. He knows everything about his reputation now, if he didn't before, and likely knows that he is even prone to murder. However, I did expect more out of him," she replied. "But don't underestimate this man. Before this trial gets much older, he will put on a good show. As you will be testifying tomorrow, be ready to get excoriated."

"I'll be loaded for bear."

Jacques laughed. "Another American expression I haven't heard. I will have my officer take you back to your hotel now."

Chapter Twenty Six

When we left the courthouse, I spotted Karn and his man entering his especially equipped van in a handicapped parking spot in a lot a half block away. But, what also caught my eye were two other heads wearing the kaffiyehs I saw in the courtroom, one a colorful red and gray and the other a houndstooth pattern. Keeping my eye on them while walking with Jacques to his unmarked cruiser, I saw them turn and stop to check *me* out before stepping into their silver Mercedes C Class.

"Do you see them?" I asked Jacques.

"Yes. And I also see them watching us. Let's see if they follow."

Jacques pulled away from his space quickly, and within seconds, the Mercedes did the same. Making a series of left and right turns, Jacques and I checked our side mirrors to see if they did likewise. And they did. At one point, he thought he had lost them, but moments later they reappeared about three hundred feet behind us.

"They're wanting to find out where you're staying."

"With fatal intentions, I'm sure," I remarked.

"We can ride all over Paris if that's what it takes to lose them. You don't need to be placed in any more danger than you might already be."

"But, you have other things to do. You have Officer Jordain there at the hotel set up as my guard, so I have no problem with you just dropping me off. Provide me with a firearm and I won't feel so naked."

"I wish I could, but..."

"Yeah, I know."

"Just stay inside this evening. Order in for dinner or take advantage of Le Fleur's two fine restaurants. And get some rest; you're on stage tomorrow. I'll pick you up myself at 8:30."

When Jacques pulled his sedan into the checkin circle to let me out, we saw the silver Mercedes pull up to the curb across the street.

"So, officially they now know you're staying here."

"It won't matter. Officer Jordain is here, I'm not going out and you're driving me to the courthouse in the morning. There are also cameras on the building and in the lobby. Not to worry."

"Okay, get on inside. I will keep an eye on them until you're in the lobby. Have a good night."

From the large window of the hotel's Cafe de la Crepe, while I dined on a plate of crabs, I kept watching the street and entrance for the two Arabs or anyone else who wanted to kill me. The Mercedes had moved on and I suspected Karn's thugs did not plan to *off* me that evening. But I knew they would be camped out there somewhere, waiting for me to take a walk. At least Jacques now knew Karn's intent on taking my life was real. He was going to take all precautions to keep me alive. I think he wanted Karn to go down as much as I did.

Once in my room, I spent about fifteen minutes on the phone with Adriana. All was well in South Florida and we both were fairly assured that Karn and his army of goons did not know where she was. He had more pressing things on his mind at the present. I gave her a capsule of the first day of the trial and that I would be grilled on the stand the next. She wished me well and that I remained safe. There was some more sugar-sweet talk that made me feel like I was in high school again and then we said good night.

The next morning, I had a banana and some yogurt, not feeling much like a more substantial breakfast. I thought maybe it was just a case of stomach butterflies in anticipation of sitting in the witness box and being verbally assaulted by Lafevre. I wasn't afraid of the man, but I was a little worried about not only making a fool of myself but also saying something that would hinder the prosecution's case.

As I stood in the lobby watching for the lieutenant's car to pull up, I thought I saw a silver Mercedes go by, but the vehicle didn't stop or park. Was I going to be wary about every Mercedes I saw on the street? However, sharply at 8:30, Jacques Allard swung his sedan into the half circle as close to the front door as he could. He was taking no chances in my taking a bullet from either someone lurking close by or from a sniper rifle. I then opened the car door and quickly slid onto the passenger seat.

"You had a pleasant night, I hope?"

"It was fine. I had a succulent plate of crabs and a telephone date with Adriana for dessert."

He smiled. "Assuming no party girls paid you a visit, then."

I laughed. "And no bad guys stormed the Bastille

trying to take me out."

"You are ready this morning?"

"I will have plenty to say about the galvanizing Monsieur Cadieux, loved, endeared and respected by so many…ten of whom we heard from yesterday."

"Julie Durand made him look less than wonderful yesterday morning. Perhaps you can finish him off today by filling the jury's ears with all the sordid details about him. Nothing like hearing it from the horse's mouth."

We were nearly halfway to the courthouse when I spotted it in my side mirror…a black Honda sedan that made the two right turns and a left, staying less than four car lengths behind us. Jacques saw it as well.

"I am sure we have a tail. But it is not the Mercedes this time. I will make another turn and see for sure."

"On my last trip here, in the two attempts on my life, in both cases their vehicles were black SUVs."

Jacques made the turn and the Honda followed. But then suddenly, when the two-lane road became four, the Honda pulled up alongside our Peugeot. When the rear side window came down, and I saw the barrel, I yelled, *"Gun!"* At the same time the gunman fired, Jacques hit the brakes. If he hadn't, the bullet would have smashed into my head. However, the round merely singed the tip of my nose but struck Jacques. He then lost control and sideswiped the perp's vehicle, the impact forcing it into a light pole. Jacques, who appeared only to be hit in the shoulder, put his foot back on the brake and guided the Peugeot to a stop. Still conscious, but fading fast, he could only say, "Stay down."

"Hang on, Jacques." Grabbing hold of his suit jacket, I reached inside and grabbed the 9 mm from his shoulder holster.

"What are you doing?" he said weakly.

I then threw open the door and ran toward the Honda, Jacques' gun leading the way. I could see that the light pole had penetrated well into the car's front end, pushing the radiator into the engine block. Steam and smoke spewed from the hood. It was like deja vu from a few weeks ago when I chased down the boys from Detroit in my woods.

As I came upon the rear of the Honda, the left rear door suddenly opened whereupon the gunman charged out, sniper rifle in hand. I neither gave him a chance to put a bead on me nor to pray about what was going to happen. The first of my two rounds struck him between the eyes and the second found the center of his chest.

Although I knew he had died instantly, I kicked the rifle away and peered inside the car. The driver's head was buried into the windshield, the rest of his body crumpled over the steering wheel. Another moron who never learned to buckle his seat belt.

As a small crowd began forming, I hustled back to Jacques who was now slumped down into the driver's seat. Blood oozed from his shoulder. After searching for a rag or something similar to stop the flow of blood, and finding nothing, I tore off my jacket and placed it tightly against the wound. Although he was ninety percent unconscious, he groaned from the pressure.

An older man then appeared at the driver's side door and said something to me in French. I shook my head. "Je suis Americaine." He nodded and pulled out his cell phone. I assumed he was calling for a rescue vehicle.

Within a couple of minutes, two police motorcyclists, in French referred to as motards, zoomed in. They saw what I was doing and one of them took over. The other officer, a sergeant, began talking in French and I again said I was American. He knew just a bit of English.

"This is a police car?"

I nodded. "Oui." I pointed to Jacques and said, "Lieutenant Allard, Seine-Saint-Denis precinct."

Seeing the Sig still in my hand, he said "Give me the gun." After he took it from me, he then began talking into his radio.

Moments later, other officers in their pillbox caps, as well as two ambulances, were at the scene. Another sergeant who spoke a fair amount of English began asking me questions. I told him the dead dudes in the Hondas had ambushed us as we were on the way to trial. He asked if it was me who pumped rounds into the shooter, and with a proud expression on my face, I told him, "Oui."

I didn't realize it but found that the tip of my nose was bleeding where the bullet had grazed me. I was that close to certain death. From my pocket, I took a handkerchief and applied pressure.

Jacques was conscious when he was loaded onto the gurney and told me the last thing he remembered was putting on the brakes. I filled him in. When the ambulance pulled away, siren blaring, the investigating sergeant resumed his questioning. However, I checked my watch and saw that it was nine-fifteen. The trial had already begun. I told him quickly I was late for court and needed to call the prosecutor. He nodded.

As I had put Julie's cell number into my phone, I dialed her.

"Bruce, where are you?" she asked in something above a whisper. "We're ready to start."

"At the scene of an ambush. Lieutenant Allard had picked me up and as we were on the way to the courthouse, a couple of goons opened on us. Jacques was hit in the shoulder and is on the way to the hospital."

"My God, are you alright?"

"Yes, but the assholes who ambushed us aren't."

"Dead?"

"Very."

"Who were they?"

"I'll give you three guesses. You'll get it on the first try."

"Karn's people. I can't believe he would order it. The jury would have to realize it was him."

"I guess I'll need to talk further with the officers here, so I won't be there for a while."

"I will get today's proceedings postponed. When you are released there, get a ride to my office."

"I will. Give my friend Jonas Karn my regards. Tell him he missed again."

Chapter Twenty Seven

Lieutenant Lucien Bain, from the same precinct as Jacques, took over the on-scene investigation, telling me he needed to secure my statement. I asked him if he could take the statement at the hospital where the ambulance took Jacques for treatment. He agreed.

When we arrived at Saint Mary's, we went directly to the trauma unit. As Jacques was in surgery, we were compelled to sit in the waiting room until such time he was taken to recovery.

Bain then pulled a mini cassette player from his pocket. "Monsieur McGowan, I will be recording your statement if you do not object."

"That will be fine."

He then turned on his recorder. "This is Detective Lieutenant Lucien Bain securing a statement from Monsieur Bruce McGowan at Saint Mary's Hospital, Paris, France. It involves a shooting of National Police Lieutenant Jacques Allard on the Rue de Chalet Boulevard at approximately eight-forty in the morning of June 26. Monsieur McGowan, would you please state your full name and provide your address."

After I provided the information, the lieutenant asked me a series of questions pertaining to my purpose in coming to Paris and how I came to be a passenger in the police cruiser Lieutenant Allard was driving. For nearly fifteen minutes I took him through the entire scenario from my law enforcement history in bringing down domestic terrorist Jonas Karn through my initial trip to Paris, including the murder of Roy Farrell, and my assistance to the procureur as a witness in Karn's trial. When asked about the actual shooting of the lieutenant, I explained there was no doubt the bullet was meant for me. Unfortunately, when the lieutenant took evasive action, it erroneously struck him.

"When the assailant's vehicle crashed into the pole and the lieutenant braked the police cruiser to a stop, I jumped out and ran toward the shooter's car. As the shooter in the back seat was getting out of the car and preparing to fire his rifle at me, I shot him in the head and chest."

"You had a gun?"

"I took it from Lieutenant Allard's holster after he had been shot."

"Did you issue the man with the rifle a warning before you shot him?"

"Hell, no. There was no time. He was going to kill me."

He had just a few other questions for me and then ended the interview.

I asked, "Will there be an inquest regarding my killing of the man?"

"I think not. The police will not only consider it as a justified shooting but a heroic action."

"I'm no hero, Lieutenant. I just don't like the idea of dying."

At that moment, a surgical nurse came through the double doors at the end of the hallway and approached our bench. She said something in French and Bain responded. I heard him say "Merci" and then she walked away.

"Jacques is in good condition after the surgery. The bullet was successfully removed, and he is resting comfortably. We can see him in recovery for only a few minutes."

After entering the doors that read 'unite de soins intensifs' we were directed to a curtain behind which Jacques lay on the surgical bed. He was pale but awake. Lieutenant Bain, obviously a friend and fellow precinct officer, began speaking to him in French. Moments later, Jacques looked at me and nodded.

"And so, mon ami, you did some target practice with my gun this morning, I hear."

"Well, I hadn't shot anyone yet today and thought, why not?"

"You managed to save both of our lives. But what happened to your nose?"

"The bullet meant for me that hit you actually caught a piece of me. A matter of inches and you'd be sending me back home in a box."

"I am surprised Monsieur Cadieux ordered another attempt on your life considering he is sitting in a courtroom defending himself against a murder charge. He should realize that a savvy jury would suspect him of being involved."

"You'd think so, but Monsieur Karn wants me dead at any cost."

"I have never seen a man so driven by hate."

"He needs to be driven, alright, off a cliff, wheelchair and all."

The same nurse appeared from behind the curtain

and told Lieutenant Bain our visit was over. Jacques then extended his left hand and I took it. "Thank you, Bruce. You will have to dine with my wife and I again before you leave."

"I'd like that. Sorry this happened to you. I feel responsible."

"Do not feel sorry. We both know who is responsible."

Before I left the hospital, one of the nurses placed a small Band-Aid on the top of my nose.

Lieutenant Bain's people had run the tag and VIN on the car in which the assailants were riding. It had been reported stolen the night before. They were smart enough to not use one from Karn's fleet just in case the attack went badly. However, they were *not* smart enough to avoid the Big Sleep.

My bodyguard, Officer Jordain, who had come to the hospital to retrieve me, drove me to meet with Julie Durand at her office at two o'clock. When I walked in, she greeted me with one of her dynamite smiles. As she was wearing a tight-fitting blue dress that accentuated every curve in her body, I knew it was going to be difficult for me to concentrate on what we were discussing. But then when I started having guilt pangs, thinking about another beautiful woman who happened to be somewhere in Florida and who happened to be my wife, while we talked, I refrained from focusing on anything south of her eyes.

"What happened to your nose?" Julie asked.

"I tried to stop a bullet with it. I guess I slowed it down or it would have done more damage to Jacques."

Julie didn't know at first if I was kidding, but

figured out in a couple of seconds what kind of joker I was; then she laughed.

After we had gotten our small talk and frivolities out of the way, I asked her, "When you advised that Lieutenant Allard and I had been ambushed on the way to the courthouse, what happened after that?"

"The judge of course postponed the trial as I requested. He reset it for tomorrow. But, thinking the jury might believe that Cadieux sent his employees to kill you to keep you from testifying, Lafevre made a statement on his behalf. I have a copy of today's court transcript. I will read it to you. "My client, Monsieur Cadieux, is very affected that someone tried to end Monsieur McGowan's life and instead wounded Lieutenant Allard. Although Monsieur McGowan is not exactly my client's favorite person, he does not wish any harm would come to him. But it does not surprise Monsieur Cadieux that this is happening considering the large list of Monsieur McGowan's enemies all over the world. There have been other attempts on his life in the United States and elsewhere. It is obvious someone either followed him here or lives here and found out he was vacationing in Paris. Again, Monsieur Cadieux condemns this attack and hopes that the perpetrators are found." So, you see that Karn is playing the sympathy card on your behalf to divert attention off of him.""

"Did you have a response to his statement?"

"I only said the two Middle Eastern men who tried to kill you are dead at the scene. And as I said that, I looked at Karn. Hearing the news, he looked like he just swallowed a guppy."

I laughed. "His only regret about the incident is that

he has lost two more of his men. He's running out of camel jockeys."

"We will need to play down the fact that you killed one of the men. Even though you shot him in self-defense, it may give substance to Karn's accusation that you are a violent man who has ended the lives of over five hundred people. Have you really done that?"

"I really couldn't tell you. I don't have notches on my firearms. Most of the men I've gone after were terrorists like him and radical Islamists who had either plotted to kill or actually did kill American citizens. But I brought *him* in and *he's* alive, isn't he? I don't relish the fact that I've had to take lives."

"Be prepared for Monsieur Lafevre to spend much time on that tomorrow to make you appear as a murderer yourself."

I nodded. "I'll make sure they see me as a choir boy."

Young Officer Herve Jordain, a strapping six-footer whose face pretty much did resemble that of a choir boy, was waiting for me outside of Julie's office. "Where can I take you now, sir?" he asked.

"I guess back to the hotel. I have no place else to go."

We walked almost at a trot back to his cruiser, which, of course, would do little to keep a sniper's bullet from tearing into me; however, I'd at least be a moving target. I didn't think Karn would send any more goons after me that day, but there was no doubt in my mind his hatred greatly overshadowed his rationality. He had already proved that. It was his worst enemy.

"You have had a most interesting day, Monsieur

McGowan."

"To say the least, Officer Jordain."

"I am sorry that Lieutenant Allard was hit and hope he will not lose the function in his right arm. I heard the talk at the hospital."

"He's going to be fine," I said. "I'm just glad the bullet didn't strike a vital organ."

"Or one of yours."

I grinned. "You can say that again."

I was back at the hotel by four. Herve would stay in the lobby until seven, keeping his eyes peeled for sinister- looking characters nosing around. Then another officer by the name of Aubert would take over the night watch.

No sooner had I gotten to my room than my cell phone rang. It was Marie de Barrere. "I am sorry I missed you when you were in our office this afternoon. I was wondering if you had plans for this evening."

"Just hoping to catch a couple of Andy Griffith reruns on French TV is all. I can't wait to see how Barney pronounces "Nip it. Nip it in the bud" in French."

"Etouffez-le dans l'oeuf. Of course, there would be English subtitles."

"So, why are you interested in my evening?"

"I would like to have dinner with you. We could also talk about what you will say tomorrow in court and what you shouldn't. One of my favorite places is Cafe Beaujolais on Rue de la Fontaine. You like our food in this country, n'est-ce pas?"

"I do."

"What do you like best? I will tell you if the restaurant has it."

"You know…all the traditional French foods like French toast, French fries, French onion dip…"

"You are very funny. Seriously, would you like to accompany me to a good dinner?"

"I think I can arrange my schedule to do that."

"Merveilleux. How about eight o'clock? I will need to make reservations."

"Will I be riding with you or Officer Aubert who is keeping watch on me?"

"I will pick you up."

"It may not be safe having me as your passenger."

"I heard. And I am glad you were spared this morning, but I will take my chances. My passenger has a reputation of being a very fearsome man."

"You're bringing someone else along?"

"I was talking about you."

"This fearsome man has no weapon."

"But I do. A .357 magnum. It has unbeatable stopping power."

A girl after my own heart.

"I hope you can drive and shoot at the same time."

"As good as your Annie Oakley."

"Then I'll be waiting in the lobby. Will have to tell Officer Aubert, though."

"I will see you about seven-fifty."

I don't do dates with women, considering I'm a married man, but as long as we'd be talking court strategy, I didn't think there would be any harm. Adriana would understand. Of course, she hadn't seen Marie de Barrere, one of the best-looking women in Paris.

Speaking of my bonny wife, I got her on the phone about an hour later. She was bored hanging around her parents in their senior living community and was planning to go home. I asked her to give it another couple of days as in my conversation with Marie, it probably wouldn't go longer than that. I told her my testimony was the next day and the defense counsel had already run through his list of pitiful witnesses. I wasn't sure if Karn was going to testify on his own behalf, but if he did, prosecutor Julie would chop him up in pieces given his history. Karn's best hope was that the jury would not connect Roy Farrell's murder with his heap of well-chronicled hate for me. She said, "okay." Maybe one or two more days of shuffleboard and bingo with her folks and their geriatric friends she could take.

Marie pulled her ancient Citroen into the hotel registration circle about a quarter till eight and I zipped from the door to her car, hopefully outrunning any bullet that was on the way to my head at 3800 feet per second. *Damn* but I couldn't wait to get home. Once inside the car, I knew my libido was in trouble. Marie looked good, smelled good and flashing her perfect set of legs all the way up to within inches of her underwear. The 'come-do- me' spike heels were not helping my lasciviousness either. Why couldn't the two prosecutors in this case have been short, dumpy, bald guys?

To try taking my mind off Marie's gorgeous gams, I

struck up a conversation about her car. "What year is your Citroen?"

'It's a 1970 M35. A classic. It won car of the year with its Wankel engine."

The ugliest car I ever saw, but I didn't tell her that. "What's its horsepower?"

"49, but gets up to a speed of over 70 miles per hour."

"Going downhill?"

"Are you insulting my car?"

"Would I do that?"

"I do not know. When I pulled up, the look on your face gave you away…looking like you had just smelled a dead rat."

I had seen rats I thought were more attractive than her Citroen. Of course, I didn't say that. "Nah. That's my look when somebody wearing a sari smelling of body odor and curry passes me in the lobby."

"And so, you are a bigot as well, Monsieur McGowan."

"Not at all. Okay, starting over. I love French automobiles and people from India."

She laughed and patted my cheek. "Let's go

get something to eat. Hopefully, we will not get ambushed before we get there."

The restaurant was not that far away, and she said we should make our eight o'clock reservation easily. Thank goodness she didn't allow me to be a male chauvinist pig by going around to open the car door for her. When she swung those legs out, placing her spikes on the ground to get out, my ticker might have gone into electric shock.

Anyway, we were ushered into the fancy dining area by a prissy garçon who didn't seem at all interested in her legs or anything else about her. She was seated and then me. Because I didn't like the way he placed the clothnapkin on my lap, I started to smack his hand. What was it with these la-di-da garçons?

I thought maybe I was a little underdressed for the restaurant's snazzy atmosphere since I wasn't wearing a tie. I did, however, decide to wear a jacket. Another garçon then appeared and took our drink order. Marie's aperitif was an autumn spiced tonic, but being the American commoner that I was, I had a Heineken.

As we waited for our dinner menu, we talked some about my harrowing morning and the fact that I was compelled to take yet another life.

"I suppose you didn't realize when you arose from your sleep this morning that someone would be trying to kill you before you arrived at the courthouse."

"Let's just say in my law enforcement history, I've never anticipated it, but I've always been prepared for the worst. Today was a bit of a surprise, however."

"But you reacted quickly by taking Jacques' gun and going after your would-be assassin." She then laid her hand on mine. "That kind of action is exciting to me. You are like the Bond character...suave, but deadly...handsome, and at times quippy."

It was then I realized she was on the make. I was in Paris, my wife in the States and she was in heat. She was trying to make me fall off the fidelity wagon. However, I was not going to allow myself to get caught in her web. I pulled my hand from beneath hers.

"Well, I'm not James Bond. I'm now just an ordinary retired househusband who seems to have once again gotten myself embroiled in a game of cat-and-mouse with an old nemesis. I'm just not sure who's the cat and who's the mouse."

I was pretty sure she took the hint. I was a faithful married guy who was not only focused on seeing Monsieur Karn go down for murder but also trying to keep myself alive. In the meantime, I was trying to *un*focus myself on her.

I ordered a plate of clams and mussels while Marie chose crawfish. Nothing about those red bugs resembled a fish to me. I wouldn't eat them in New Orleans and sure as hell wasn't going to eat them in Paris. They ranked right up there with the French snails. After a little conversation about the trial, they brought our food…quicker than I thought. Had it been cooked? But, although my dinner was okay, seeing what was going on across the table, I had a little trouble putting it down my swallerpipe. In watching her bite off the tails and sucking the brains out of the heads of those roach-looking critters, my stomach was turning.

"What do you think Karn's chances of prevailing are?" I asked her.

"Right now, I would say 50-50, maybe leaning a bit further to our side. I believe it all comes down to whether the jury likes you or has sympathy for him. I don't think they will like him. They will not like his voice; nor will they like the fact that he has been a terrorist most of his life. But people can also be both sympathetic and forgiving. If he shows remorse for his past, they may like him better. Some of the jury will also not want to see him sitting in a wheelchair behind bars. He is already in a bodily prison."

"So, how do you think the jury will perceive me?"

"A well-spoken man with charisma and movie star looks. Remember, six out of nine of the jurors are women. What is not to like? You are something between the Jackal and an international man of mystery. Once Julie showcases your history to the jury, they'll think you are Monsieur Bond straight out of the movies."

"I know you're being complimentary, Marie, but I don't want to be perceived as such. Sure, they will find out I served in federal law enforcement and with a Department of State counter-terrorist unit. However, I think they need to see me as a retired, ordinary citizen who once worked in defense of his country but then being duped by a madman out for revenge set me up for the kill. They should be in sympathy for *me* and what I've had to put up with. Years ago, my daughter was kidnapped, my wife shot and almost killed, and now, for the past two months, he has tried several times to send me to the boneyard."

She once again laid her hand on mine, this time squeezing it. I then said, "I don't think you ever told me about yourself. You know that I'm married and have a thirty-three-year-old daughter who's with the FBI. How about you? Married? Kids?"

"I am divorced and have two teenage girls, fourteen and seventeen, both of whom think they are twenty-one.'

"How long have you been the chief prosecutor?"

"Three months. I was one of the deputy

procureurs for eight years before that."

"I had heard from Jacques that you were a force to be reckoned with. Put away lots of people. The French mob especially fears you. They call you Barracuda de Barre, he says."

"I suppose I do have a reputation. The criminals are tough and I have to be tougher."

"Okay then, tough lady, put away this maggot who has been a festering boil on my backside for over three decades."

She smiled. "Julie Durand and I together will do our best."

Chapter Twenty Eight

The barracuda and I sat for another hour after we finished dinner talking some more about the case, but also about other cases we both had over the years. When the evening was over, she took me back to the hotel. However, before I exited her car, she leaned into me, gave me a hug, and kissed me on the lips. That's when my olfactory senses discovered she was a closet smoker. I could smell and taste it on her. But then she righted herself in her seat and smiled. The last thing she said as I opened the door was, "Too bad things aren't different, Monsieur Bond. We could be great together."

I then said, "Good night, Marie. See you tomorrow."

If I had given in to the old libido, the night would have ended in a sexual frenzy. But my marriage would have been over, and I would have carried pangs of guilt with me all the way back across the ocean. What some guys don't realize is the power of the little brain over the big one is fatal to the marriage. An hour or two of pleasure can turn into a lifetime of pain for a guy. But as one who's had to resist temptation a number of times, I was the better man for it.

When I entered the hotel, Officer Tristan Aubert stood and greeted me. "Did you have a nice evening, Monsieur McGowan?"

"Yes, I did, sir. Thank you."

"I was much concerned that you were out and that I did not accompany you. My lieutenant would not have liked that."

"There was no threat that I could see. Anyway, there was a barracuda protecting me."

He gave me a puzzled look which a lot of people do a lot of the time.

The next morning, at eight twenty-five, my door rang. Through the peephole, I saw that it was Herve Jordain. "Are you ready to go, Monsieur McGowan?"

I opened the door and nodded. "Ready, Herve. After you."

As I had lost my sports coat, stopping the blood flow from Jacques's arm, I only had one other set of dress clothes appropriate for trial…my gray suit with the faint pinstripes. I usually don't wear a tie, even to church, but that day I did. If I do say so myself, I looked rather GQ. Maybe it would help me look less 'vicious' as Lafevre had referred to me.

When I stepped into the courtroom, Julie let out a low whistle. "Hello-o-o, Monsieur McGowan," she said in an almost sing-song. "As you Americans say, you clean up real nice."

Standing beside her, Marie smiled. "Monsieur Bond, I presume."

I returned her smile. "Just a plain old run-of-the-mill American private citizen these days, ladies."

"Are you ready for the grill?" Julie asked me.

"Let's do this."

That day, both Marie and Julie sat at the prosecution table. Across the room, Jonas Karn sat glaring at me. On his face was an expression that screamed "Why can't I kill this man?" Or maybe I was only imagining it.

After the "All Rise" command was issued by the bailiff, Judge Sartre told us to take our seats. "Madame Durand, you may call your first witness."

"My only witness, your honor. I call Monsieur Bruce McGowan. You may take the stand, sir."

The bailiff administered the oath and I sat down. The glare from Karn's eyes turned into a burning sear. I supposed he thought he was being intimidated.

"Monsieur McGowan, would you please state your full name for the court?"

"Bruce Tavish McGowan."

"You are an American?"

"Yes."

"Please give the court a capsule of your work history."

"After college, I served as a commissioned officer in the United States Army for twelve years. I was then recruited by the FBI and finished out my twenty year career as a Senior Special Agent. Again, I was recruited, this time by the U.S. Department of State where I worked in its counter-terrorism department for another eight years."

"What was your job description there?"

"I profiled foreign and domestic terrorists who plotted against the United States government and its citizens."

"Can you be more specific?"

She was going too far. I didn't think she would. However, I thought perhaps she was trying to broadly get things out in the open before Lafevre did. He would dig hard. But as my missions were mostly top secret, there was just so much I could divulge.

"I was sent on missions to neutralize terrorist threats."

"Did that mean you were compelled to take lives as necessary?"

"Sometimes. Especially when the terrorist or terrorist elements were attempting to take American lives."

"When you were with the FBI, were there times that you took lives in your capacity as an agent?"

"Very few."

"Do you remember exactly how many?"

"Every one of them. Six."

"And with the Department of State?"

"Certainly not over five hundred as Mr. Lafevre claims."

"Can you estimate?"

"No, I cannot."

"Would you say over four hundred?"

Julie was pushing my buttons. But, again, she was only doing what Lafevre would be doing.

"No. I have never kept score. It would be callous and soulless to do so." I practiced saying those words as I knew they were coming; however, I thought they'd be asked by the defense.

"You told me you had arrested Monsieur Cadieux when he was known as Jonas Karn. In what capacity did you do that?"

"The first time was thirty or more years ago when I was with the FBI. He had reconstituted the domestic terrorist organization known as the Weather Underground. He had engaged a number of dissidents to set bombs in government buildings in Washington, D.C. and other cities with intent to destroy America's government infrastructure, kill members of congress and the military, and create widespread anarchy."

"Objection, your honor. How does Monsieur McGowan know what Monsieur Cadieux's intent was? My client's activity in the United States can only be described as necessary to stop American imperialism, further the civil rights of Black Americans, and halt the Vietnam War where America's young men were getting slaughtered daily."

"Monsieur McGowan's testimony is supported by a number of documents on record at Interpol that have previously been presented to this court.

Monsieur Karn's actions were traitorous, violent and criminal."

"Over-ruled. Continue on."

"You arrested the man seated there at the defense table and whose name was Jonas Karn."

"Yes. He resisted and I was compelled to take him down personally."

"Then what happened when he was released from prison?"

"He kidnapped my daughter Caroline, coercing me to come for her so he could kill me out of revenge."

Lafevre again objected. "It is only Monsieur

McGowan's opinion my client wanted to kill him. Monsieur Cadieux did not kill him as you can see. He was only wanting to make a point. He has since regretted the taking of Caroline McGowan and has openly apologized for the act."

The judge thought for a moment, then said "Sustained."

Julie continued. "What ensued from that point?"

"I was able to escape with my daughter, but having found evidence of a bomb-making factory in rural Colorado, in my government capacity, I was part of a task force that moved in on the warehouse. Jonas Karn and several of his fellow terrorists seeing us coming, blew up the building, killing several of his own people. Karn, however, ran from the building before the explosion. Several of our team were badly injured."

"And what further occurred?"

"As you spelled out in your opening statement, I was marrying my current wife on the grounds of her Bed and Breakfast. Before that, and while I was out of town, Mr. Karn, pretending to be a country inn reviewer, was staying at my fiancée's inn. At the wedding ceremony, as we were saying our wedding vows, he appeared from the woods and fired a single pistol shot. The bullet that was meant for me struck my wife in the back, critically injuring her. My special agent daughter, who was in the audience, then pulled her pistol from her purse and shot Mr. Karn, causing the paralysis he has now. Now, seventeen years later, still holding a grudge for everything in his life he himself caused, concocted a scheme to bring me here by purchasing…"

"Objection, your honor. That is his speculation and

not supported by fact. In my opening statement, I explained that Monsieur Cadieux has expressly denied purchasing a tour for Monsieur McGowan."

"Sustained."

"You have been to Paris twice over the past two months. What have you experienced on both occasions?"

"Attempts on my life. Three times the first and second week I was here, and just yesterday when two men shot a police lieutenant who was escorting me to the courthouse. The bullet was meant for me…" I then pointed at Karn…" and that man there in the wheelchair ordered it."

"Objection."

"Sustained."

Julie's face said she was not pleased with my theatrics, and she was right. However, what I said would hopefully stick in the jury's mind.

"No further questions, your honor." She returned to her table.

"Your witness," the judge said to Lafevre.

He then slowly rose from his chair and with unwavering eyes fixed on me, walked toward the witness stand as though he were a lion stalking its prey.

Chapter Twenty Nine

"Monsieur McGowan, how are you today?"

"Doing well, thank you."

"First of all, my client, Monsieur Cadieux, is pleased that you were not injured or worse in the heinous attack on the car in which you were riding yesterday. He abhors what happened. I assume you were not injured."

"The bullet fired actually burned across the tip of my nose and all that remains is a small scab. I don't call that an injury compared to Lieutenant Allard's wound."

"Monsieur Cadieux expresses his concern for the lieutenant and hopes he recovers well."

Sure he does, I wanted to say, but didn't.

"You have been wounded many times I understand. How many?"

"Probably five or six. The one that brought me closest to death was when Jonas Karn's mother, of all people, shot me in the back."

"You beat me to the punch, as you Americans say. I was soon to ask you about that. The information I have is that you broke into Madame Karn's home and terrorized her, firing a pistol within inches from her head. Do you admit that?"

"Your client had forcibly taken my daughter and I was trying to get information from her on where she was."

"Again, Monsieur Cadieux regrets the day he took

your daughter Caroline. He was driven by the pain and unnecessary violence you inflicted on him years earlier and wanted to get your attention. What you did to him when you captured him was inhumane. You nearly kicked him to death and in doing so, it affected his…manliness."

"Again, he resisted…"

"And as you are a bigger man, instead of merely restraining him, you decided to scar him for life."

I didn't reply.

"As a matter of fact, you have a history of apprehending suspects with violent use of force, sometimes shooting them in a non-vital part of their body to inflict pain."

"If you know that, then name one such incident."

"Your take-down methods are well-documented, Monsieur. On three occasions, you either shot or cut with a knife Islamic suspects to get information from them. I hold here in my hand those reports of your apprehensions. Read them to the court."

"*You* read them, counselor."

"Your honor, I will now need to treat Monsieur McGowan as a hostile witness."

"Ask your questions, Monsieur."

"It is little wonder why so many victims and family members come after you, Monsieur. It seems at least one of your victims who has drawn you here to Paris has you in his sights."

"And he sits right there in his wheelchair."

"Mesdames ey monsieurs of the jury, you see that my client has no capability of doing anything but turn his head. We contend that if someone is trying to kill Monsieur McGowan, the person or persons doing so can drive vehicles, handle weapons and otherwise pursue him without any limitation."

"Your client has quite a few such capable people working for him that carry out his orders, many who are documented Islamic radicals such as the one who sits there beside him today."

"Monsieur Abu is a trained and certified caregiver who tends to Monsieur Cadieux's physical and medical needs. But it is you who are on the witness stand. I ask the questions and you must refrain from making your accusations. You mentioned earlier that on three occasions there were attempts on your first trip here to Paris. Can you describe the attacks?"

I knew where he was going with that. He was planning to draw me into admitting I had fended myself against al- Tajir in one of the attacks. I had broken into Karn's party to do that.

"The first attempt was with an automobile. While my wife and I were walking on the street, a van drove straight toward us, compelling us to jump down an embankment on the Seine. The second time, I was walking near my hotel, and from the open window of a large vehicle, someone fired several rounds at me with a rifle. He was obviously a bad shot."

"And the third?"

"The very reason we are here in this courtroom, Counselor. Although I wasn't at the scene, Mr. Karn and his man killed a new friend of mine named Roy Farrell. The knife was meant for me."

"Your honor, I ask you to squelch Monsieur McGowan's last statement. There was no involvement by my client in that murder."

"So he claims, your honor," I said.

The judge then admonished me. "Monsieur McGowan, please refrain from making such statements. Just answer the questions without making your opinions known. The jury will disregard."

I looked at both Marie and Julie who tried to stifle their smiles. But it was Marie who wagged her finger at me to stay on course.

"Let me ask you about the invitation for you to come to Paris without any cost to you. Was it signed by my client?"

"No."

"Did it allude in any way to my client?"

No."

"Why do you think my client was somehow involved?"

"Because out of curiosity, I went to the travel agency here to find out who paid for it."

"When you got there, did anyone offer to tell you who?"

"No. I was told the person wanted to remain anonymous."

"Again, why do you think Monsieur Cadieux was the one who arranged it?"

"I saw his name in the agency's computer screen."

"Did they show it to you?"

"No."

"How did you see it, then?"

"When the person I was talking to left the room, I looked at the screen."

He grinned. "Mesdames et monsieurs, this is the devious character of the man sitting here. He feigned to be ill so that the person helping him would leave her desk to get him some water. Then he views something confidential that belongs to the agency."

"Objection. Who told Monsieur Lafevre this? Our office secured Cadieux's name through records subpoena."

"I can give the court the name of the clerk who divulged this. Again, it goes to show how Monsieur McGowan will go even to dishonest and beguiling means to get what he wants."

"Objection. Counsel is using character assassination to try proving his point," said Julie.

"Sustained. Jury is to disregard."

"What we contend is that when you recognized Monsieur Karn was coincidentally on the same tour as you, you yourself had so much hate for him for kidnapping your daughter, you embarked on a vendetta to claim he was in fact trying to kill *you*. Perhaps these attempts on your life did not happen. Maybe you yourself killed Roy Farrell and blamed it on Monsieur Cadieux. As you have killed so many, what is another life?"

Julie jumped up from her chair and practically screamed "*Objection!* This is an outrageous supposition! It is also a ridiculous ploy to take the focus off his murderous client and place it on Monsieur McGowan. This bullshit concoction is so absurd and far-fetched that it is obvious counsel is grasping at straws."

The judge nodded. "Monsieur Lafevre, Monsieur McGowan is not the one on trial here, but your client is. Please stick to defending the charges and not make unfounded allegations. And Madame Durand, please refrain from using profanity in my courtroom."

"All right, Monsieur McGowan, what did you think when you saw that Monsieur Cadieux was on your tour?"

"I actually didn't recognize him at first. His looks had greatly changed through the years. He has grown the beard and added those thick-lens glasses, not to mention putting on a lot of weight. As he wore a red beret the entire time we were on the tour, he reminded my wife and I of Santa Claus. Not knowing his name, that's what we called him."

Most of the jurors then looked across the room at Karn to validate what I said, and a couple even smiled.

"Let me go back to the statement I had made before, leaving my allegation out of it. You yourself despise Monsieur Cadieux, don't you?"

I looked at Karn and then shook my head. "The man I know as Jonas Karn has paid the price for his crimes against the American government and although he is a fugitive from justice by escaping from prison and fleeing to France, in a way he has also paid for kidnapping my daughter since it was her bullet that placed him in that wheelchair. Rather than hate him, I more so feel sorry for him."

"But it was in his hospital room you were seen

placing the muzzle of a gun to my client's head, ready to pull the trigger."

"Hmmm, you called me vicious and inhumane. Yet your client is alive here in this courtroom, isn't he? Yes, I was angry. He had just shot the woman I was to marry. But whatever you may think of me, I would never pull the trigger on a man who helplessly lays unable to move in a hospital bed or wheelchair. However, as long as he has a mouth, he will order people to go after me. It will be them I'll have to deal with."

"As you killed Monsieur Cadieux's longtime caregiver…?"

"Objection, your honor. Again, this is a wild, unsubstantiated claim on the part of counsel. The matter to which he is referring, was duly addressed by the National Police as well as our office."

"Sustained."

Judge Sartre then asked Lafevre, "Counsel, do you have further questions for Monsieur McGowan?"

"Not at this time, but I reserve the right to recall him at some point in the trial before it ends."

"So granted. I see the morning is about over and we will recess for the lunch hour. Monsieur Lafevre, the testimony of Monsieur Cadieux is scheduled for tomorrow, but if your client wishes to testify this afternoon, we can move it up."

"We can do that. Is it alright with you, Madame Durand?"

"Yes. We are prepared."

"Very good. We are in recess."

Chapter Thirty

There was a two-hour lunch break and so the ladies and I decided to catch a quick lunch at a sidewalk cafe near the hospital. I wanted to see how Jacques was doing. Marie and Julie were good with that. As they each had worked cases with him over the years, they had become close. After parking in the hospital's covered garage, we checked at the information desk for Jacques' room number.

Moments later, we tapped on the door of room 328. When Jacques yelled out "entrez" we went in.

The grin on Jacques' face was gleaming. "What are you three doing here? Are you not supposed to be in court?"

"The judge let us out for good behavior," I quipped. "Seriously, we're on a lunch break."

"Did you testify?"

"He did a very good job," Marie said. "I believe when the jury compares Bruce with Karn, they will think the man in the wheelchair is nothing but a scoundrel."

"It doesn't hurt to have an all-woman prosecution team putting on a case before a mostly female jury, either," I remarked.

Julie said, "I'm glad you think so, but it doesn't always work out that way. But we think the jury will get the case as early as tomorrow. Unless Lafevre has something up his sleeve."

"So, it is moving along well."

"Yes, but we came here to see how *you* were doing, not talk about the case."

"I have been up walking around today, but as you can see, my right arm is in a sling. It will be weeks before I'm able to do anything from shaking hands to swinging my golf club."

"We hope they'll let you out soon," I said. "Nothing like having tender loving care at home."

Julie checked her watch. "Sorry to make our visit short, but I think if we want to have lunch at the cafe, we must get on."

"Heal up, Jacques. Hopefully I'll see you again before I leave Paris." I thrust out my left hand and he extended his.

"Good luck in getting this maggot on wheels convicted."

Our lunch was light but good. No one had a drink except tea and water. It would not have served well to go back to the courthouse with alcohol on our breaths.

We were back in our seats just before two. The judge returned to the bench, we all rose and then sat back down.

"Monsieur Lafevre, I believe you plan to call your client to the stand."

"Oui, your honor. Monsieur Cadieux, would you please roll your wheelchair there by the witness stand?"

It took a few moments, but for the benefit of the jury, he blew into his straw and maneuvered his chair forward, around in a semi-circle and then up against the stand. His large Arab caregiver in the keffiyeh helped him. When he was in place, the aide placed a blanket over Karn's legs and wiped his mouth with a handkerchief.

Nice little theatric, I thought.

Lafevre swore him in and asked him his name. "Henri Cadieux," he replied.

"Monsieur Cadieux, you are the owner of a place called Ramatuelle, is that correct?"

"Yes, just like the city not far from here." His womanish voice crackled through the courtroom like a shrill bird. I saw members of the jury looking at one another. I didn't know if they were about to laugh or merely react in pity.

"Monsieur Cadieux…"

Karn suddenly cut in. "Before you begin, Monsieur Lafevre, would you be so kind as to let me make a statement?"

The interruption seemed to surprise his attorney, but he nodded, "Yes."

"Even though some of you in the courtroom know *of* me, I would say few actually know me personally. Therefore, you have never heard me speak.

You may think my voice is comical and it probably is; however, my voice has not always sounded like this. Every time I hear myself talk, the image of the man who made me this way comes into my brain. It was the man sitting behind the defense table, Bruce McGowan, who in arresting me over thirty years ago, brutally attacked me. It is embarrassing to tell you this, but besides crushing my windpipe, he kicked me between the legs so hard that I lost my testicles. As I could no longer perform sexually, my wife who partnered with me in the Underground left me. I was a broken man for years. My passion as a crusader for civil rights in America was also affected.

"You may ask how I became known as Monsieur Cadieux. I will first take you back to my years as a crusader. You see, I was an idealist…wanting the best for my country and my fellow citizens. I along with my friends knew things were not right in the United States…a war going on in a country we had no right being in…thousands of American young men getting butchered every year…Black Americans still being discriminated against and deprived of their rights even a hundred or more years after they had been freed. My friends and I knew it was time for these wrongs to be righted. Yes, I did things I'm not proud of. But it wasn't the first time a group of young revolutionaries rioted for their freedom. Two hundred years before that, as a result of the revolution, those oppressed colonies became what is known as the United States. "But then I was punished for my crimes. Unfortunately, as a misguided felon, I harbored ill feelings about Monsieur McGowan. I wanted revenge. And as a result, I became the person you see here. When I left the United States, I wanted a clean break from that life. Having remorse for these new crimes, I wanted to devoid myself of that life…and of being who I was. I wanted to become a respectable citizen in my new country. In essence, a new me.

"I don't want anyone to feel sorry for me. I either sit in this chair or must be laid in the bed every day by my companion. Monsieur Abu you see there is new at the job but does a very good job helping me. My longtime caregiver who I loved was murdered by the man you see near the prosecution table, Bruce McGowan, after he forced his way into my home…"

And so, he got it in. But he didn't provide the particulars.

"…you cannot realize what I go through every day. My caregiver must bathe me and help me in the bathroom. I have no control over my bowels and bladder which you may observe before today is over. Now, I am not faulting Monsieur McGowan for that. To protect her father and future stepmother from certain death, the woman, Caroline McGowan, had no choice. I am a quadriplegic because of my own bad decision. I have no hatred for her.

"You may ask, do I hate Monsieur McGowan? I hate no one. I must say that he is not my favorite person in the world, but I am not a murderer. I was concerned about the officer as well as him yesterday when I heard they had been ambushed. I bear no one any ill will." He then looked back at Lafevre. "You may now ask your questions, sir."

I watched the jury during his soliloquy and must admit, I thought some of them appeared affected. I had to hand it to him; he put on quite an emotional performance. But, would anyone see through his line of happy horseshit?

"Thank you, Monsieur Cadieux," said Lafevre. "That was very moving, and you covered in your statement much of what I was prepared to ask. However, I will ask you some specific questions pertaining to what transpired back in April of this year. Did you pay for Monsieur McGowan's tour to Paris?"

"I did not."

"But your name was on the travel document as the payor."

"I don't know why. Perhaps someone who is out to frame me and who knows about my troubles with Monsieur McGowan did that. Maybe he did it himself. I believe he harbors as many hard feelings about me as I do about him."

"Objection. Speculation."

"Sustained."

"You've lived in Paris for just under fifteen years. Why did you decide to take the tour of Paree?"

"As you can see, I have limitations and have mostly stayed at home, never seeing much of the history and beauty of Paris. Most venues have not been handicap friendly. I heard about this particular tour last year and that it made proper arrangements for people like me. So, I signed up for a spring tour.

"When did you realize Monsieur McGowan and his wife were in your tour group?"

"He may not have recognized me, but I knew it was him immediately after the tour group got together."

"And what was your reaction?"

"I have to admit…a fiery bolt went through me."

"Did you want to kill him?"

"Monsieur Lafevre, I've never wanted to kill anyone. Even when I was a rebel in those early 1970s and then later revived the Weather Underground, I wouldn't think of taking a life. I was just all about bringing the government to its knees, to realize they had not only abandoned our civil rights, but rights guaranteed under the U.S. constitution."

"So, I must ask you this question, Monsieur Cadieux, did you kill or arrange the murder of Roy

Farrell?"

"I did not and on my mother's grave I swear it."

"Was it you who made the statement at Monsieur

Farrell's murder scene to the effect that Monsieur McGowan was not so invincible after all?"

"No, I did not."

"Thank you, Monsieur Cadieux. I have no further questions."

Judge Sartre then said, "Cross examine, Madame Durand?"

"Thank you, your honor. Monsieur Cadieux, when did you change your name from Jonas Karn to what it is now?"

"I can't remember exactly, but it was about a year and a half after relocating here."

"Which was after you escaped from your minimum-security prison in the United States. Are you not a fugitive from justice?"

"I don't see it that way, Madame. I consider that there *was* no justice in the U.S."

"And shortly after fleeing to Paris, your rich uncle died leaving you a fortune. Now you live comfortably and in high society."

"Madame Durand, I have not lived comfortably for the past seventeen years. You see what I am. How comfortable do you think that is?"

"You know what I meant, Monsieur. Financially comfortably."

"I don't want for anything…except arms and legs that work."

"I present to the court Exhibit number one. Whose legal signature is this?"

"That's mine. You must have gotten it from one of my bank records you subpoenaed."

"Obviously, you weren't able to sign it yourself. Who did?"

"My poor dead caregiver, al-Tajir signed all my legal documents."

"I now present a different document. Is this the same signature?"

"Yes, it appears so."

"Monsieur Cadieux, this document is the contract and payment to Saint-Amaury Tours for Bruce McGowan's trip here to Paris."

There was a groan from the twenty or so spectators in the courtroom.

"If that is the case, the signature was forged. I explained that someone has had it in for me and is trying to frame me."

"I had the signature compared with those in your bank records and other business dealings by two handwriting experts and they attest they are identical. Your honor, I present their affidavits, Exhibits 2 and 3, into evidence. If necessary, both experts can be brought in to testify. Now what do you say, Monsieur?"

Karn stared at the signature but said nothing.

"Now that we've established that it was you or your caregiver who arranged to lure Monsieur McGowan here, let's talk about what happened at the murder scene. I also introduce Exhibit 4, the sworn statement of Elizabeth Farrell, widow of Roy Farrell who was murdered three blocks from the restaurant where you dined and from where you left with your caregiver minutes before the Farrells did. She swears the person who taunted her dead husband, thinking he had killed Monsieur McGowan, had a high-pitched voice, much like yours. She remembers hearing someone in the tour group who sounded much like the killer but couldn't put her finger on it. Shall I read what she reported the murderer said?"

"I heard what she was claimed to have said in your opening statement and when Monsieur Lafevre questioned me."

"How can anyone not believe it was you who directed the murder? You lured Monsieur McGowan here and you set him up for the kill..."

"Objection, your honor. Counsel is no longer questioning my client; she has stooped to making accusations, unfounded as they are."

"I agree. Sustained."

"As Monsieur McGowan and the decedent resembled one another in stature, hair color and wearing similar clothing, on a dimly lit street in the fog, the murderer killed the wrong man. I will ask the same question as your attorney...Monsieur Cadieux, did your man who regularly escorted you everywhere you went kill Monsieur Farrell at your direction?"

"I haven't changed my answer, Madame Durand, no and *hell* no."

"Then how many men with high-pitched, raspy

voices like yours would you think there would be in a five or six block area on the night of the murder?

There was your voice in the same restaurant where Monsieur Farrell dined and one at the scene of his murder. A little coincidental, wouldn't you say?"

"I can't answer that, Madame. But there have been other coincidences occurring in this matter. I did not kill Monsieur Farrell or order Monsieur McGowan killed and I have not been involved in any alleged attempts on his life."

"You told the court only minutes ago that you never killed or even wanted to kill anyone, yet you tried to kill Monsieur McGowan at his wedding seventeen years ago. You missed then and you missed that Friday night in early May when your caregiver killed the wrong man."

"Your honor, again I object. Madame Durand is back to her accusations and is no longer questioning my client. I consider this badgering."

"Monsieur Lafevre, I must this time disagree. She is making her points based on the evidence presented. However, Madame Durand, please stick to questioning and not making declaratory statements."

"Yes, your honor. I only have one more Exhibit. It is a video of the court proceedings from two days ago. Could you have the bailiff play it on the screen?"

Julie handed off the tape. A few moments later an image of the courtroom appeared on the screen with the date of 25 June at the bottom. I knew exactly what it contained. It was the information I delivered to Marie at our dinner. It would be the coup de grace in the case that proved Karn was a liar. Maybe when all was said and done, the jury would see through his lies and believe the evidence. Believe he had not only planned my murder but attempted a number of times since the death of Roy Farrell to end my life.

Julie then began. "Mesdames et monsieurs of the jury, I direct your attention to the screen where on Day One of this trial two Middle Eastern men came into the courtroom and sat behind defense counsel and Monsieur Cadieux. You will note that when the court day was done, Monsieur Cadieux and his aide nodded to the two men, and they quickly left the courtroom. There…see it? After leaving the courthouse and entering their vehicle, they followed Lieutenant Allard's police car, with Monsieur McGowan riding as a passenger, to the hotel where he is staying. On the morning of the 26th, Lieutenant Allard picked Monsieur McGowan up at the hotel around eight- thirty. On the way to the courthouse, these same two men, now driving a stolen car, ambushed Lieutenant Allard's vehicle, shooting from the rear driver's side window, narrowly missing Monsieur McGowan but striking the lieutenant in the right shoulder. The driver of the assailant vehicle then lost control and struck a pole. Quickly and heroically, Monsieur McGowan secured Lieutenant Allard's pistol and went after the shooter. When the would-be killer swung his rifle around to finish his target, Monsieur McGowan fired, hit and killed the man. Exhibit six are the death photos of these two men and as you will see, they are the same men Monsieur Cadieux acknowledged in the courtroom."

I watched the jurors faces. A couple of them sat with their mouths open while two others whispered to one another. To me, the case was a slam-dunk, but one never knows how a jury will digest the evidence.

Karn's and Lafevre's faces registered their shock.

Karn scanned the faces of the jurors and Lafevre's eyes were focused on the floor. Lafevre sat stroking his chin with his fingers.

The judge asked, "Madame Durand, do you have further?"

"The prosecution rests, your honor."

"MonsieurLafevre?"

"The defense also rests."

"Do either of you have additional testimony or evidence to present?"

Both Julie and Lafevre answered "No, your honor."

"It appears we get a break today, mesdames and monsieurs, we are done early. Court will convene at ten tomorrow morning for closing arguments. You are dismissed."

Marie then hugged Julie. "Outstanding, my dear. As perfectly presented of a case if I ever saw one."

"I agree, Julie," I said. "You took down one of the most high-powered lawyers in all of Paris. When you put up the film, I saw the agony of defeat on both of their faces. They obviously know what's coming."

We watched as Karn and his caregiver rolled out of the courtroom. Neither looked in our direction. When the three of us gathered ourselves up, Marie said "I'll take you back to your hotel."

I didn't see Officer Jordain waiting for me in the hallway, since court concluded for the day at threethirty, so I said "That would be great. I'll be back before he even leaves to pick me up."

Chapter Thirty-One

In the Valley of Bones

This time as I rode with Marie, the fact that she was wearing her court attire and looking all professional-like in her pant suit, her shapely legs weren't exposed up to her ya ya. But she was still rather frisky, occasionally touching my hand.

After she had swung her car into the registration circle of the hotel, she said, "I will see you at the courthouse at ten. I hope you will have a good night. This time she squeezed my hand but didn't offer a kiss. Since I had given her no response from the kiss the day before, she left well enough alone.

"Good night, Marie."

After I had gotten out, I heard her cellphone ring. So that she wouldn't be talking while driving, she gave me a wave and then pulled into a parking spot near the hotel canopy. No sooner than I had turned around to walk inside, a vehicle pulled up within inches of me. When the sliding door of the black van opened, a large Arab- looking man jumped out and swung some kind of club at my head. It was the last thing I remembered.

"Bonjour, Monsieur McGowan. I trust you had a nice nap." His screeching voice was like fingernails down a chalkboard.

"What the hell?"

"A place you will see before the day is over. "

I knew I was riding in some kind of vehicle but

couldn't see because of the cloth around my eyes. My hands were also bound by duct tape.

"Why keep this over my eyes? If you're going to kill me, I'd like to see a little daylight before dying."

I then felt someone's hands on my head and the cloth came off. It *was* still daylight and after checking my watch, it was four-twenty.

Karn's wheelchair was locked in place in the back of the van. The Arab dude who slugged me was in a seat by the sliding door and I was sitting on the floor with my back against the opposite side of the vehicle. Another kaffiyeh-clad hombre was driving.

Karn sat grinning at me like a Cheshire cat. "I just figured as many times as I have tried to kill you, McGowan, I might as well see that it is done personally. Can't trust anyone these days."

"You tried that a couple months ago and killed the wrong man."

"And I regret that. This time I'm looking right at you and there will be no mistakes. When my men throw your corpse down into the Valley of Bones, no one will find you or even find out how you disappeared. Tomorrow, I will be sitting in the courtroom smiling, thinking about the buzzards feeding on your flesh." "Well, what do you know? You *do* hate me after all, Karn. That means you perjured yourself today. Actually, every time you opened your lying mouth you perjured yourself. How many years will that be on top of your murder conviction?"

That was when the Arab dude who slugged me at the hotel backhanded me in the mouth.

Karn laughed gleefully and then looked out the

van's window. "We're almost to Kota Ridge and the dreaded valley. Famous place, McGowan. You should feel honored ending up there."

"Why is that?"

"It's where French royalty and noblemen who pissed the people off ended up after they lost their heads on the guillotine. And then more recently, when the French Mafia have made people disappear, that's where they toss their carcasses. No one, not even the police, goes down there looking for the dead. Pretty Adriana will never know what happened to you."

I could see out the side door glass that we were up high…not as high as Montmartre, but somewhere isolated outside of Paris. The driver had pulled off the road and stopped the van on a large, flat rock. I suspected there was a cliff at the end of the rock.

"Fahid, slide open the door and escort Monsieur McGowan out. If he tries to run, shoot him."

Fahid did as ordered and then waved his pistol toward the door. "Get up and step out. Do not try anything."

I would have been a bit handicapped to do so, considering my hands were taped together, but I thought perhaps I could throw a roundhouse kick and knock the gun from Fahid's hand. However, I saw that the driver had exited the van and was standing outside the sliding door with a pistol of his own trained on me. The ramp then dropped and as I slowly walked down it, Fahid told me to "get down on the ground."

And I did. It appeared I was going to be shot execution style.

While Fahid stood over me, the driver went back

inside, unlatched the wheelchair and rolled Karn down the ramp.

"That's right, McGowan; I wanted to personally see the bullet go into your head." He blew into the straw and circled around me toward the edge of the cliff. I thought "one little miscue and he could end up down in the Valley of Bones." I would liked to have seen that before I died, but I couldn't be that lucky. Of course, being dead is not lucky either.

Karn continued. "Which one of you gentlemen would like the honor…Fahid? Abdul? Fahid, you have the 44 magnum, but Abdul, your pistol is only a 9-millimeter. I want to see brains and blood painted all over this rock. So, you do it, Fahid."

I closed my eyes tightly and said a quick prayer, hoping that in spite of all my misdeeds and sins, the Good Lord would have mercy on me. And then I heard a shot. *Heard it.* Three seconds later, Fahid's body plunked down beside me, his eyes staring at me in death. When I lifted my head from the rock, I saw Abdul looking this way and that, trying to find out where it came from. But then there was another shot and a second. Abdul's body tumbled off the cliff and disappeared.

I got to my feet and looked around, seeing no one. Did I have a guardian angel out there somewhere? I then looked at Karn. His mouth was in a grimace, and his eyes were firing lasers. *"Why can't you die, McGowan? Why the hell can't you die?"*

I then got to my knees in front of his chair. "You know something, Karn? I lied in court as well. I said I would never end the life of a helpless, handicapped person. I didn't pull the trigger when I placed the muzzle of my pistol against your head seventeen years ago. That was then…this is now." I then grabbed hold of the arms of his chair.

"What are you doing, McGowan? Take your hands off this chair."

With all the strength I could muster, I shoved his motorized wheelchair toward the edge of the cliff. It was muscle versus hydraulics. The fear in his eyes was an expression I had not seen on his face since I held the muzzle of my pistol against his temple in his hospital bed seventeen years before. "How does it feel to know you're this close to death, Karn?"

I saw the sweat beads on his forehead that were even fogging his thick-lens glasses. His eyes appeared even greater magnified.

"You wouldn't."

I wanted to. However, for some reason, I couldn't.

But then what happened was either an accident or intentional on his part. He suddenly blew into the plastic straw, and the wheelchair lurched backward, rolling off the edge of the cliff. Although I made a feeble attempt to tighten my grip on the chair's arms and hold it, its electric momentum was too powerful.

I watched as he and the chair plummeted and bounced into the jagged rocks, listening to his screams all the way to the bottom. "McGowan… nooooooooooo!" And then there was nothing but silence. For a long moment, I stood not so much in horrified silence as I did in relief. In his state of panic, did he accidentally propel the wheelchair in reverse? If so, it was either God or karma.

I then turned around and looked in the direction

from which the bullets came. "Okay, whoever you are, you can come out now."

I expected one of my police bodyguards, like Herve Jordain, but I didn't expect Marie de Barrere.

"Marie, how…?"

"I had parked off to the side in front of the hotel to make a phone call. Just seconds later, in my rear-view mirror, I saw the van pull up: then someone came out of it and hit you with a club. He pulled you into the van and it took off. I started to go inside and get the officer who was looking after you, but in doing so, knew I would lose them. I followed them here, parked over in the trees and after hustling up here, hid behind their van. Then when I saw Cadieux's man place his gun near your head, I pulled the trigger. For good measure, I also shot the other guy."

I walked toward her and gave her a long hug. "Thank you, Marie."

"I haven't had any target practice for weeks. Felt good."

"Who else did you see?"

"That's it."

"Are you sure?"

"There were only two of them, I am sure."

I looked into her eyes and couldn't tell if she was lying to me. She not only had to have seen Karn in his chair but me with my hands on the chair's arms when he went off the cliff. And if so, did she think I pushed him over?

I looked back toward the edge of the cliff. "I heard people call this the Valley of Bones."

"Yes, I know about it. I was fearing you would end up down there."

I turned and looked at Fahid lying on the huge rock with a .357 magnum bullet in his chest. "Well anyway, nice shot, Annie Oakley. But his carcass needs to join his partner in crime at the bottom of the ravine."

"It will make for a clean end to something we will not have to explain."

"Then this didn't happen," I said.

"I know nothing about it."

After I dumped Fahid's body off the cliff into the Valley of the Bones, I restarted the van, faced it toward the edge of the cliff, put it in drive, and let it roll off the edge as well. I stood watching it crash and bounce against the rocks below like a large toy until it disappeared two hundred feet down into the trees.

"Can I get a ride back with you?" I asked with a smile.

"Monsieur McGowan, I will take you anywhere you want to go."

It was a nearly wordless trip back to the Hotel Le Fleur. I guess we were both quietly reflecting on the parts we had played in the events of that afternoon. There was little more that we *could* say to one another. I assumed she had never killed another human being and maybe that was why she was so silent. Then again, maybe she was thinking about how she had witnessed me killing a helpless old man in a wheelchair. I guess I as much did, but I would just let her form her own opinion on that.

When she deposited me at the front door of the hotel, she smiled at me through the open passenger side window for a few seconds with her knowing eyes. "See you tomorrow, Bruce." I nodded with a smile of my own and gave her a two-finger salute. She then she pulled away.

Upon entering the lobby, I found Herve Jordain pacing with his hands behind his back. "Monsieur McGowan, I was very worried. I wish you had told me you were with Madame de Barrere. When I went to the courthouse to pick you up, I couldn't locate you."

"I'm so sorry, Herve. I should have thought about you and that you'd be coming after me. As court ended early, I was going to meet you here in the lobby to tell you. But, as the trial will be over tomorrow, you'll be free to get back to your regular duties."

He grinned. "I liked *this* duty. Maybe you can stay a little longer."

I took a hot shower, put on a fresh set of clothes and then walked down the street a few blocks from the hotel to have a nice, celebratory dinner at a French pub…alone. It felt good not having to be looking over my shoulder every time I left a building. Adriana could also rest easy.

I took my time eating my baguette and drinking my Heineken while recounting what had occurred that afternoon. The image of Karn disappearing over the edge of that cliff was sticking with me. Yes, I *wanted* to kill him and wondered if pushing him that close to the edge, I actually did. I have always agreed with Clint Eastwood that I only killed those that *needed* killing. And Karn was one who did need it. Anyway, his body was mostly already dead; but it was his evil mind that had to die.

I also wondered what would happen at trial the next

day. Monsieur Cadieux would not be showing up and there would only be two people in the courtroom who knew why. Would Lafevre go ahead and do his closing argument without him, or would the judge postpone what was left of the trial and send the authorities to look for him? But what the hell did it matter? I had another beer.

Back in the room, I made my nightly call to Adriana.

"How was your day, sweetheart?" she asked me.

"Fine. It ended well. How about yours?"

"Please tell me I can go home."

"That bad, huh?"

"Mom is driving me crazy...telling me I need to do this and need to do that. She keeps saying that my marriage is obviously in trouble, or I wouldn't be staying with them by myself. Dad is eating himself into another heart attack. Refuses to eat the healthy foods that I cook. He and Little Debbie are now going steady. Mom fusses at him constantly and tells him one day he won't wake up. Other than that, I'm having a wonderful time."

"Then go on home."

"Do you mean that? Will I be safe at home without you being there?"

"Jonas Karn is dead."

"Dead? How?"

"He went out on a cliff with some guys, got too close and his wheelchair went over the edge."

"Hmmm. I don't know whether to feel sorry that it happened or be elated that he's out of our lives."

"I'm thinking that last thing."

"Wow, that's pretty crazy. What about the trial? I assume it's over and you can come home."

"There are some matters to wrap up with the trial, but yes, I should be home in a couple of days."

"And I can't wait."

"I'll let you know the plans. Pack your bags and call the airlines. Go home, my dear."

"Gladly."

Chapter Thirty-Two

Epilogue

"Good morning, Herve."

"Good morning to you, Monsieur McGowan. Did you have a good night?"

"Slept like a baby."

"I understand today is closing arguments in the trial."

"Yes. It will be the last day I'm sure."

"Then there will be the verdict."

"That's the way it works. You should sit in on it."

"I believe I will. I will ask my sergeant."

When Herve and I arrived at the Palais de Justice and entered the courtroom, we were surprised. Jacques Allard was sitting on my bench behind Julie Durand and Marie de Barrere. His arm was in a sling, but he looked good.

"Jacques, you're here," I said.

"Ah, you noticed."

"How do you feel?"

"My shoulder is still sore, but the therapy I went through at the hospital helped."

"Should you be here?"

"I have to be somewhere."

It sounded like something I would say.

Julie then remarked, "This will be the day Monsieur Cadieux goes down."

I looked at Marie, but neither of us gave it away with our faces. I wanted to say, "He *already* went down."

Julie glanced at the clock on the wall. "It's one minute till nine and Karn isn't here yet. Monsieur Lafevre keeps looking back at the door."

The judge then entered the courtroom and the "all rise" command was given. When he sat down, he looked around the courtroom. "Monsieur Lafevre, where is your client?"

"I do not know, your honor. Maybe his vehicle is stuck in traffic."

"Have you spoken to him by phone this morning?"

"I am troubled that his caregiver neither answered his phone last night nor this morning."

"I will give him fifteen minutes and if he is not here, I will hold you *and* him in contempt."

"Yes, your honor."

Judge Sartre then returned to his chambers. When Lafevre pulled out his cellphone, in my mind I said, "Give it up, counselor. He's not coming…ever."

"I wonder what happened to him." Julie said.

Jacques answered the question. "Maybe he knew what the verdict would be and as our American friend here would say, he flew the coop."

"He flew all right," I was dying to say.

When the fifteen minutes were up, Judge Sartre reappeared with a sour look on his face. "Monsieur Lafevre, I see your client is still not here. You are both in contempt. We cannot proceed without him. If you do not hear from him within the hour, I will send the police after him. If they do not find him, he will then be a fugitive from justice. Do you understand this, Counselor?"

"I do, your honor."

"Madame Durand, Madame de Barrere, the court apologizes for this delay," the judge added. "Monsieur Lafevre, you will notify me when you finally hear from your client."

Of course, Lafevre did not hear from Karn. The judge swore out a warrant for his arrest and the police were dispatched to Ramatuelle at one o'clock that afternoon to apprehend him. When they arrived at the house, the officers only found the cook and one Middle Eastern employee. Neither had seen Monsieur Cadieux nor two other of his employees since the morning before when they departed for trial.

That evening, Julie, Marie, Jacques and I met for dinner at yet another swanky restaurant called Republique. It was Jacques who picked me up this time and not Marie. The last time I rode with him, the experience was not so good. On the way to the restaurant, we only spoke briefly about that. This time there would be nothing to worry about.

For the better part of an hour before even ordering our food, the four of us sat and talked not only about where Karn could be but whether the judge could render a directed verdict without the jury. I think by the time we did order our food, we were all a bit loopy from our before-dinner drinks.

It was then I told them I was going home that next day, that is if I could get a flight out. "For nearly twenty- four hours, Karn hasn't surfaced. All that is left are closing arguments and the verdict. I don't need to be here for that. Julie, you can send me an email letting me know the results."

Marie, of course, secretly knew why Karn was AWOL. She went right along with me. "Bruce, you are correct; you don't need to stay. It could be that Cadieux, AKA Karn, will never be found. He was a fugitive from justice in the United States and maybe he has now left France."

He not only left France, he left the world. No, I didn't actually say that.

"I will miss you, Bruce," Julie said. "You were very helpful in this trial and I enjoyed both our conversations and company."

"I'll miss you all as well," I said. "We may have started out as associates on the case, but I'm glad we became friends along the way. And each one of you worked hard to take down a monster. This guy was a boil on my butt for too long. Three times I've had to contend with him…only this time from a wheelchair."

"I have a feeling you have seen the last of him, Bruce," Marie said facetiously, and with a knowing smile. "You won't be stalked by him any longer."

I smiled back. "And I am sure you are right."

Jacques added, "But, if he has escaped prosecution by leaving France, he may resurface in your life from somewhere else…maybe change his name again."

As Julie and Jacques continued to speculate on Karn and his whereabouts, Marie and I glanced occasionally at one another but added very little. We both shared a secret about which we would never speak. We both knew a scourge on society had been eliminated and that was all that mattered. Three bodies lay in the Valley of the Bones and she had put two of them there. I continued wondering from her vantage point if she thought I had pushed Karn over. If she thought I did, so be it. One thing for sure, there would remain between us a perpetual bond. I don't keep secrets from Adriana. However, it wasn't a *carnal* secret that would be a threat to my marriage; it was just something she didn't need to know about. It would not serve well for her to know that I was two seconds from certain death and that another woman had saved my life.

The ladies and I said our goodbyes. Both gave me hugs, but Marie's included a kiss, again on the lips. For her it may have been a wanton kiss, but I took it as a seal to our covenant.

When Jacques took me back to the hotel, it was a few minutes past ten. We sat for a few minutes in his car chatting idly and then he said, "Methinks our chief procureur is, as you Americans say, warm for your form."

I laughed. "You're really into our American idioms, aren't you?"

"Are you dodging my comment?"

"She's a very lovely lady…smart, professional and insightful. She's also single and probably lonely. Maybe I was just someone who, in our conversations, made her feel good about herself. Yeah, I could sense that she needed companionship, but she knew that I am happily married, and so she appropriately kept her distance."

He grinned. "And I perceive if there was not a Madame McGowan, you might have responded to her differently."

I grinned back. "One never knows."

"Well, good night, Bruce, and goodbye. I hope you can get a flight out tomorrow. Vivienne and I do plan a trip to the United States, and we will be sure to put your Wolf Laurel on our list."

"I hope so, Jacques. And if we ever decide to return to Paris…on a trip that *we* will pay for *ourselves*…you will be the first people we'll look up."

"You'll be back. It is inevitable. Once you get a taste of Paris, you can never stay away for good."

We shook our left hands and in my best French, I bid him adieu. "Au revoir, mon ami. My best to the lovely Vivienne."

I then returned to my room and after making several calls to airlines, to my surprise was able to get a flight out the next day at one-forty in the afternoon. While lying in bed, waiting for the sleep that would eventually take over, I began reflecting on yet another action adventure I had lived through, wondering how many more of them there could possibly be. It seemed they kept coming through no fault of my own. I wanted my retirement years to be filled with golf, hanging out with the few friends I had at the country club, and frolicking as much as I could with the lovely Madame McGowan. Although at times my Paris experience was harrowing, even near fatal, I enjoyed both its beauty and the Parisian friendships I had cultivated. Contrary to the conventional myth about the French, there was nothing rude I had found in its people. I found them delightful. I even owed my very life to one of them…Marie. Beautiful, sensuous, but unobtainable. I wished her well…but most of all, I wished her love.

It was an uneventful trip back home. Flights were on time, I was not sandwiched in my seat between two beefy bozos with halitosis, and the lovely Adriana who herself had just arrived on a flight at Yeager airport, was waiting at the gate for me. We took an Uber back home and found the old country inn just as we had left it. Any of Karn's goons still lurking around who had not heard of his disappearance had not booby-trapped or set fire to our home. The Karn reign of terror was over.

A few days later, I came home from one of my club's golf tournaments to find that Adriana, who was once again coming up with new patterns for making her clothes, had gotten from the Belk store another outdated mannequin to replace her old friend Eunice. When she pulled out the naked, life-size doll from an upstairs closet to show me, the shock I experienced turned quickly to laughter. She was the spitting image of a real person. But not just *any* real person. Her new mannequin wore the unmistakable, beautiful but frozen face of none other than Madame Marie de Barrere.

Praise for

Provocation: Return of the Weatherman

This is the second book in Lee Martin's Bruce McGowan series and it does not disappoint! McGowan is still my favorite Clint Eastwood meets James Bond meets John Wayne cowboy type hero. I loved this novel! It kept me engaged and I could not put it down. It is a terrorist thriller as can only be told by a true patriotic hero himself. I love the way justice is dealt by McGowan. I suspect that events such as are told in "Provocation: Return of the Weatherman" actually happen but we civilians never hear about them or the true heroes. Reading this series makes me feel like I have an "in" on the action. Great read.

JCL

SEE WHOLE SERIES ON OUR WEBSITE: I.E.R. Media

http://www.colonelleemartinbooks.com